A Novel

JOURNEY to HOPE

JUNE A. CONVERSE

A Novel

JOURNEY to HOPE

JUNE A. CONVERSE

Heart Ally Books
Camano Island, Washington

Journey to Hope
Copyright ©2020 by June A. Converse
www.JuneConverse.com

All rights reserved. This book or any portion thereof may not be reproduced or used in any manner whatsoever without the express permission of the publisher except for the use of brief quotations.

Cover design: Deranged Doctor Designs

Published by:
Heart Ally Books
26910 92nd Ave NW C5-406, Stanwood, WA 98292
Published on Camano Island, WA, USA
www.heartallybooks.com

ISBN-13: 978-1-63107-029-7 (epub)
ISBN-13: 978-1-63107-030-3 (paperback)
Library of Congress Control Number: 2020914167

10 9 8 7 6 5 4 3 2 1

Dedicated to all of us who need hope.

Hope
Smiles from the threshold of the year to come
Whispering 'It will be happier'...
~Alfred, Lord Tennyson

LEESIDE MOUNTAIN NEWS

SPECIAL EDITION ♦ DECEMBER 25, 2012 ♦ LEESIDE, NC

Family Annihilation in Leeside

By Jeffrey Rileson – Leeside Mountain News

Six members of a Leeside family were murdered in their home on Christmas Eve in what the police are calling a family annihilation. The Lee County Sheriff's department arrived at 932 Leeside Mountain Drive Thursday at 10:12 pm. Police found the bodies of Seth Bridges, age 52, Brice Bridges, age 32, Amanda Lopez-Bridges, age 32, Courtney Bridges, age 24, Kiley Bridges, age 9, and Lucas Bridges, age 7. Marcia Bridges, age 50, was the only survivor.

"Marcia Bridges was taken to the local hospital, where she was stabilized and sent by a life flight helicopter to a hospital in Charlotte," said Sheriff Johnson. At press time, there was no report on her condition.

The 911 operator received a call at 9:42 pm from the Bridges' neighbor, Stephanie Culberson. According to reports, Culberson entered the home when she was unable to reach members of the family by phone. Ms. Culberson could not be reached for comment.

According to Johnson several suspects have been identified. The North Carolina Bureau of Investigation, the Georgia Bureau of Investigation, and the Keys County Police (a suburb of Atlanta) are working together to apprehend these suspects. Johnson refused to give the suspects' names at this time.

"There is no danger to the citizens of Lee County. Based on the evidence, this horrific crime appears to be directed specifically at the Bridges' family," Sheriff Johnson said in a phone interview earlier this morning. No motive or other details are being provided by the sheriff's office.

LEESIDE MOUNTAIN NEWS
DECEMBER 27, 2012 ♦ LEESIDE, NC

Family Annihilation Arrests

By Jeffrey Rileson – Leeside Mountain News

Four arrests have been made in the brutal slaying and torture of the Bridges family on Christmas Eve. Sheriff Vince Johnson announced the arrest of Michael Jenkins, age 24, Andrew Hughes, age 24, Chase Darnell, age 26, and Joshua Simpson, age 28. Simpson is the nephew of the only survivor, Marcia Bridges.

The four men are being held without bond in the Keys County jail until they can be transferred to Leeside. Sheriff Johnson said, "The Keys County Sheriff and Police Departments have been instrumental in the apprehension of these men."

According to arrest records, each suspect has prior arrests for possession, manufacture, trafficking, and distribution of methamphetamines. Simpson is also awaiting trial for burglary and domestic violence.

"We found several key pieces of forensic evidence and witness statements that point to these men," Sheriff Johnson told reporters. "We received a valuable tip from a woman in the Keys County area."

Johnson is confident all the perpetrators have been apprehended, but he declined to give further details regarding motive and evidence.

Regarding the condition of the only survivor, Marcia Bridges, Johnson said, "She is in critical but stable condition. She suffered a variety of injuries to her torso, her hand, and her head. At this point, we have been unable to contact Mrs. Bridges. She is at Charlotte Memorial and as soon as the doctors allow, we will obtain her statement."

The Bridges Family

Many people in our small community know and respect the Bridges family. Marcia volunteered in our school's literacy programs. Her husband Seth sat on the Leeside School Board and was an avid golfer. Their son, Brice, and their daughter-in-law, Amanda, were both law enforcement officers in Keys County, a suburb of Atlanta and could often be seen using local mountain trails for triathlon training. Brice and Amanda's two children, Kiley and Lucas, attended Keys Elementary School where they excelled academically.

Courtney, the Bridges' 24-year-old daughter, had finished her graduate work to become a registered dietitian. She had been planning her spring wedding at the Mountaintop Lodge before she settled in the Chicago area. Her fiancé, Eli Watts, was not in Leeside at the time of the crime and has been unavailable for comment.

No information has been provided regarding funeral or memorial services.

Kathleen

Hurrying out of the bitter, unrelenting Minnesota wind, Marcia Kathleen Bridges stepped gratefully into the manufactured warmth and welcome solitude of the greenhouse. She took a minute to breathe it all in—the soil, the herbs, the fertilizer, the flowers—before flipping on the overhead lights. Pots of all shapes, sizes, and colors cluttered the shelves and tables. A dusting of potting soil littered the concrete floor. Underneath the heat lamps, as if on a stage, sat a royal blue resin pot. *Hippeastrum*, the label sticking out of the dirt announced.

"The world would call you a Christmas lily, even though you aren't a lily at all." She walked to the next pot and read the label. *Saintpaulia.* An African violet, a flower that wasn't a violet at all, either. Idly, she wondered what they would have called themselves if they'd had a voice in the matter. Would Saintpaulia have labeled herself a violet, as if saying it made it so? Who knew there were so many identity crises in the plant kingdom?

At least they had that in common. For thirty years she'd been Marcia Kathleen Bridges. She was just Kathleen now. Like tearing off a label, she had ripped *Marcia* from her life. Marcia no longer existed.

But a new name didn't make her a new person. A new name didn't make her a person at all. People liked to call her a survivor. But calling her one didn't make it so. No, this new person, this Kathleen Bridges, was nothing more than an empty shell who stubbornly refused to quit breathing.

An empty shell who was staring, unseeing, into the corner where a single, stunning, bright-yellow-and-red daylily bloomed. Kathleen shook herself back into the moment and, for the thousandth time, touched the scarf hiding her scars, the sunglasses covering her eyes, the headphones keeping her mind engaged on anything other than herself. Matt believed she was ready to stop hiding behind walls, to put away her barriers, to face mirrors and engage with people and be in the real world. But what if he was wrong? In order to enter the real world, she would have to relive the past. Was it worth it?

Was he worth it?

She tilted her face toward the sun shining through the greenhouse ceiling and, for the first time in almost four years, she allowed a memory to filter in with the light.

"Grammy! Look! Fairy dust." Kiley's small finger, with its nail painted princess-pink, poked into the dust floating in the sunbeam. "Are you sure it's fairy dust?" Kiley turned her deep brown eyes to her Grammy's bright blue ones. "Mommy says it's just dirt floating around, looking for a place to land and make a mess."

Marcia hooked her finger around the nine-year-old's pinkie and guided her hand to the bottom of the sunbeam. With their fingers interlaced, they drew a heart on the table.

"If the fairy dust was just dirt, our fingers would be dirty." She flipped their palms up. "See? It's fairy dust."

"But what does fairy dust do?" Her precocious Kiley twirled her hand through the sunbeam, watching the dust dance around her fingers.

"Fairy dust makes wishes come true. Make a wish and then blow."

Kiley squinted and scrunched her little nose in deep concentration before she blew as hard as her little-girl lungs allowed.

"What did my big girl wish for?"

The child turned towards her, placed her palms on Marcia's aging cheeks, and squeezed. "Grammy, I wished Lucas would turn into a frog and hop away."

Behind her, the greenhouse door clicked shut and Kathleen's memory floated away on the fairy dust. She squeezed her eyes closed, trying to recapture the girl's face and to smell her peach shampoo.

"I don't need a babysitter," she said, without turning. Matt's every-fifteen-minute check-in was both wonderful and wearying. But what she needed was some time alone to convince herself she was ready to go back into therapy. Intensive therapy hadn't helped her before. How would this time be different? If she couldn't, or wouldn't, do the work, did she have any hope for recovery?

"That's not what I'm doing." Matt's voice held the never-ending tenderness that she both loved and hated.

Refusing to face him, she said, "You haven't left my side for three days. What do you call it if not babysitting?" He didn't deserve her bitterness, but he needed to leave her alone, give her a few fucking minutes.

"Kath, will you face me so we can talk about this?"

For four years, she'd barely spoken to anyone, never let anyone into her home, never allowed thoughts of yesterday or dreams for tomorrow. She'd not reached out to another soul. Then she'd met Matt and everything had changed. She wanted to reach out to him now. She just didn't know how.

"Your therapist said..." Matt started.

"Dammit! I know Lisa told you to keep an eye on me. You've been a good boy. Take a break. I have the plants. I have my headphones. You'll just be across the yard." The look on his face forced her anger to flee. None of this was his fault. He was not the enemy, but he did not understand what he was asking her to endure. She took a deep breath, held it for five seconds, and said, more softly, "I'll come get you if I need you."

"Why don't we compromise? We leave for Charlotte tomorrow, and there are some decisions I don't want to make without your input. How about we work through those and then we'll have breakfast?" His dark brown eyes pleaded with her. She could see where his fingers had been making tracks in his hair. Seth had done the same thing when Marcia was being stubborn.

Kathleen hesitated. "What if I decide not to go?" The words were part question, part dare. What if she did decide not to go?

After her family was murdered, Marcia had spent two months in the hospital before being transferred to an inpatient psychiatric facility called The Center in Charlotte, North Carolina. She hated every moment of it. She had gone to group, and to art, and spent an hour a day with her therapist, Lisa. She'd rarely spoken and then only in monosyllables. Like an old dog, she had obeyed her masters, ate what and when they told her to, followed them from room to room. And when her master sat, she disappeared into a fictional world like a dog disappears into sleep.

The hospital had been days and days of physical pain. But the nurses had never asked her to talk. At The Center, she had been surrounded with people who wanted her to remember, to grieve, to interact. The hospital had probed physical wounds. The Center probed emotional ones.

The other residents, and even some of the therapists, had been scared of her. She could still remember the looks and the whispers. "Isn't she that lady whose family was murdered?" "How does she stand to live?" "Do you really think she was tortured?" "What do you think is under all those bandages?" "Do you think they kept her finger as a souvenir like on *Criminal Minds*?" The staff tried to keep the talk to a minimum, but even they looked at her with interest—and with pity.

Lisa had eventually coaxed her to share small memories, but each time the topic got close to that Christmas Eve, Marcia withdrew. She'd go days without opening her mouth. Finally, unable to bear it anymore, she left The Center, stopped calling herself Marcia, and escaped to her beach house in North Carolina. Marcia had promised Lisa she would find one public place to go regularly, and Kathleen kept Marcia's promise. She went to the same restaurant every night and ordered the same meal. Once a day, Kathleen surrounded herself with people but stayed wholly, untouchably alone.

Then a tall man with salt-and-pepper hair, penetrating brown eyes, and shirt emblazoned with a Minnesota Gopher sat, uninvited, across from her. His presence had been both strong and gentle. He seemed to see something in her no one had seen in almost four years. He was willing to wait patiently for her to let him into her loneliness. He brought love and a dogged determination.

But now the memories were brewing and bubbling out of her subconscious, and even his love could not protect her.

"Kathleen, we have to go to Charlotte. We have to get you help. The nightmares are happening every night. More and more I find you staring at me but not seeing me." He glanced down at her hands, and she knew he was looking at what used to be a finger but was now a mangled reminder of what her nephew had taken from her. He ran his thumb over the bloody scratch marks. "And you keep hurting yourself." He raised his somber gaze to hers and dropped his voice to a gentle whisper. "We need professional help."

"You don't get it." She practically spit the words in his face. "To you this is some sort of adventure, some sort of project you can manage. To me it's life or death." She leaned closer to him. "I know my life was limited at the beach. But I could breathe. I had found a way to endure." She shook her head several times, trying to find the words that might convince them both that returning to Charlotte was a mistake. "I wasn't happy. I don't expect or deserve happiness. But I was managing."

"That's bullshit and you know it. I've spent hours pulling strings to make sure you get to go home at night. No one else there gets to do that!" He paced around the small space, obviously searching for his own mix of words. After several trips back and forth, he stopped and cradled her face in his palms. "Kath, you rarely talk. You only eat enough to survive. And you sleep in a fucking closet. Four days ago you were restrained in a hospital bed because you had clawed yourself to shreds. Your knees and elbows were raw and bleeding from crawling. Since then, you've either slept or kept yourself mired in a fictional world." He swallowed, touched his forehead to hers. "Kathleen, you were *restrained.* That is not managing."

The table shook with the force of her hold. "And whose fault is that?"

Matt jerked as if she'd slapped him. He dropped his hands and took one step backwards.

She leaned her back against the table, gripping the edge until her fingers ached. "I'm sorry I said that. I know none of this is your fault. But I want it to be your fault. I want to take this anger and hurl it at you."

"I wish it worked that way." He moved back to her and placed his hands near hers. Leaning in, he kissed her forehead. "If attacking me helped, I'd gladly suffer the assault. But every time you strike out at me, you become more angry."

"I don't know how to stop it. It's alive in me." She sagged and let her head fall into his chest. "This is why I live in books. When I take a step into the real world, I lose control. Anger flashes out of me before I even recognize I'm angry. I want to hurt everyone around me."

He lifted her chin so he could stare into her dark lenses. "You said you don't want to start over with a new therapist. Lisa has been waiting over three years for you to finish what you two started." He paused. "Love, how many days since they died?"

"Don't. Please."

"You can dig into my skin as hard as you need to," he whispered into what was left of her ear.

She dropped her hands and let her arms dangle at her side. "One thousand four hundred thirty-one," she whispered. Tears threatened but she would not allow them to fall. Crying was the release she did not deserve.

Matt stroked her jaw. "You are many things. Strong. Courageous. Beautiful. But you've had one thousand four hundred thirty-one days without peace."

She shifted out of his embrace. Turning to one of the larger plants, she jerked the plant out by its roots, scattering dirt across the table. "I'm scared."

"Me, too. But it's not a question of *wanting* to do this. No one would want this. The question is, are we *willing* do this? Are we *willing* to see this through?"

She turned to glare at him. "You act like we walk down a path and come out on the other side. I will never be *through* this. Do you expect me to stop missing them? Do you expect me to be normal? That's not even the goal. If that's what you expect, I'll head back to the beach right now."

Matt lifted his hands in apology. "Listen to me for just a second. Okay? When my mom died, my dad really struggled. He went to a grief therapy group and it—"

Silently, she pleaded with Matt to stop comparing, stop pretending he understood, stop applying the pressure.

Oblivious to the stillness that overtook her, Matt kept talking. "Dad tells me that he was surprised to feel guilt and anger. Guilt at working so much. Anger because Mom didn't do the trial treatment. Even angry that she died. The point is, counseling helped. The Center in Charlotte—Lisa—will help you. I will help you."

"Stop it." The words shot out of her mouth. "Your father sits in that house knowing you and your sister are safe." She heaved in a deep breath, not searching for calm but fine-tuning her rage. "I will not see my children at breakfast. At lunch. At a football game." She lowered her voice, and finished on a thick, painful whisper. "I will never give another gift. I will not laugh over memories. I..." She couldn't look at him, didn't want him to see her shame. "I crawled into a closet and *survived*."

She crumbled to the ground, shattering the pot containing the Christmas Lily into fragments. She looked up at him. "I don't think I can do this."

He sat down across from her and checked her palms for cuts. She shifted until their knees touched. "I got up one morning as a mother, a grandmother, a wife. I was Marcia Bridges." She swallowed back the burn in her throat. "Now I have no idea who I am. Who I'm supposed to be. Or even who I'm allowed to be. I'm so filled with—"

"You're so filled with what?"

"Rage." It felt strange how calm the word sounded when her body was a cauldron.

"Do you want to live that way?"

She wanted to go back. To redo. To undo. "What I want and what I deserve are not the same." She scooped up a handful of dirt and let it waterfall through her fingers. Marcia could grow beauty from a tiny seed. Marcia could grow beauty from anything. Could Kathleen?

She stroked his cheek with her dirty fingers. "If I go to Charlotte, if I go to The Center and back to Lisa, the goal will be to excise the hate." She found her sunglasses where they'd fallen among the broken pots, hid behind the dark lenses, then stood and began to pick up the jagged pieces.

From his place on the floor, he lifted his arm and silently asked for her hand.

Instead of taking his hand, she looked at the sun through the greenhouse ceiling. She raised her hand into the sunbeam, watched the dust dance over her fingers. "My granddaughter called this fairy dust. I used to tell her to wish on it."

Matt stood, wrapped one arm around her waist, and lifted his hand to join hers in the sun. "What would you wish for?"

Marcia had been comfortable with love and afraid of anger. Kathleen was comfortable with anger and afraid of love. "You want me to wish away the hate. But, Matt, all I am is hate."

Matt

Matt Nelson pushed through the back door of his parents' home, moved through the mudroom, and walked to the bay window overlooking the backyard greenhouse. The smell of coffee and sizzling bacon barely registered. For the last three days he'd stayed close enough to hear Kathleen call out to him. Now they were separated only by a backyard and he still didn't like it.

His dad, Joe, wore his ubiquitous flannel pajama pants and a shirt so ancient the only thing left of the Minnesota Gopher logo was the buck teeth. The normalcy of the scene helped to settle Matt.

"Sit down," Joe said, with a voice only a father could perfect. "You can see the greenhouse from the chair. Trust me, I know. I often watched your mom from here during her final weeks."

Matt accepted the coffee and joined his father at the table, shifting his chair to face the window. His father had been by her side when his mother was dying of cancer, but Matt couldn't bear to watch her suffer. He hadn't stopped carrying the guilt of not visiting her enough. Would he do any better with Kathleen? Was emotional pain easier to watch than physical pain? He wished his father could tell him how to help Kathleen recover.

Matt sighed and looked out the window again until he saw Kathleen's shadow move inside the greenhouse. His mind wandered back ten weeks to the first time he ever saw her, hiding on that beach. He'd been wearing flip-flops instead of wingtips, and he'd sat on a barstool on a beach in North Carolina watching his Minnesota Twins, eating wings, and trying not to admit to himself how much he had come to dread most aspects of his life, how he hated being a tax attorney and having his name on the front door of the family firm. He was 51 years old and just now discovering how unhappy he was in the real world.

He didn't even know what he was doing on vacation—the first one he'd taken in a decade—except that his mother had written him a letter before she died. In it she begged him to come to this very restaurant on this very beach to look for a mysterious woman. How could he not?

He was sitting there feeling foolish when this petite woman, wearing a blue dress, dark sunglasses, and a wildly colored scarf, had stepped onto that deck in that restaurant on that nowhere beach and changed his world. For the first time in his life, Matt saw someone he wanted—needed—to know. Kathleen's brokenness called to him on a level he didn't bother to question. And since then, it had been ten weeks of discovery, of love, of crisis, of chaos. But why would his mother trust him to stand by Kathleen better than he had stood by her when she needed him most?

Matt shifted his gaze from the greenhouse to his father. "She has these nightmares," Matt whispered, remembering the fresh marks on his arms where she'd clawed at him. Without warning, Kathleen would roll out of bed in the middle of the night and crawl toward the closet. When he tried calling her name—first Kathleen, then Marcia—she stumbled and paused as if she heard something but couldn't find the source. He tried grabbing her and holding her to his chest. He tried shaking her and using a firm, commanding voice. But she never saw him. Never seemed to see anything.

"Dad, she can't stand to look in her own eyes because they remind her of her son." Matt knew he was violating Kathleen's privacy, but he needed to tell someone. "When she's awake, she reads one novel after another. I can only get her to sleep if I read to her." Matt stopped. He didn't want his father to see his Kathleen as only this broken person, and he didn't want his father to see him floundering. Floundering was not in the Nelson family culture, and it shamed Matt to be stumbling, but he had to say what was true.

"She's not getting better." For months, Matt had watched his mother suffer terrible physical pain. But his mother had been able to rest and receive pain medicine and, more important, she had understood what was happening to her. This—this unknown, frightening place that Kathleen was facing—was worse. He could hold her and love her, but he could not give her a prescription for inner demons.

Every day, she withdrew further into some fictional story, and every night she disappeared into terror. He couldn't watch her continue to fight unseen monsters, and he could not fight them for her. "The only solution I can see is in Charlotte."

Matt looked around his mother's kitchen. His father had changed nothing in the months since she'd died. Her collection of silly coffee mugs still lined the top of the cabinets—mugs that had become less whimsical and more brazen as he and Patti grew. He studied the mug in his hand, the one with *Shuh da fuh cup* winding languidly around it in elegant calligraphy. For the last several years, it had become a competition between him, Patti, and his nephews. Who could find the most asinine mug? There was considerable incentive: the winner didn't have to help clean the breakfast dishes and earned a year's worth of bragging rights. Last Christmas, his nephew Joey had won with a mug that said *I do not spew profanities, I enunciate them clearly like a fucking lady.* His mother had used that mug even when all she could stomach was water. Matt hadn't realized it until he'd met his Kathleen, but he missed fun. He wanted fun traditions back in his life. Fun traditions he and Kathleen would create, that were theirs alone.

Would that ever be possible?

With his fingertips, he reached beneath the table until his fingers found the words he had carved into the wood with the small pocketknife his grandfather had given him: *Matt Nelson is the bomb.* He'd been about twelve. His mother had found him there, wood dust on his face. She'd been angry for a day and then she decided that the carving would be a great way to embarrass him with a future girlfriend.

Matt wondered what stories Kathleen had to tell. What crazy things had her kids, Courtney and Brice, done? What were they good at? What made them laugh or cry or get angry? How had they spent their Sunday mornings?

He rose and refilled his coffee cup, then his father's, before returning to his guardpost. "She's so tired. I don't see how she keeps moving. A weaker person would have collapsed already." The strength she exerted to keep everything buried, to keep breathing, astounded him. Humbled him. From the moment he'd seen her across that beach restaurant, a protective instinct he'd never known existed beat in his heart and demanded that he gather her to him.

"You need rest," Joe said.

Matt almost scoffed. When was the last time—or the first time—he had considered his own needs? His pattern was to move from one responsibility to the next. Even if he did know what he needed, Kathleen's needs had to trump his.

Hoping his weariness didn't show, Matt stared at the table before he looked at his father. "At her beach house, she has this room. It's at the top of the stairs and it's locked. *Locked* locked. Seven locks. One for each person she lost, even the

Journey to Hope

dog. On the wall next to the locked door, there are these tally marks. I didn't understand at first. Then, God, Dad, when I got it."

His dad didn't respond except to look at Matt with compassion and support.

"She was counting the days. Can you imagine? Every day, her only way to remember them was to make a black mark on the wall."

Matt pointed to the family pictures his mother had scattered everywhere. "Kathleen has twenty-five pictures in her living room, all of them turned backwards." Matt swallowed. "Until she met me, she'd not once said their names. She's afraid of them. How do I help her get her family back?"

Joe grabbed Matt's forearm, leaned closer to him. "Matt, I agree she needs to get help. But it's not your responsibility."

That unexplainable protective instinct moved into Matt's chest, giving his voice a defensive edge. "I'm not abandoning her. If she insists on going back to that half-life on the beach, I'll go with her. I'll pick her up when she breaks. I'm just trying to prevent that."

Matt buried his face in his palms and scrubbed at his eyes. At work, he told people what to do and they did it. And when he gave instructions, he knew he was making the right decision for his clients and his employees. But he played games with people's money, not their very lives. Now, he was playing with Kathleen's life and he was fucking scared. She'd already told him twice that sometimes she wanted to die. He didn't believe she would hurt herself, but what if he was wrong? What if whatever the therapists forced her to confront in Charlotte tipped the scales? What if she made that one final decision because of him?

"When are you planning to leave?" Joe asked.

"Tomorrow." Matt wasn't sure if he felt relief or dread.

"Tomorrow?" His sister's voice echoed his words. She spoke from the hallway, her tone shrill and accusatory.

"Good morning to you, too," Joe said, rising to make his oldest child coffee.

Patti ignored her dad and kept her eyes on Matt. "If you leave tomorrow, how in the hell will we properly transition the cases?"

Matt chose to ignore Patti's tone. The last time he had seen his sister, he had proudly introduced his Kathleen. Patti had treated her like a contagion and dared to ask Kathleen how she could stand to be alive. It was no wonder Kathleen had bolted and found a closet to hide in. It was Patti's fault that Kathleen had had to be tied down in a hospital. It was Patti's fault they were in this crisis mode. But he wouldn't fight with her. Fighting with his sister seemed ridiculous with all the other problems swirling around him. "It's more complicated now."

Patti took the coffee from her dad but stayed on the opposite side of the kitchen, using the island as a buffer between them. "You can't give me a few days?"

"It's at least a three-day trip if we allow for rest along the way."

Patti pointed at the ceiling. "Planes, Matt. You can make the flight in four hours."

"Yes, Patricia." He knew he sounded condescending, but he didn't care. "There are planes. But I need to have my car and I need to take more clothes than I can carry in luggage. Plus, I'd like to spend the time with Kathleen."

"Fine, drive. But give me one damn week."

She was being such a bitch. If he didn't know his sister better, he'd believe she was jealous. "I can't and, quite frankly, I don't want to. This place we're going to has a three-month waiting list. Because they have a history with Kathleen and because she is in crisis, they are willing to get her in sooner.

I cannot—will not—call them now and ask for more special treatment."

"She's been alone for a long time. Why can't you put her on a plane and then get there after you help me?"

"Patti, I am not leaving her." Matt pointed across the lawn. "She's in the greenhouse and even that feels too far." Even if he could leave her alone, he didn't want to go to the office. He was over the sixty-hour weeks. He was over working weekends. He was over going home alone. He'd been over it for years.

"My God, Matt, you've only known her for a few weeks!"

His sister didn't get it. Kathleen was trusting him with all of herself. The first time they'd made love, she'd been rigid, her fists balled into the sheets, her face white with dread and the certainty of his disgust. But she'd also been desperate to be seen and heard and loved. She'd allowed him to unbutton her top and look at what was left of her torso. He'd touched, stroked, and kissed each scar. Everything about her astonished and humbled him. Her bravery. Her strength. Her vulnerability. He, too, was desperate to be seen, to be heard, to be loved. He was privileged to be in her life, to learn from her and help her return to life. "Patti," he said, with the calm conviction of the one thing he was certain of, "I love her."

His sister's shoulders dropped and she huffed out a loud, annoyed breath. "All I'm asking for is one more day." She turned to their dad. "I'm sure even Dad agrees with me. Nelson Nelson and Jones is the family firm. Dad's legacy to us."

Joe looked toward the greenhouse. "We don't get to choose what others need, how others suffer, how others recover. All we can do is hold their—"

Patti slammed her mug on the table. "I'm so sick of him getting all the support around here! Matt, you call me from a beach in the middle of nowhere, tell me Mom sent you on some errand and that you've fallen in love. Now you're moving to North Carolina with a woman you've known for a total of ten weeks? You're acting like an eighteen-year-old."

Matt watched his sister closely. Her fingers were white where she gripped her coffee mug. Her eyes were wide, and she sat with her shoulders thrown back as if she were waiting to pounce. What the hell? He and Patti had a great relationship. He enjoyed time with her and Dave and the boys. Patti was compassionate. Or at least she had been. This venomous person was not his sister.

He tried to ease the tension in the room. "Patti, I'm not heading off to join the circus. I'm helping the woman I love face something you and I can never understand." Patti needed to back off and give him some of that compassion. Kathleen was spiraling but so was he. He needed to catch his breath and he could only do that once Kathleen was safe. Safety meant going to The Center in Charlotte.

Tears sprang to Patti's eyes. "You think taking care of this woman is what Mom wanted? Is this your penance?"

Penance? Matt hadn't spent as much time with his mother as Patti had, but he had been taking care of the family firm. He had been making sure his dad could stay home and not worry about the family legacy. Now he wanted some time off. Patti lived in California—away from the much busier home office. She played golf on the weekends. She sat in the board meetings. But Matt prepared board meetings. If anyone needed to pay penance, it was his sister.

She stood to leave. Matt could see that she was fighting back tears. "Did you forget your promise to take Jake and Joey to the football game this weekend? Don't worry, Mattie. I'll explain you have to finish your humanitarian project. Wear your halo. I'll keep taking care of things. It's your life you're ruining, not mine."

The sound of Kathleen's shuddered breath forced Matt to spin around. His Kathleen stood at the entry to the kitchen, staring at him as if she didn't quite know who he was.

"I don't want you to break promises because of me," she whispered. "I don't want to be a humanitarian project."

"Love." He was afraid that if he moved toward her, she'd collapse. He extended his hand, palm up. Kathleen stood utterly still. Seeking guidance, Matt risked a look at his dad. But Joe gripped his coffee cup and watched Kathleen as if he was ready to catch her if she fell.

She gripped the doorframe and, even from across the room, he could see her body shudder. Her throat worked and Matt understood that she was trying to stay in the present and not let memories drown her. Finally, she said, "I've ruined enough lives."

Matt moved to stand before her. He didn't touch her, but he stood close enough to hear her ragged breathing. He wanted to take off her sunglasses, but he wouldn't take that away from her right now.

"I have to go to Charlotte, but you don't have to go with me."

"I'm not going because I have to. I'm going because you are my world." He kissed her forehead but otherwise didn't touch her. After several long, tense seconds, she fell into his chest, clutched his waist and held him with whatever strength she still had.

He wasn't paying penance. But he was going to do things differently. This time, he was going to stand next to the person he loved. She needed him and he needed her. He would be her place to rest.

He wrapped her in his arms, bent to her damaged ear, and added, "And it's not *you*. It's *we*."

Kathleen

"The trees are still pretty," Kathleen said. "I never thought I'd see these colors again." Fall in the mountains had always been her favorite time of year. The crisp air. The myriad of colors. Fireplaces and burning leaves charring the air. Kathleen rested her head against the car window, felt the warmth of the sun and the warmth of Matt's hand in hers.

"I had no idea Tennessee was this mountainous," Matt said.

"Other than coming to my beach, what traveling have you done?" She knew the conversation was superficial. But she appreciated that he seemed to understand they both needed a break from the drama. She wanted to prove to him—and to herself—she could be more than a snarky bitch or a sad weakling. She was practicing normal even if it tasted funny on her tongue.

Matt shrugged. "Business trips. Visits to Patti after she moved to California. Would you like to do more traveling?"

His question was innocuous enough, but the topic conjured memories of Seth. They'd had dreams. They had wanted to hike the national parks, see Scotland and Ireland and Australia, take family cruises. They'd talked about becoming expats in Italy. They would never move that far from the kids, but it was fun to practice bad Italian and drink Italian wines. Under that last Christmas tree, wrapped in Mickey

Mouse paper, had been a trip to Disney World for the entire family. "Marcia liked to travel. I'm not sure what Kathleen likes," she said.

It was their third day on the road, and Matt seemed to relax as they moved further and further away from Minnesota. It was the opposite for her. They were now past the halfway point, and it was taking more and more effort not to panic. Every mile brought her closer to The Center, closer to having to sit with Lisa, and Lisa pushing her to relive that night.

"Why don't you close your eyes and sleep?" he said. "We don't hit our next stop for about two hours. I'll just listen to the book, and when you wake we can see if I'm getting any better at figuring out whodunit."

She stroked his thumb with her own, closed her eyes, and let the gentle swaying of the Escalade lull her into a half sleep and a full memory.

She was back at the beach restaurant on what was supposed to be her last visit. She had arranged everything she would need. The pills. The bourbon. She knew how and she knew when. One more dinner. One more look at Seth's favorite beach. One more sunset. She would be dead and with her family by morning.

Then an older woman wearing a Minnesota Vikings shirt and a matching dark purple scarf plopped herself at Kathleen's table. She introduced herself as "Betty from Minnesota," as if being from Minnesota was critical information. The audacity of a complete stranger doing this stunned Kathleen into silence. Betty talked about her cancer, about her bald head and side effects, about how much she enjoyed wearing 'funky' scarves. At first, she didn't require Kathleen to talk. She jabbered about her kids, her grands, her greenhouse in Minnesota. When she asked Kathleen about unique ways to tie a scarf, all Kathleen could imagine was Betty's horror if Kathleen were to peel off her scarf and show the carved flesh, the burn scars,

Journey to Hope

the missing ear, the tufts of hair protruding from the mutilation. Part of Kathleen wanted to do it, to see this woman run away screaming. Part of her savored this tiny penetration into her loneliness.

Eventually Kathleen spoke. Not about her family or her loss. She spoke about gardens and favorite flowers. As she always did, at ten o'clock, Kathleen stood to leave. Betty grabbed her arm and Kathleen flinched. No one had touched her in three years. Not since she'd left The Center. Betty must have noticed Kathleen pull away, but rather than release her, she tightened her hold.

"Whatever you're thinking of doing, don't. Someone will come and help you and give you something to fight for. Will you promise to wait?"

Kathleen didn't want to wait. She was tired. Just so fucking tired.

But Betty, this stranger who seemed to see into Kathleen and who had braved the animosity, continued, "There's no hope for me, but there is for you. Let me give you my courage."

Kathleen stared at the dark ocean, the white breakers and white sand, the full moon. She could hear her granddaughter Kiley shriek at the cold water. She could see her grandson Lucas try to catch the minnows. She could see her son Brice's sunburnt nose. She could smell the hamburgers Seth always grilled. She took off her sunglasses and showed this stranger her eyes. Eyes that matched Brice's. Eyes that were as blue as a cloudless sky. She opened her mouth to tell Betty to mind her own business but instead heard herself say, "For over three years I've waited. I can wait a few more months."

She didn't know what Betty saw in her that night. Despair. Desolation. Determination. But it was as if meeting her caused a space to open inside her. She'd gone home, destroyed the pills, poured out the bourbon. She never understood why she'd agreed to the stranger's request, but she kept the promise.

Betty's son Matt arrived on the tenth of September. One hundred five days before her Christmas Eve deadline. Hoping to scare him off, she'd shown him her disfigured body. But he hadn't recoiled. With his caramel eyes, he'd looked at her with acceptance and love. He'd told her she was strong and that he wouldn't let her go. And now that he was in her life, her family, her precious family, had started talking to her.

"Moms, what's your favorite leaf color?" Courtney asked.

"I've never been able to decide. I'll see a brilliant orangey-red and think that's the one. Then, one leaf will have every shade of yellow and I'll change my mind. What about you?"

"This year it's the ones that are red or yellow but look like they've been burnished. What's that called? You and Stephanie did it with that table."

"Do you mean antiquing?"

"Yeah, antiquing. I like the leaves that look antiqued. Is antiqued a word?"

With her eyes closed, Kathleen laughed. Courtney had an amazing ability to turn any word into a verb.

Then, without warning, Courtney's smile faded, and Kathleen saw her daughter's body drop off the kitchen stool with a thud near her feet. Before she could go to her, Courtney's eyes lost their light.

"Auntie, are you having a lovely Christmas?" Josh straddled Courtney's body and spat in Marcia's face. "Why didn't you invite me for your famous Christmas Eve lasagna? Are you too good for me?" His voice was a horrific combination of menace and excitement, as if he were a little boy at a carnival.

Kathleen's eyes popped open and she saw again the glorious masterpiece of colors. The smoke clouds draped over the ridges like a woman's shawl were achingly familiar. She and Seth had sat on their deck every morning and every evening watching this same mist move around the valley. She sat up straighter and blinked, but she wasn't dreaming. Looming before them was Leeside Mountain, her home, the last place she'd seen her family alive.

"Pull over, pull over, pulloverpullover." A convulsion shook Kathleen's body, sweat bloomed on her forehead and coursed down her spine. She clamped her hand over her mouth and started to whimper, to pray to an entity she no longer believed in. She prayed for rescue from the sickness permeating every pore of her existence.

The car swerved across the highway and down the exit ramp. Before the Escalade came to a full stop, Kathleen opened the door, fell to her knees, and lost the battle. Vomit splattered onto the asphalt. She tried to gulp in fresh air but only succeeded in triggering violent dry heaves.

She jolted when a hand touched her neck. "Seth?" She tucked her chin deep into her neck and focused on breathing through her burning nose.

"Kathleen," an unfamiliar voice called.

Drool leaked from her mouth. "We should have been happy here," she mumbled. "Instead we were destroyed." She watched as the drool dripped from her chin into the mess.

"What's your name?"

She shook her head. What a stupid question for Seth to ask. "Marcia. Marcia Bridges."

"Love, I need you to sit up and give me those eyes."

Love? Seth didn't call her that. He called her hon. *Hon, can you get us another cup of coffee? Hon, do you want some more wine? Hon, I love you.* Where was Seth? It was Seth who held her hair back and soothed her when she was sick. It was Seth who brought her ginger ale.

Hands grasped her forearms and pulled her into a kneeling position.

"Kathleen, open your eyes."

Keeping her eyes closed, she reached up to grasp the hands touching her face. "Seth, why are you calling me that?"

She pulled her head away from the strange touch and tore at the painful itch where her ear used to be.

"It will help if you open your eyes." The voice sounded as afraid and confused as she felt. "Please, tell me your name."

She didn't understand. "My name's Marcia." She shook out of his hold. "No, no. That's not right. I was Marcia. But Marcia died." She opened her eyes and glanced behind the man. "I don't want to be here."

The man's hands cradled her neck as if he knew her intimately. She looked into his wide, tear-filled eyes. He was being so very gentle. But she didn't deserve gentleness. She tried to pull away, but he held her with his thumbs tracing the pulsing veins under her ears.

"Keep your eyes on mine. Don't look anywhere else." His voice was a tender command.

When his face came fully into focus, her thoughts slowed and became more manageable. She knew this man. This man was safety. This man ran her a bath every night. This man read to her so she could sleep. This man saw her scars and still held her when she slept in the closet. "You're Matt Nelson. Your mother sent you to my beach. You wouldn't go away." She frowned at him for a few seconds before she snuggled her cheek into his palm.

He breathed out a long breath, touched his lips to her forehead. "And I won't be going away now or ever."

She looked again at the mountain where her home used to be. She and Seth had bought the cabin years before he retired. They'd spend weekends on the mountain, dreaming of the day they would retire and enjoy the oasis full time. "We grew blackberries. Seth made blackberry pie and blackberry wine and even tried to make blackberry beer. I would spend hours in the kitchen making jars and jars of jam."

Her nephew Josh had loved the blackberry ice cream. He and Courtney would sit on the deck, their little legs swinging, shoveling the treat in as fast as they could. No matter how much ice cream he ate, Josh would want more. Marcia had watched him grow into his gangly legs while his freckles faded and he became a handsome young man.

"He ate my blackberries," she whispered to herself before she stuffed Josh's image into the pit of anger.

Matt carefully lifted her from the ground, moved them away from the mess. He settled against the car and pulled her into his lap, wrapping his arms tightly around her. He continued his caress, moving his fingers into her hair. When she shivered, he said, "We need to get cleaned up."

Kathleen didn't shift. "I've always been afraid of vomiting. Seth said I become a three-year-old. Even at my age, I usually cry and literally beg my body to behave. I used to pray and try to bargain with God." She'd served God with time and money. She'd taught her kids to love Him. She'd had a sincere faith. But God had abandoned her while her family died and she was tortured. If He existed, then she hated Him. When she thought of God, that ever-present fury burned hotter in her throat. She had Matt. She had herself. She had help in Charlotte. She did not need a mythical god.

Her head tilted toward the mountain. "The cabin was only twenty minutes from here. This was my village."

Matt looked shocked. "I swear I didn't think of that. I just planned the most scenic route."

She placed her cheek on his heart and focused on his warmth. "Their ashes are scattered up on that mountain. Stephanie—she was my best friend." She paused, thinking how little Matt still knew about her. "She brought their urns to the hospital. But, I—" She pulled her head back and found his eyes again. "I didn't want them sitting on a window ledge in the hospital." She glanced back at her mountain. "So Seth's family spread them on the trails behind our cabin." The same trails she and Stephanie had walked together every day. Now that was lost to her, too, just like everything else.

Matt trembled but he didn't speak. It was as if he knew she needed his arms but not his words.

She shook her head, twisted her fingers into the cotton of his shirt. Focusing intently on his eyes, hoping he could see her conviction, she said, "I should have died with them. I should be scattered on that mountain, too."

Matt

Matt stroked Kathleen's hip as she slept next to him on the bed. Her translucent skin and the deep purple circles under her eyes plagued him. "I'm sorry," he murmured. "If I'd known, I would've been more careful."

He had found them a luxury hotel in downtown Asheville. As advertised, it was lovely, with a large living area and separate bedroom. After a hot bath and a minimal meal, she'd climbed into the bed, curled into a fetal position, and fallen into the deep sleep of someone physically and mentally exhausted. Matt had sat with her until the sun dipped below the horizon, pretending not to be terrified about Kathleen's reaction on the mountain. Now he clicked off the lamp, pulled the blanket up to her chin, and kissed her cheek.

She had worn the scarf to bed for the first time since he'd first slept with her. Not wanting her to hide from him, he carefully untied the knot and slid the fabric away. With the lightest touch, he traced her bumpy flesh. "I'll just be in the living area. The light will be on but all you need to do is say my name and I'll be here." He knew she wouldn't hear him, but he wanted the words in the air as if they would drift down and cover her.

The first days of the trip had been so beautiful—the scenery and the companionship. They'd argued over the clues in the audiobook. They'd found silly tourist attractions to visit.

They'd held hands and made love. It was normal. It was perfect. And then his thoughtlessness, his incompetence, had shattered their peaceful bubble and sent Kathleen to a place he didn't understand.

She didn't stir as he rose from the bed and retrieved his phone from its charger. When he left the room, he kept the door open an inch so he could peek in without disturbing her.

He wanted to call his father. But there was nothing his dad could do except worry. He wanted to call his sister, but he was still angry that she, in the last few days, hadn't asked, even once, about how he and Kathleen were doing. Instead, she'd left messages whining about clients. Not knowing what else to do, he paced in the living area and dialed the number for The Center in Charlotte.

"The Charlotte Center answering service, my name is Tammy. Is this an emergency?"

"My name is Matt Nelson and I need to speak to Lisa Barnett."

"Is this an emergency?"

Matt looked toward the bedroom and considered how to respond. "I'm calling about Kathleen Conners. Lisa was—is—her therapist. She's not in any imminent danger but I really need to speak to Lisa."

Matt heard a keyboard clicking before Tammy spoke again. "Well, you're in luck. Lisa Barnett is the on-call therapist tonight. I'll contact her and she'll call you. Please give me your number and repeat the patient's name."

Matt provided the information, ended the call, and peered in to make sure Kathleen had not moved. He just needed someone to tell him what to do. And, though he was loath to admit it, he wanted reassurance that he could handle this.

The phone buzzed in his palm, jerking Matt from his worry. "Lisa?"

"Is everything all right? Kathleen okay?"

"Yes. No. Shit, I don't know."

"Matt, can you take a deep breath."

"Am I hurting or helping? Am I asking her to face too much?"

"Whoa, hold on for a second. Let's focus. Are you on your way to Charlotte?"

"Maybe she's right. Maybe the beach is the only place she can have any type of life."

"Tell me why you encouraged her to make the trip to Minnesota." Lisa was using the same technique he used with clients who had been summoned by the IRS. Get the client to relax by redirecting the conversation.

"There were a few business things I needed to do. I didn't want to leave her alone and I truly thought getting away from the beach would be good for her. But she's crumbling." He took a deep breath and told Lisa about the afternoon's disaster.

"You told the answering service this wasn't an emergency. You're wrong. The dam is being battered and will soon—very soon—collapse. Where is she now? Update me on how she's been since then."

"She would only nibble at the food I ordered. The usual six bites but the smallest bites she could create. She hasn't spoken much. She didn't read or even want to listen to a book. I've been reading to her at night and she shook that off, too. She just wanted to bathe and go to sleep."

"Being physically ill in and of itself is hard on the body. Add to that the trauma of facing her mountain—well, I think she's doing all she can right now. Sleep will help. You'll be here soon. Just try to get her to eat, sleep, engage. Keep conversation focused only on light topics. Matt, unless she mentions her family, steer clear of the topic until you get here."

"Lisa, what if you're wrong?"

"Matt," she started in her consummate therapist tone and then annoyed him further with a long pause. "It doesn't matter where she is. It's time. It's past time. Here's the truth of the matter. The small snippets of memory—the mountain, these conversations with her family members—we keep saying she's starting to remember. But that's not accurate—she's not remembering. She's reliving. The sights, the sounds, the smells, the words, the pain—it's as if she's catapulted backwards. That's the confusion you've seen; her mind and body go to that place again. It's not uncommon in her type of PTSD. And it will continue—and get worse—until she gets help."

Matt thought about his mother and her last few days of hospice. The nurses couldn't quite manage the pain. His dad had suffered. Patti had been trying not to cry. He'd had to act like he had it all together. He compared that to what Kathleen had to face. Her pain—physical, mental, emotional. Her family's pain. Those final moments. The last words spoken. The last words *not* spoken. That last eye contact. Guilt. Regret. And rage—so much rage. Of course she was scared.

"I'm at a loss for what to do, how to be."

"Exactly. You're at a loss because what she's dealing with is bigger than you, bigger than her. Look, Matt, coming here isn't just about her. It's a balancing act all PTSD families struggle with. How to be supportive and protective. How *not* to enable in an unstable environment. And, in some ways, it's harder for you because you're accustomed to stability and you've been thrown into the deep end. Is she sleeping in the closet?"

Matt leaned back against the couch, stared at the ceiling. Sighing, he answered her, "In Minnesota, we slept in the closet three out of four nights. Since we've left Minnesota, it's been every night."

"How does she explain that to you?"

"She just slips down to the floor and crawls away. Her eyes are open but I'm sure she's not seeing anything. I do know she makes no noise. I join her and when we get up we both pretend nothing is amiss."

"What about nightmares? Crying?"

Journey to Hope

After letting out a frustrated breath, he said, "I assume it's a nightmare sending her scrambling to the closet. But as I said, there is no outward sign of a nightmare. No thrashing. No crying out. No moaning. She's there one minute and in the closet the next. She never cries."

"Tears and crying serve a very important function. But it's not only the lack of crying. In the hospital she went through serious physical torment with no help at all. You can't make a patient take pain medication if they don't want to. If she could refuse it, she did."

"Why would she do that?"

"She wanted—needed—to suffer."

His chest tightened with his own tears. He couldn't imagine the pain she must have endured.

"She acts like that night is gone—as if she hit a delete key and erased the fact that she was there. But she was there. She saw everything. She crawled to a closet that night for survival. She's doing the same thing now. She believes facing the horrors will destroy her. When she gets here, my job will be to show her the opposite is true. Are you sure you want to help her out of this closet? It will be quite difficult to watch." Lisa was gentle with the question. She would not judge him if he bolted.

"I'm not some cheesy, romantic type. I would have scoffed at anyone who said what I'm about to say. But from the first moment I saw her at the beach—sitting there so alone, so lovely in a blue dress, staring at the ocean—my entire body reacted. I sat 50 feet away from her and felt her enter and leave that restaurant. She felt me, too. She took off those damn sunglasses and those blue eyes pierced me—heart and soul." His laugh was humorless. "Then she ran—literally. And so did I. It freaked me out. While I waited for a cab to take me to the airport, I opened another one of the letters from my mom. That letter directed me to a specific restaurant and a specific

37

woman. She wanted me to find Kathleen, but I already had." The miracle of that coincidence had sealed his love and his commitment to Kathleen. What freaked him out was his overwhelming desire—need—to enter her brokenness—to live there, if that's what it took to be with this woman. He'd not been looking for love or a relationship. But now that he had met Kathleen, he understood just what a gift love is. He understood his parents' unwavering commitment to each other. He understood his place with Kathleen. He paused, took in a deep breath. "Just give me some advice on how to help her."

"You can't make her come here, but you can make it clear you are limited in your ability to help her. You can let her know you're drowning, too."

"I'm not drowning." Shit, maybe he was, but it was his job to keep them both afloat, not weigh Kathleen down with his problems and doubts and worries.

"Then why are we on the phone in the middle of the night?" Lisa's tone was gently challenging.

He let the question sit between them while he checked on his Kathleen. The bed was empty. She was huddled asleep in the closet, shivering on the cold floor.

"Because she deserves more than this." What he didn't admit to Lisa was that he couldn't live like this. Worried all the time. Afraid of every move, every decision. Never sleeping. If The Center was what she needed, then he'd get her there. "We'll be there Monday."

He tossed the phone on the bed and made a place for himself behind Kathleen in the closet. He tucked her against him and whispered, "I can't do this alone." He was scared for her. For himself. For all the mistakes yet to be made. But he'd promised to stand next to her. He would keep that promise no matter the cost.

Journey to Hope

Matt woke in the closet. Alone. Kathleen's pillow was gone, and she had wrapped the blanket around him much like he had for her the night before. He slowly rolled over, listening to his middle-aged body complain. After talking to Lisa, he understood that getting to Charlotte was imperative and could not be delayed. It would take two hours to drive to Charlotte and then another 48 hours before they would check into The Center. He promised himself he'd make damned sure she relaxed. He would do everything in his power to keep her safe for two more days.

Before he'd fallen asleep, he'd put together a plan. They were both used to daily exercise and that had been forgotten. This morning, they would go to an outdoor supply store and buy boots and socks. Backpacks. Protein bars. Water. They were going on a hike. If she was afraid to go into the store, she'd be safe in the car with her earphones. While there might be other people on the trails, there would be no expectation of interaction. It would be her and him and the crisp air. Tomorrow, they'd drive to Charlotte, settle in a hotel. They would go to the movies. They'd hide in the dark, eat popcorn, drink soda. He could find her a bookstore. Without saying a word, he would show her what their lives could be like.

Excited to get going, Matt rose, yawned, and went in search of his Kathleen. The bed was empty. The bathroom light was off. The living area was in shadows. "Kathleen," he called. Where was she?

He found a note in her messy handwriting tossed on the bed. *The fitness center—K*

He pulled on sweatpants, snagged his room key, and pursued her to the rooftop fitness center. Maybe he was acting as a babysitter, but after yesterday he didn't care.

Stepping out of the elevator, he could see her through the glass door as she ran on the treadmill. Her outfit was exactly what she wore when she walked the beach—black yoga pants, black shirt, scarf, earphones. He smiled at the Gophers scarf his father had given her. He craned his neck and saw a towel and her sunglasses sitting on a weight bench. She was beautiful, with muscled legs and tan skin. He'd always dated tall women, but her petite five-foot frame fit perfectly under his chin. He loved how her eyes were blue as a Minnesota sky. She never let anyone behind those glasses. She never showed anyone her anguish. No one except him.

Paying closer attention, he noticed her legs quivering, the bright red of her face, the strangeness of her gaze. Something was wrong. She was all-out sprinting.

As he opened the door, cold air and the rancid smell of sweat assaulted him. "Kathleen," he called. Her eyes were wide, unblinking. She didn't slow or turn in his direction. "Kathleen?" he said louder.

She ran on.

"Kath," he raised his voice almost to a shout.

She ran on.

He reached over and gently tugged the earphone out of her left ear. No reaction. Carefully he touched her wet shoulder with his fingertip. "Kathleen."

She jolted, and her body collapsed to the mat. She flew backwards and slammed into the floor. Her head cracked against the linoleum.

Rushing to her side, Matt checked the back of her head for blood. "Talk to me. Tell me where you are." He tried to sound calm.

Kathleen shook her head from side to side as if trying to shirk off his touch. Her eyes darted to him, to the mirror, to the treadmill, to the weights. She opened her mouth, closed it. Her eyes shot back to his and he watched as her disorientation shifted to anxiety.

He kept his hands underneath her head to cushion it from the hard floor. "Relax. Keep your eyes with me."

Her eyes held his as if he was a tether.

"Where are you? Who is with you?"

She looked left, right, and back to him. "The fitness center."

He heaved out a long breath and fought the desire to pick her up, throw her in the car, and race to Charlotte. "Are you hurt?"

She looked at him as if the question made no sense. "I think I'm fine." She touched her head and winced. "Bruised, maybe." She lifted her left leg and looked at the exposed area of her calf. "Road rash."

"Stay down for a few more minutes." He checked her scraped calf. Checked her other leg, her elbows. Nothing antibiotic cream couldn't handle. But Lisa was right. This was a fucking emergency.

"Let me get up," she said hoarsely, "I feel stupid lying here like this."

He wound his arm around her waist and guided her to the elevator, trying to hide his fury. All he wanted was for the next 48 hours to be drama-free. A hike. The movies. No trauma.

Once they were in their room, he steered her toward a chair before he found some water in the bar. "Drink."

She took the bottle and began to drink as if her body screamed for hydration.

He walked to the closet, yanked the blanket off the floor and covered her shivering body.

"I'm sorry," she said with a trembling voice.

His anger melted away. None of this was her fault. Dropping to his haunches in front of her, he took the empty water bottle and held her hands. "Don't apologize. You did nothing wrong. It just scared me." He handed her the fresh bottle of water. "Drink more, please."

After she took several gulps, he asked, "What time did you get up? Did you go straight to the gym?"

"Four, four-thirty or so. I couldn't go back to sleep, so I thought exercise might help."

Matt looked at the clock. "Almost two hours." He took in a deep breath, looked back to Kathleen. "Can you explain what happened?"

She picked at the water bottle label instead of looking at him. "My book quit playing and I couldn't get it fixed." Her nails scraped against the plastic, the sound like fingernails on a chalkboard. "No book. Nothing but me. I thought about Lisa, about The Center, about…." She choked but continued to speak, "After yesterday, I just—."

He tilted her chin so their eyes met. "You just what, Kathleen?"

"I want to run away." She dug her fingernails into his forearm. "Don't you see? I can't stop the voices."

"I thought you liked talking to your family," he said. When she'd first told him she heard their voices, he had been alarmed. But then his father had told him he continued to talk and listen to his mom. They'd spent fifty years together, his father had explained, and talking to her was still the best part of his day.

Kathleen looked at him with wide, haunted eyes. "Not them. My nephew and his friends. He taunts me, laughs at me, accuses me."

Matt knew very little about that Christmas Eve. She'd asked him not to dig for the details. She wanted the opportunity to tell him when she was ready. But he did know that her nephew was the ringleader of the drug-addled, murderous gang of men who entered her home that night. "That's why we need to get to Charlotte," he said.

"I want to go to the beach first."

That was not the right answer. He stood and paced in front of her. "Fuck, fuck, fuck," he muttered.

"Matt —"

"Just give me a second to calm down." He tried to take the bite out of his voice but wasn't sure he succeeded. "I made us a promise." He bowed his head and whispered, "I do not know how to help you. You can't expect me to keep fucking this up and causing you more pain. But I can't seem to get a handle...."

"A handle on me? Is your project not going as planned?"

He blew out a breath and kept his mouth shut. He didn't deserve her venom, but she depended on him to be rational. He would have to fake it.

She stood and the blanket fell, pooling at her feet. The water bottle crumpled and sloshed water down her arm. "I did not ask you to come to my beach. I did not ask you to approach me." She shoved her finger into his chest, poked him with each sentence. "I did not ask you to sit on my porch. I have not asked you for one damn thing."

He gently caught her finger, lowered her arm. "Kath, let's both calm down."

She pulled her arm out of his hand and hurled the bottle past his head. "I was managing. I had a life. I was making it."

Unable to stop himself, he shouted, "You were not. You did not have a life. You were one step into the abyss, and you know it. YOU KNOW IT." He rested his palms on his knees and fought to put the anger away. "You were either going to fall over the edge or someone had to pull you back."

"Who designated you to pull me back? Maybe I didn't want to be pulled back."

He forced himself not to grab her by the shoulders and shake. He didn't want to hurt her—never that—but he wanted her to see the truth. "Bullshit. You could have gotten rid of me at any time. You could have simply locked your door. Shit, Kathleen, you wear a fucking sign."

"And what does this sign say?"

Her sarcastic tone re-lit his barely tamped fuse. "'Stay the Fuck Away From Me or Suffer the Consequences.'" He shook his head, unclenched his fists. "Kathleen, I'm sorry. That was…" He needed to get his shit together. Yelling at each other was not going to help. They needed to pack and get their asses to Charlotte.

When she spoke again, her voice was more curious than angry. "Why didn't you stay away?"

Her blue eyes blazed and reminded him of the first time he'd seen her at that nowhere beach. He still felt that desire to stand alongside her, to be her knight in shining armor, no matter what it cost him.

Exhausted, he sat down in one of the chairs. "I wanted to. I bought a one-way ticket as far from you as I could get." He wondered what she saw in his eyes. "I couldn't do it. I couldn't leave you." Maybe he should have gotten on that damn plane. But, even with all the drama and pain, he still wanted her next to him.

"You can leave now." She pointed at the door. "I don't want this."

"What do you want?" He felt like he was in a negotiation with a difficult client. The most important negotiation of his life, about their life together.

"I want my hair to grow! I want to sleep in a bed! I want the voices to stop." She crumpled into the chair next to him. "I want my family back."

He stroked her cheek and lowered his voice, "I can't give you that…" He lifted her chin so they were eye to eye. "Have I told you my vision of us? We are laughing and traveling to all the places in the world we've never seen. I see us digging in the dirt in our backyard, in the home we create together. Your pictures are on our wall and we add more. I see my family becoming your family and yours becoming mine. I see us together. I see a happily ever after."

Wrapping her arms around her waist, she pulled away from him.

He dropped to his knees beside her. "I can't give you back what you've lost. But I can give you love and a safe place to rest and to remember." She stiffened and remained silent. "My dad told me my mother refused an experimental treatment that might have extended her life." He stopped because he needed to swallow back the emotion clogging his throat. "I've never given much thought to heartbreak. I haven't had to. But now I know what heartbreak is. When you want *more* and the one you love doesn't."

"That was different. It's not fair..."

"It is different. They had over fifty years together. A lifetime behind them. What you're doing is worse."

She sucked in an audible breath, but he kept talking.

"We have a lifetime *ahead* of us. But we can't have that without Lisa and The Center. We can't have it unless you want it."

"I'm not giving up. I just want to rest for a while. Prepare myself."

He knew there was no preparing for what lay ahead. He also knew that if she went back to that beach, she'd never leave again. He stood and stroked her cheek, "What will we do, spend our days pretending there is no world? Keep all your memories behind a locked door? Pretend Seth and Brice and Courtney never existed? Hope the voices stop?" He leaned over, snuggled his cheek to hers and whispered into her mangled ear. "I'm trying to decide what to do if you give up now. *My* happily ever after seems out of reach."

She turned so they were toe to toe. "Do you know what my life will be like? Sitting in a dreary room listening to women tell their pathetic stories. Sitting in Lisa's office while she carves me apart. They won't be happy until I see it, taste it, smell it. LIVE IT AGAIN. Every word, every gunshot, every scream. That's what you are asking me to do. I couldn't do it last time. What if this time is no different?"

"You were alone last time. Now you're not. You have me. I have you. Can we at least try? As crazy as this sounds, I believe your family and my mother orchestrated this. They're all tired of watching us live these half-lives."

She studied his face for several seconds before whispering, "She told me you were my gift."

He took two steps away from her. "I want us to find out what we're meant to be. But I want all of you—the past, the present and the future. If you don't want that—if you can't do that—well..." He didn't know how to finish the sentence because her refusal was untenable.

"And if I can't do it?"

He swiped at his wet eyes. "I'll get you safely home. Then, I'll figure out my own life."

Quietly, he went into the bedroom, changed into running clothes, and grabbed his headphones. When he returned to the living area, Kathleen's palms rested on the cool window as if that pane of glass kept her prisoner. She didn't turn toward him when she said, "I feel like you're threatening me."

He kissed the crown of her head. "No, love. It's not a threat. It's the reality of the situation. We get in the car and drive to Charlotte together. Or I drive you to the beach."

He left the room without another word.

He cranked the volume on Led Zeppelin and tried to outrun his sense of powerlessness. He ran as fast as he could, but the defeat in her eyes haunted every mile. They'd come so far, but he didn't know if they'd make it through this. He'd left his home and his job. Would he have to leave her, too?

Kathleen

Kathleen closed her eyes and rested her head against the uncomfortable wingback chair in the hotel room. Matt had asked her what she wanted. She wanted to read for pleasure and not escape. She wanted to spend a full night in a bed. She wanted to tell Matt her family stories. She wanted to be able to remember the beauty before that night. And she wanted her best friend. She wanted Stephanie.

She'd met Stephanie at church twenty-five years ago, serving snacks and listening to children's complaints at Vacation Bible School. Together they had lost and gained the same ten pounds, tried new foods and new places and new hair colors. They'd parented together and sighed with relief when Courtney, the youngest, walked across the college stage. When she and Seth had decided to move permanently to the mountains, Stephanie and Mitch had bought a cabin on the same street. They weren't just friends. Stephanie was her sister in every way but DNA.

If Kathlene were still Marcia, she and Stephanie would be heading to the big apple festival held every October in Leeside. As soon as they would arrive, they would go in opposite directions and the Great Competition began. Whoever found the tackiest creation had to buy the other one coffee. And, to make it worse, the loser had to display the item on her mantle for the entire year. Kathleen had lost that final year. Stephanie had found a Last Supper painting made of velvet, complete with Christmas lights at the disciples' and Jesus's eyes. Jesus's eyes had been blue, and every time Kathleen looked at that hideous display, she'd laugh.

It was Stephanie who had found her that Christmas Eve almost four years ago and Stephanie who had come to the hospital every day for two months. Together they had learned to tie a scarf. Stephanie had shed the tears Kathleen could not. If she were here now, Stephanie would not let her get away with wallowing in self-pity. She would shake Kathleen and force her out of the bubble she had created for herself. But Stephanie was Marcia's friend, and Marcia had died. In order to become Kathleen, she'd had to cut ties with Stephanie. She had shoved her into the same box where her family lived. In one night, Marcia had lost herself, her family, her faith, and her friend.

Now she was pushing Matt away, too. She was tired of being alone, but she wasn't sure she knew how to do relationships anymore. After her years without contact, she no longer knew how to manage conflict. Her anger was too hot to control, and that beast wanted to lash out, hurt others the way she hurt. The beast ruled her mind, keeping her thoughts and memories and emotions tangled and knotted like Kiley's curly hair.

Matt was the first person who hadn't flinched when he saw her missing finger or her scarred body or heard pieces of her story. Even Stephanie had recoiled and looked away whenever some new horror was exposed. But not Matt. With words and with touch, he told her she was beautiful and precious. Her Matt never flinched.

He said he loved her. But how could that be? He didn't know her. She didn't know herself. He thought The Center was the only way to fix her. But The Center would dig into her guilt and rage. They would push her to excavate her emotions so she could find love. What if, in the process, she lost Matt? She'd lost every person she'd ever loved. Could she survive one more loss?

She closed her eyes and began to count backwards from one hundred while she let a memory slide in.

Her boy, her precious four-year-old grandson, barreled into the house, smelling of little boy sweat and excitement. He tugged on her leg until he had her full attention.

"Gwammy, guess what!" Lucas's excited voice entered her mind even as she continued her count. "Daddy signed me up for To Kick A Doe! I get to kick people. And I won't get into twouble."

Marcia burst out laughing. "I think you mean Taekwondo." She sobered, ruffled his messy brown hair, and added, "You do realize that means they get to kick you, too."

The little boy's face scrunched up and he twisted his lips with his chubby fingers. "The stringway didn't mention that."

"Stingray?" she asked with a huge grin.

"Yea, you know. The leader guy."

"I think you mean Sensei."

He gave her the proverbial 'whatever' look and went on. "He wears white pajamas and a black belt. I get to wear the pajamas too, but I have to wear a white belt. Those pajamas are called G—like the letter in the alpabet. You'd think they could come up with a cooler name."

"Lucas, it's called a gi." She said the word a few times and he practiced with her. "And, it's al-pha–bet."

He plopped down on the floor, crossed his legs, and rested his elbows on his knees. "I'm kind of scared, but don't tell Daddy."

In the memory, Marcia mirrored his position, placing her knees against his. "Scared of what?"

In the hotel room, Kathleen also sank to the floor, but she kept her eyes closed and the memory close.

"It's going to hurt. Those punches and kicks."

"There's an old saying, 'No pain, no gain.' Do you know what that means?"

He shook his head and stuck out his little bottom lip. Lucas did not like to not know things.

"If you want something in life—a black belt or anything else—you'll only get there after you go through some pain. Anything worth having is worth the struggle. If you don't suffer through the pain, you can't gain whatever it is you're trying to achieve."

"No pain, no gain. That sounds awful."

"That's just the way life is. Always has been. Always will be. You appreciate things more if you have to work hard to get them. Every challenge you accept will require sacrifice. Choose your challenges carefully."

"Huh?" He looked like a confused puppy. She was feeding him too much information, but he needed to get this message if he got nothing else from his Gwammy.

"I assume you chose Taekwondo. You chose the challenge. Now you have to suck it up and face the hard work—even when someone's kicking you, especially when someone's kicking you. My point, darling boy, is to choose challenges you are willing to work for. Once you've made the choice, you can't give up. That's quitting, and we do not raise quitters in the Bridges family."

Brice's shadow moved in and loomed over them. "Hey bud, Grammy giving you the suck-it-up speech?"

Marcia and Lucas tilted their heads and looked up into Brice's blue eyes.

"She said I can't quit even if they kick me in the balls."

Marcia and Brice laughed. "That's not exactly what I said but that about sums it up."

Kathleen, sitting cross-legged and alone in a hotel room, laughed at the memory.

"He earned his blue belt," she said aloud. "And he learned to face the fear and take the pain. But he never learned to say alphabet." She let his little face fade away and then said to the room, to herself, and to her family she believed was listening, "We don't raise quitters, do we?"

Without even realizing it, she'd already found the courage to love Matt. When he came back from his run, she would stand up straight, give him those three crucial words. "I love you," she practiced. "I love you." The words frightened her. But she couldn't—wouldn't—live scared to love. "I love you," she said once more.

But he'd been gone over an hour. Maybe he wasn't coming back. He had been so angry. What if he climbed in his car and drove back to Minnesota? Would she be sitting here alone when the sun went down? She'd forced Stephanie out of her life. Had she forced Matt's hand too? She should stand up, pack her own bags, be ready to say goodbye. But she didn't want to let him go. She wanted him and all his hope and his assurance and his promises.

When Matt walked in, sweaty from his run, Kathleen wanted to weep in gratitude. But she stayed on the floor, gazing at her lap, afraid of what she'd see in his face. "Are you okay?" she asked him. Three ordinary words that could determine her future.

Like Lucas used to do, he sat on the floor, his knees to her knees. He placed his palm on her leg, waited for her to look at him, and said, "I'm fine."

Fine. Fine. FINE. She hated that word. "Do you know what *fine* means?" she asked. "It's a throwaway word. It's a step back. It means you don't care enough to dig deeper and share yourself with me. It means you want me to say I'm fine, too." Kathleen began to parrot the conversation of the unengaged. "Hi, how are you? I'm fine! You? Oh, I'm fine, too. Thanks for asking. How's the weather?"

"Wait, hold up." He reached out to her, but she pushed his hand away.

"You know when people say they're fine? When they don't give a shit and they don't think you give a shit either. It's the best way in the world to keep everything superficial." She sighed. "*Fine* is a stop sign. *Fine* is not what people who love each other say." The last thing she had said to Stephanie was, "Go home. I'm fine."

Matt grabbed her wrist. "For me, *fine* is a habit. Most of what I've had in my life has been superficial," he said as he laced his fingers with hers. "Please ask again."

She stared into his eyes for a long time and saw sincerity and willingness. "How are you?"

"I'm not fine. I haven't been fine for a long time and I'm just admitting it. I'm worried and afraid. I'm hopeful. I'm glad you're still here and you're safe. It's a weird place for me, an uncomfortable place." He stroked her cheek. "I will never put up the stop sign and I'll never tell you I'm fine again."

She hoped she deserved his kindness, his goodness, his hope. He'd left his content life for her and all she'd given him was worry and fear. She should say it now—*I love you*—but the words were still stuck behind a clump of doubt. Marcia loved. But could Kathleen? If she gave him those precious words and she couldn't reclaim her life, she'd only hurt him with a promise she could not keep. She wrapped her arms around his neck and buried her face into his neck, silently pleading with him to wait for her, and to hold her heart.

Matt

Matt smiled at the bag of books Kathleen clutched when she climbed into the Escalade. He'd hated pulling her away, but after five hours in a bookstore, food was a necessity. They'd spent the last two days sequestered in the hotel room, watching TV and ordering room service, apologizing and reassuring each other with their bodies. But this morning, Matt had to get out of that room. He was unused to a sedentary existence, and the thought of one more movie, even with Kathleen in his arms, was more than he could stand.

"How many books did you buy?" he teased.

"Only nine."

"Nine? How long will it take you to read nine books?" The smile on her face made Matt want to put a bed in that bookstore and give her an unlimited credit card.

She shrugged. "At the beach, I'd read one a day. I suppose it will depend on how much free time I have after tomorrow."

This was the first mention of The Center since their argument two days before. In his professional life, he confronted conflict face-to-face. But this situation was as fragile as hand-blown glass. One wrong move, one crack in the glass, and she might run back to the beach with or without him. The Center would control their days and their destiny. The Center would shatter the glass. For the next fifteen hours he didn't want anything to burst their little bubble of peace.

"What do we want for dinner? I'm sick to death of room service." He could only eat so many bagels and salads. He needed a taste, just a taste, of normalcy. He wanted to eat a steak and watch sports on fifty screens.

She pinned her sunglassed eyes to his face but otherwise remained still. A laughing couple walked past their car. That's what he wanted for his life. Laughter. Easy affection. He needed to prove to himself, and to her, that they could be an ordinary couple in an ordinary town enjoying an ordinary meal. But maybe suggesting dinner out was one step too far.

"What are you thinking?" he asked, holding his breath.

"You want to eat in a restaurant?" Her tone was flat. Not angry. Not fearful. Just flat.

"Yes, Kath, I'd like to eat in a restaurant. We can tuck into a back table if that makes you more comfortable." He'd just spent the last five hours sitting in a wooden chair, creating a stress-filled to-do list while she lost herself among the bookshelves. His back hurt. His ass was asleep. He was tired, physically and mentally. Yes, he wanted to go to a restaurant. He wanted a loaded baked potato and a chicken wing appetizer. He wanted a freshly poured draft beer.

She looked out the windshield and asked, "Where would you like to go?"

He reached over the console, laced their fingers together. "You choose. I want anything not brought to me on a cart."

Without looking at him, she clutched his hand. "Before this happened, when I was still Marcia, I made all the household decisions. Now, I don't make any. I eat the same thing every day. I don't even shop for my own food. The grocer puts my items in bags, and I pick them up."

She turned her head to face him but before she could continue, he said, "Can you take off the sunglasses, please?"

She pulled off the glasses and clutched them to her chest. He was struck by the sadness reflecting from her beautiful blue irises.

"I went to the grocery store when I first moved to the beach. I covered myself and went very early in the morning. When I got to the aisles, I couldn't make any choices. Everything on the shelves screamed at me." Her eyes pleaded with him to understand. "I ordered catalogs from the stores I liked when I was still Marcia. The multitude of choices swamped me. I ordered five of each item in neutral colors. Five pairs of pants, five shirts, five simple dresses, five sets of exercise clothes." She paused for several seconds and searched his face. Apparently satisfied, she added, "It's scary not to be able to choose between a red shirt and a white one."

Matt replayed their time together. She wore black or blue or beige. Her clothes were lovely and well-made but simple. Today she wore black slacks and his Gophers sweatshirt. Her scarf—the one element of color she allowed herself—reminded him of a child's finger painting. "The scarves?"

"I buy every scarf in every catalog. I hang them in the closet on a tie rack. I wear whichever scarf is up next." She wound the Gopher's scarf through her fingers. "This one was on rotation."

Matt couldn't imagine not being able to make choices. He ate Raisin Bran but knew he liked Cocoa Puffs more than Frosted Flakes. He liked microbrewed beer and hated any diet drink. His closet was filled to the brim with suits and silk ties and shoes. Matt lived in color. Kathleen lived in a monochromatic world.

"I eat bagels and cream cheese because that was what Courtney liked. Brice and Seth liked sandwiches so that's my lunch. Dinner is always a salad because Amanda wanted Lucas and Kiley to eat something green."

Running his thumb over the dark circles under her eyes, he said, "Maybe it's time we figure out what Kathleen likes to eat."

Her eyes widened. "I have no idea. I don't know Kathleen. She's just a body forced to move in this world."

Matt watched as she squinted her eyes, scrunched her nose and bit her upper lip. When she felt safe, his Kathleen was animated and adorable. She shrugged and rewarded him with a shy smile. "Hamburgers. Swiss cheese. Mushrooms. Hand-cut fries. Lots of ketchup."

He leaned across the seat and put his lips next to her missing ear. "Burgers sound perfect." He put the car in drive but before he could pull out of the lot, she grabbed his forearm and said, "What if we don't like Kathleen?"

You don't even know her. Matt remembered his sister's words but refused to let Patti's warning ruin this small success. "I love you," he said. "I love the parts of you that are Marcia, the parts that are Kathleen, the parts that you've yet to develop." He put the car in gear. "Time to feed her hamburgers."

Matt found one of those gourmet burger places with twenty televisions and thirty beer taps. The smell of cooking grease reminded him how much he missed going out. Kathleen didn't take off her sunglasses, but she sat across from him, eating and talking and smiling. With each bite of his hamburger, Matt's tension eased, and his confidence grew. Normal was within reach.

"Good?" he asked.

"Better than I remembered." She coated another fry in a mountain of ketchup, leaned over her plate and slurped it into her mouth. A glob traveled down her chin and plopped on the table.

Matt laughed. "Like ketchup?"

"Not really. Lucas did." Using her index finger, she scooped up the mess and put it in her mouth. "He wanted his fries to swim. They made him wear a bib but that didn't deter him."

Normally he loved when she shared her family with him, but right now he wanted to enjoy their time together without ghosts and drama. "I'll order you more fries if you promise to cheer for my Vikings in tonight's game." He pulled a fry from her plate, ran it through the ketchup and shoved it into his mouth.

The ridiculously young waitress appeared with a fresh mug of beer and a glass of tea. As she set the glasses down, she turned to Kathleen and said, "What happened to your finger?"

Matt jerked his head toward the girl. Had she just asked that? Had she been so rude? So stupid? "Bring me the check." He wasn't polite and he didn't care when the waitress sputtered and bolted away.

"Matt, stop," Kathleen said. He saw Kathleen's spine straighten. She pulled off her sunglasses and showed him those amazing eyes. "You want normal? This is what normal will look like. People will always stare at me. They will make hurtful comments." She placed her disfigured hand on his forearm. "People will notice a missing finger and mutilated hand. They will notice the scarves. I hope to smile and laugh and love. But I will always carry sadness and regret that strangers can see and feel. When people find out who I am, I'll get looks of pity and even accusation. If I do this, that will be my new normal. Can you live with that?"

He'd woken this morning desperate for fresh air, sunshine, beer. Simple pleasures he'd taken for granted. He hated that one challenging meal left him so discouraged. And he hated that his sister's words kept chipping away at his confidence.

You'll never have a normal life with someone like her.

Matt would prove his sister wrong. He stood, tossed some cash on the table and reached his hand out to Kathleen. "I'm sure you bought a new mystery. I'm ready to snuggle into bed and flex my whodunit muscles."

Kathleen

Willow Lodge loomed before Kathleen. It was an innocuous building, painted yellow. Three other identical buildings circled the large cul-de-sac. To the uninitiated, the place appeared to be a tranquil resort, but instead of a relaxing spa experience, each building held twenty-four women trying to create life out of shattered pieces.

The buildings were long single-story rectangles, each painted a soft pastel color. In front, The Center had placed elegant signs. Willow Lodge. Elm Lodge. Oak Lodge and Maple Lodge. Each lodge had ten windows and a covered patio with rocking chairs. If positioned correctly, the rocker on the far corner on the left could not be seen from the front windows. The first time she'd stayed here, no matter how cold it was, she'd hidden in that chair with her headphones and her fictional friends until she was dragged back inside.

She'd spent last night in a closet, but she was here now. She wasn't ready, but she was willing. She was this odd mixture of confident and uncertain, proud and petrified. Matt stood next to her and, with him by her side, she'd step into the depths of her memories and hope she survived.

Before Kathleen's feet touched the carpet under the portico, the door swooshed open and Lisa stepped out. The medicinal smell common to all healthcare facilities engulfed

Kathleen. She stumbled, slammed her eyes shut, and held on to Matt's waist as the smell pulled her into the past.

"Mrs. Bridges," a voice pulled her awake and into pain. "Mrs. Bridges, I need you to wake up for me." The stranger patted her arm, jiggled it, pressed on the needle feeding oblivion into her veins. "I need you to tell me how much pain you're in."

Cold hands pulled her eyelids apart, flashed a bright light into each eye.

"I'm Dr. Lee. Do you remember me?"

The sheet was pulled down, her gown was moved, and cold air froze her skin. She jerked away from the fingers peeling her bandages off.

"I just need to check your wounds."

Marcia tried to burrow into the mattress. She tried to swat his hands away, but the restraining straps held her in place.

"The burn specialists will be down later today to debride again. Later we can talk about rebuilding your ear."

"Kathleen," Matt's frantic voice snapped her back to the present. She touched her scarf, adjusted her sunglasses, and fought to ground herself anywhere but in that hospital room. She'd refused pain medicine so she could feel the worst of the physical pain. It was the only penance she had.

"Good morning," Lisa called from just outside the door.

Kathleen had hoped this would be easier. Other than the slight situation at the restaurant, she had been feeling rejuvenated, strong, and ready. Now, Matt stepped in front of her, blocking her view of Lisa and her view of that door. She dropped her forehead into his chest and felt the heat of his arms slide around her and pull her deeper into his embrace. "I want to go home."

"We did not come this far to stop now. We are going to fight for our happily ever after." He leaned back and cradled her face in his hands. "Let's take this journey. Together."

Yesterday he'd bought her a tote bag with Curious George holding the Man in the Yellow Hat's hand. Her children had loved Curious George, and the bag made her smile. She'd packed paper, pens, and three books—one she'd read so many times she could recite it, and two new ones by a favorite author. She squeezed his hand, allowed herself two more deep breaths, and faced Lisa.

The younger woman looked exactly the same as Kathleen remembered. Courtney would have said she had the perfect figure, the perfect wardrobe, the perfect makeup, and absolutely the perfect shoes. As always, Lisa wore shoes with a four-inch toothpick heel. Today they were a red patent leather with a gold medallion on the toe which matched her silk multi-color blouse. Her medium-brown hair was in a messy bun that looked casual but actually took patience and skill to achieve.

"I'm very glad you're here. I promised when you left that I'd be here when you were ready."

"I'm trying to be ready." She clutched George to her chest. "I want to be ready."

"You are ready. You're strong. You are in a better place this time. And, most important, you have support that doesn't remind you of everything you've lost." She shifted her gaze to Matt. Her voice changed subtly, became more formal, more professional, a bit stern. "Matt, it's nice to see you, but you can't come in today."

Matt pulled Kathleen against his body as if to tie him to her. The heat of his words matched the heat building in her chest. "What do you mean? I'm walking her in, helping her to get settled. You cannot expect—"

"She has to find the strength to do this on her own. This choice has to be hers."

Matt stiffened and Kathleen silently pleaded for him to scoop her up, race to the car and peel out of this damn place.

Instead, his deep brown eyes held her and he touched his nose to hers and said, "I love you." Then he sighed and lowered his shoulders. He was going to leave her here. Alone.

What if he never came back? If one of her kids was dating someone like her, she'd beg them to move on. If he didn't return, what would she do? Could they force her to stay? Until she signed the intake documents, she was free to walk out, find a taxi, find an airport, find her beach. She had money. She was not trapped.

She twisted the bag around and around until the blood no longer reached her fingertips. She relished the way her fingers burned, then tingled, then cooled.

"Kathleen," Lisa gently touched her arm. "What's in the bag?"

Kathleen untwisted the bag and thrust it at Lisa. "Books, headphones, a new Ipod, pens, paper."

"You can bring in the pens and paper and the journal. Not the books, headphones, Ipod, or sunglasses. If you come in, you cannot do so hiding behind sunglasses and books. Group begins in ten minutes in room A. I hope you come in." She turned and disappeared into the mouth of Willow Lodge.

Kathleen held her sunglasses to her face and prepared to walk to the car. This was too much. Too fast. Too cruel. It was one thing to take down walls brick by brick. It was another to bulldoze them. They'd find another solution.

"Was every piece of advice you gave me growing up a bunch of bullshit?" Courtney's angry voice pierced Kathleen's consciousness.

"First day of kindergarten, first day of Girl Scouts, first day of camp. Do you remember? My first day anywhere, I'd stand there just like you are now. All bent over trying not to puke my guts out. You'd rub my back for all of one minute and then you'd tell me to, and I quote here, 'suck it up and walk through the door.'"

Her daughter's voice became warm and tender. *"You used to tell me that every time I found the courage to face my fears, I'd find the courage to make my dreams come true. It was so cheesy. I hated it. I mostly hated it because you were right."*

"All my dreams include you," Kathleen whispered.

"I know, Moms. I know. Do you remember the time I wanted to start riding horses? I was all gung-ho to become the next great Olympic Dressage athlete. You told me no. I was furious. I threw your words in your face. I was such a beastly kid sometimes. Why did you tell me no if that was my dream?"

Kathleen almost smiled at Courtney's habit of jumping around in a conversation, hoping the listener could chase her randomness. *"You have an allergy—a serious allergy—to horses. I told you that some dreams have to be altered to fit the truth of the given situation."*

"You also told me that dreams are like Play-Doh—we can reshape them into something new as often as we want. Remember, we went to the store, bought every color, and molded dreams all afternoon."

Kathleen crouched down, rested her head on her knees, and listened to her daughter's sweet challenge. *"Josh took away your chance to see your dreams come true."*

"Am I allowed only one dream? I have a new dream based on new circumstances. My dream is for you to move on and take us with you."

From what seemed like a great distance, she heard Matt call her name and felt his touch on her back.

"Moms, I know you dreamed of my wedding, of more grandkids, of getting old with Dad and hiking all over the world. Get out your Play-Doh and let's do some reshaping. Just like you always helped Brice and me, we'll help you now. What do you want this new dream to include?"

"I want to open those boxes and look at your smiles and I want to stop looking forward to death."

"Take his hand, Moms. Open your eyes, stand up and go through that door. Learn to trust yourself again. We'll be with you on the other side."

Kathleen reached her hands out to Matt.

He helped her to stand, picked up her dropped bag. "I don't know what to do or to say. I wish I could take you away from here. But, Kathleen…"

"I have to go through that door. I know I do. Courtney said she'd be on the other side."

She stood on her tiptoes, put her mouth to Matt's and said, "Get Play-Doh. Every color." She took the bag from his hand, pulled out the books and headphones. After one last deep breath, she pulled off the sunglasses, shoved them at Matt.

She kissed him hard before saying, "Please don't be late." With Courtney's promise echoing in her mind and Curious George on her arm, she darted through the door of Willow Lodge and onto the path of hope.

Matt

Matt blinked at the closed door before turning slowly back toward his car. He understood why Kathleen couldn't have the books. But the sunglasses? Did they have to take everything before she even entered? Could they not let him see inside the building?

"Mr. Nelson?"

Matt spun and found a man about his own age moving in his direction.

"Ken Richardson." The man extended his hand. "I'm the director. Did Marcia—I'm sorry, Kathleen—get in all right?"

The man before him was a few inches shorter than Matt's six-foot three frame. He wore what Matt called weekend business. Khakis. Blue button-down. His tie, however, shattered the businessman image. Wile E. Coyote lay splat on the ground and the Road Runner was giving his thumbs-up. He added to this silliness with high-top sneakers. Matt stuck out his hand and knew it was petty when he squeezed the director's hand too hard. He held up Kathleen's sunglasses. "I spoke to Lisa for a long time last night, and not once did she hint I wouldn't be allowed in or that Kathleen would not get to take her sunglasses and books. It all seems so…" Matt struggled to find the best word and finally settled on, "harsh."

Ken looked at the sunglasses. "Why don't we take a walk? Maybe I can make you feel better and answer any questions you have."

"The glasses?" He wanted an answer, not a walk.

"That's not going to be possible. But I can explain our program and help you understand the decision."

Ken walked toward the wooded area surrounding the property, motioning for Matt to follow. "It's hard, isn't it?" he asked. "When we have someone we love who needs a place like this. Watching them face a war where they must fight alone."

Ken was right. Everything was hard with Kathleen. But the way she smiled at him, the way he felt when she wore his t-shirt to bed, the way he lost himself when they made love was worth the struggle. He was creating a new life for himself and her and them. This was day one of that new life. Standing taller, he said, "I'll handle it."

Ken kept walking and, even though he kept his voice comforting, Matt could sense his skepticism. "The women you see here don't get to go home at night. There's a reason for that. We can intervene in a crisis and we can give the family a rest. It might be easier on both of you if she had that full-time support."

"How do families do it? Lock someone away in a place like this?" He had only known Kathleen for ten weeks, but he couldn't imagine leaving her here around the clock. She wouldn't agree to stay and he wouldn't ask that of her because he didn't want it, either.

"As I'm sure you've learned over the last few weeks, taking care of someone with major trauma issues is exhausting and frightening. These women and their loved ones are desperate for help."

Ken paused and looked at Matt closely, as if he were reading tea leaves. "Why did that make you angry?"

Matt glanced at the man. "Why do you think I'm angry?"

Ken looked pointedly at Matt's hands. "Look at your fists. Your shoulders are almost implanted into your ears."

Matt shook out his hands and forced his shoulders back into place. "I'm angry at myself. I can't believe I brought her to a place I know so little about. And I didn't ask Lisa the right questions. I made assumptions and that is not like me. This may be rude, but I have no idea if this place is any good or if there's somewhere better." They walked along a well-worn trail littered with bright yellow leaves. The remaining leaves would fall soon; the trees would be bare and exposed to the winter cold. This would be his first winter somewhere other than Minnesota. He wondered if he'd miss the snow.

"Our program is comprehensive and varied so that we can create a personalized treatment," Ken said. He greeted a young woman walking up the sidewalk before continuing, "Our therapists are the best and the most dedicated. Lisa is no exception. Last time, because of the medical issues and recency of the trauma, we let Kathleen guide the process. This time she will be challenged *to do the program*. What we are asking her to do will not be easy."

Matt reached up, broke off a small branch and switched it in front of him, channeling the energy building inside him so he could respond calmly. "What will this path look like?"

"I can't discuss Kathleen's specific situation until she's signed all the privacy forms. She might decide to limit your involvement. Many patients make that choice." Ken straightened his tie in a gesture less necessary than reverential.

Matt closed his eyes, blew out a long breath, and continued to slash at the air with the stick. Until this moment he had not considered that she might not want him actually involved in her care. Maybe she only wanted him to be a taxi service or a landing place to avoid staying here. He shook off that doubt. She had not allowed anyone except him to see her scars or touch her body. She'd trusted him and given him a glimpse of her pain. She would sign those papers. "What *can* you tell me?"

They walked past a large gaggle of geese fighting over food someone had sprinkled on the lawn. On the right, Matt heard horses whinnying. These surroundings were a tranquil enclave in the middle of a growing city.

Ken led Matt to a bench where they sat facing the water. "We only treat women over 21 years old who *choose* to be here," Ken said. "That's a key component. No one is forced to be here."

Matt listened intently, wanting to trust this place, this man, this process, and wanting to know his role was vital. A Canada goose drifted on the water, creating perfect circles like the geese in Minnesota. He wasn't in Minnesota and he wasn't in a boardroom or courtroom, but he wasn't in a foreign land, either.

"During the interview process—which is another step you bypassed—we determine who is the guiding force of treatment. The patient has to be in the driver's seat. If it's mom or dad or husband or *boyfriend* demanding or cajoling the patient, then we make other suggestions for care."

Matt wasn't sure if that was a warning or an admonition. "What about the first time Kathleen came?" She'd told him only that she'd spent two months in the hospital and then four months at The Center. He knew she hadn't been in a mental state to make a decision about continued care.

"She'd stopped talking, mostly stopped eating. She'd blocked all visitors. She agreed to come here because she believed she had nowhere else to go. That is not a motivation to get help. We'll have to delve into her true motives this time. If she wants to work through the trauma, we'll help. If she doesn't, there is nothing we can do."

"She's had the chance to give up for years now. She hasn't because that's not who she is and not what she really wants."

He wanted to sound confident. Instead he hated that his voice asked for reassurance. "That's why I want her to have the sunglasses. Give her time to adjust and settle."

"Her family was killed almost four years ago. When do you want us to start?" He wasn't being sarcastic. It was rhetorical and yet demanded a realization of the circumstances.

Unused to not getting his way, Matt swallowed back a smartass retort. He was here because it was time to start. He just hadn't expected the uncompromising environment.

Ken shifted on the bench so he looked at Matt and not the lake. "It's totally normal to feel relief."

"That's not what I feel." His defensiveness was loud and clear even to his own ears. He *was* relieved and desperate for a break, for a chance to relax, for a chance to process his new world. Not wanting to be so exposed, Matt refused to speak.

"Just say it," Ken encouraged. "I can't help you if every time I ask something you stop to weigh your words."

Matt kept his gaze on the geese creating circles on the lake. "*I'm* not looking for help. I just want to know about this place, about my role, about how you will help Kathleen."

Ken sat silently and Matt knew he was patiently waiting on him to be more truthful. Matt pulled in the deepest breath he could and let the words tumble out, "When she disappeared behind that door, I felt like I could breathe for the first time since I met her. What does it say about me that I am relieved to have some time away? I'm so relieved to let someone else deal with her?"

"Taking care of someone like Kathleen—or any of the women here—is daunting. It's a constant balancing act. Why wouldn't you be relieved? If you didn't feel some level of relief, I'd be worried about you."

"I want to be there for her. I do love her. I wish—" He wished he knew what he was doing. He didn't want to be at NNJ, but in his office he was captain of the ship. The Center was in another ocean and he wasn't even allowed to touch the controls.

"You will be there for her. Recovery is a family process. It's best for you to get some rest from all of this. She'll need a healthy you at night."

"What do I do today? How do I spend eight hours worried and unable to get to her? For the last several weeks, she's been my world and my job." He shut his mouth in embarrassment. He had plenty to do. He had three pages of notes for NNJ. Three pages he desperately wanted to avoid. What he should have asked was, *What do I do today that will make this easier?*

"Kathleen will be taught to use her emotions and her intellect to choose the next best decision. You need to do the same."

All of his life Matt had known what was next. He was not impulsive by nature. But without notice he'd quit his family's firm and moved from the only city he'd ever known. Without real thought, he'd agreed to once again manage the firm he was ready to leave. He'd fallen in love with a woman he just met. He was estranged from his sister. He sat here with no personal goals, no plan beyond Kathleen's treatment and no idea how to form one. Kathleen didn't know who she would become. Neither did he.

Ken stood and together they followed the trail toward the car. "Do you have a support system?" Ken asked.

Matt wasn't sure if Ken was referring to something specific or support in general. He had his father, but Joe was still grieving the loss of Matt's mother, and Matt didn't want to worry him. There was his sister, Patti. She might be angry with him, and he with her, but she'd be there for him. He could depend on her, and that released some of the building pressure. Matt shrugged off the question and asked one of his own. "What can I expect when I pick her up?"

"There is no instruction sheet. Every person, every situation, every day is different. What works today won't work tomorrow. It's very difficult and disconcerting. Let her guide the evening. Within reason. Be sure she eats and takes some time to de-stress. She'll want to pretend her day is over. She'll want to hide in one of her books, but she'll have a homework assignment every night. Help her to face that." Ken shook his head and added, "I'm still not convinced it's in her best interest to leave at night. We have trained staff to watch, monitor, and assist when necessary."

"I've done a pretty good job taking care of her these last several weeks." This one area was non-negotiable.

"Matt, this will be different," Ken warned.

"I'll do whatever you say *except* leave her here. That's not an option for her. Or me. That hasn't been an option since I first met her." Matt stopped at his car, extended his hand and said, "I can learn how to take care of her."

Ken ignored Matt's outstretched hand and said, "Let me finish."

Matt's gut turned over like it did when a jury rose to give its verdict.

"If she fully engages here—which she needs to do this time—we are going to open some very painful wounds. Wounds she doesn't even know she has. We never know how a patient will respond. Anger. Despair. Shutting down or lashing out. Hiding in corners. Hurting themselves. The list is endless and is unique to everyone. Her safety—mental and physical—is at risk."

"I understand." He faced Ken exactly like he would face a judge or the IRS. He pretended he was prepared and sure of victory. But since he'd stepped on that beach, his life had been one out-of-control experience after another. He wasn't prepared and he wasn't sure of victory. He was keeping that detail to himself.

It was Ken's turn to extend his hand. "Get a support system. This process can suck you under and it's up to you to take care of you, regardless of what she needs."

Matt nodded even though he didn't agree. He couldn't be sucked under, and her needs trumped his.

Ken walked away. Matt looked at Willow Lodge but couldn't see through the tinted windows. He clicked the locks of his car and began to climb in when Ken called to him from across the parking lot.

"Oh, and Matt, freeze some oranges."

"Freeze oranges?" Matt asked.

"When she's terrorized, and she will be, put one in her hands."

Matt fingered the sunglasses still in his pocket. Ken seemed to be someone who was careful with words. He hadn't said *frightened*. He hadn't said *angry*.

He'd said *terrorized*.

Matt climbed into the Escalade, searched for a Walmart on his GPS. He would buy an orange and all the Play-Doh on the shelves. It wasn't much, but it was something.

Kathleen

Kathleen was the first to arrive at the morning group session. She sat in the same recliner she had sat in three years ago. It was well-worn leather that might have been brown but was now colorless. Stuffing had been picked from the armrest, making it look like a shorn sheep. The best feature, however, was its rotating base. Kathleen could—and would—turn the chair away from the group and look out the window.

She had work to do; she understood that. But hearing an alcoholic's story would not benefit her. Listening to someone who refused to eat or who took a razor blade to her arms would not help her, and her problems were none of their damn business. Her memories—the good and the bad—were not for public consumption.

From her corner chair, she could see women in the Lodge's living area move around, chat, and gather their bags for the day's sessions. The Willow Lodge building included a central commons area everyone called "the big room," with comfortable sofas, matching chairs, and a large fireplace. Smaller seating areas dotted the big room. In one section, a couple of women were playing a game, and in another, a woman sat on the floor, furiously coloring. With its paintings and carpet and plush furnishings, it could have felt like a family's large living room. Shattering the illusion was the large windowed, soundproof office. The therapists used the space for phone calls and note-taking and resident-watching. Big Brother was monitoring, taking names, deciding futures.

Kathleen sat in one of four dedicated group therapy rooms that circled the big room. The space reminded her of Sunday School classrooms for middle and high school students. Bright fluorescent lighting completed the classroom ambiance. Instead of bible verses, posters for suicide prevention shared the walls with posters about attitude and self-determination and mindfulness. Someone had drawn a mustache and glasses on the face in the suicide prevention poster.

Kathleen frowned at the huge feeling wheel painted on the front wall of almost every room on the property. It was a staple of The Center. Consisting of three concentric circles, the seven basic emotions wrapped around the center. More complex emotions formed rays like pie pieces. Happy and all its associated synonyms were yellow. Surprised was purple. Bad was green. Fearful, orange. Angry, red. Disgusted, grey. Sad, blue. She hated being asked over and over again how she felt. There might be twenty-five different ways to say it, but *angry* worked for her.

Women began to shuffle into the room and settle into the chairs. A young woman walked past the empty sofas and an empty chair. With her feet dragging and her face down, she walked toward Kathleen. When she stood next to her, the woman lifted her face for only a second and muttered, "Mind if I sit on the floor here?" She tapped the rug near Kathleen's leg.

Everything about this woman—this girl—screamed despair. Hair so dirty the color was indeterminable. Dirty fingernails and clothes that were two sizes too big and two weeks past due on a good washing. Kathleen looked at her own outfit. Black leggings, black athletic shoes, white socks. She'd decided to wear Matt's overly large sweatshirt because it smelled like him and, more important, she could pull down the sleeves and cover her missing finger. A Duke Blue Devils scarf covered her scarred head. Kathleen had been—was still—in a state of despair. But her clothes and body were clean and her fingernails were never dirty.

As much as she wanted to tell this girl to move on—to find an actual seat—she couldn't do it. A minuscule compassion peeked through her anger and her fear. She moved her legs to the left and made room for the sad creature to lean against her recliner.

Laughter pulled Kathleen's attention to the front of the room. Two young women were shoving each other and laughing loudly.

"Maybe we can convince that one to take a bath," a very young girl sneered. She wore a t-shirt and shorts that allowed a butt cheek to peek out.

The girl at Kathleen's feet jerked and then leaned into Kathleen's legs. She was frantically picking at the skin around her nails and it dawned on Kathleen that the dirt under her fingernails might be dried blood.

"Missy," the tag-along one said, in an immature combination of shock and admiration. "That's so mean."

Missy's brown hair, with its bleach-blond tips, resembled tiny daggers. A tattoo climbed up her arm. Roses? Hearts? Feathers? Kathleen looked at her face and took in her pockmarked skin, caved-in cheeks, yellowed and chipped teeth. This girl was a meth-head! Kathleen was sharing space with a person as hideous as her nephew. She pinched and twisted the flesh on her wrists, praying the pain would keep her in the present, even as a memory pulled her under.

"Hey, man. We don't need to kill them. We just need to find the money," the boy with wide bloodshot eyes and oozing acne said.

Seth stared at the gun and moved to block Courtney. Marcia was unable to understand what was happening and unable to make her feet move.

"We can give you all the money we have," Seth said.

"Money," her nephew sneered. "Too late for that."

POP. Crash. Brice's body fell. More blood.

"Daddy!" Lucas's little, loud, terrified scream.

Marcia watched the blood of her son part around Seth's feet and spread across the floor.

"Good morning, ladies," Lisa's loud voice pulled her out of the darkness. "Welcome to Monday."

A stream of sweat trickled down Kathleen's back, leaving her cold and slightly nauseous. She was back in Willow Lodge, but the remnants of the memories stuck to her like barnacles. She tucked her chin into her chest, twisted a fingernail into her palm and hoped Lisa would not expect her to participate today.

"Let's start with introductions and emotions," Lisa said. "Tonya, why don't you get us started?"

"Tonya. Proud and ready."

"Joyce. Irritated."

"Debra. Sleepy."

"Misty. Amused and disgusted."

"Gloria. Worthless." This was the girl sitting at Kathleen's feet. She'd spoken the words to the floor and, even sitting next to her, Kathleen barely heard her.

Kathleen was next and if she didn't speak, she'd bring attention to herself when what she wanted was to stay as hidden as possible. She pulled in a deep breath, shoved the fingernail deeper. Once she gave her damn name and picked an emotion, she could turn around and disappear into her fictional stories. Lisa may have taken her books, but Kathleen knew the stories and the characters. "Kathleen. Anxious."

The introductions continued but Kathleen quit listening. She faced the window and began to count the leaves as they drifted and floated.

"Moms, life is not going to stop, and you've ignored it long enough. Turn around, face the room, and be part of this," Courtney whispered.

Kathleen fought back a bitter, sarcastic response. Like a recalcitrant child she spun her chair around and slammed her arms across her chest. She focused her gaze one foot above Lisa's head.

"I'd like everyone to open their binder, take out a piece of paper, and find a pen," Lisa said. "In this assignment, jot down anything that comes to mind."

The White Binder. Kathleen thought of it as a proper noun. One of the therapists had given it to her before the lodge door fully closed behind her. Her weekly schedule had been placed behind the plastic cover. Beginning at 8:00 a.m., every minute was choreographed. DBT, ACT, EFT, Anon—a cornucopia of acronyms, each hoping to be the panacea for Kathleen's trauma. Even at 5:00 p.m. the work wasn't over. Someone would hand her a homework assignment.

The binder was filled with blank paper, assignments, articles, guided journaling, and, of course, a feeling wheel.

Some of the women groaned. Some of them sat straighter, as if the principal had spoken. Kathleen snatched up her bag and was surprised to find Matt's pen. Other than the letters his mother bequeathed him, the pen was his most prized possession. A Montblanc his father had given him when he passed the bar and joined the family firm twenty-seven years ago. Kathleen traced her finger over the inscription. *Let's Get To Work.*

"Every week you ask, 'When can I go home?' And every week I tell you the same thing: 'That's up to you.' The process of recovery begins and ends with you. It begins with how you choose to focus your energy, your mind, and your heart. There is no hurry. You have to let your body and mind guide you," Lisa said, pulling everyone's attention to the front of the room.

"Do we ever fully recover?" someone asked.

"Recovery is a forever, full-time job. But you do find ways to live and protect yourself. Which nicely leads me to the first part of my little weekly speech. Before you can move forward, you have to accept where you are. Life has dealt each of you a set of circumstances that just are. You don't have to like them. They don't have to be fair. But they cannot be changed. Can one of you give an example?"

Women squirmed and looked at their laps. Kathleen remained perfectly still, her eyes wide and focused on the suicide prevention poster until the image began to blur.

Lisa waited, and when the room felt thick enough to blow the windows out, one woman finally said, "I accept that I'm an alcoholic."

Everyone turned to look at the speaker as if she were the bravest person in the world. Or the stupidest.

"An excellent place to begin," Lisa said. "Tonya, why do you turn to alcohol?"

Tonya maintained eye contact with her lap until the woman beside her reached over and linked their fingers together.

Rather than pull away, Tonya's fingers turned white with the force of her grip. Rather than swallow back her tears, she let them fall. Rather than run, she sat up taller, looked Lisa straight in the eye, and said, "My father molested me as a child. I'm ashamed. I'm disgusted by my body. I'm afraid of men. Those are my facts."

Empathy, an emotion Kathleen never expected to have again, rolled over her in waves. How could a father do such a thing? Seth had been a wonderful man. Patient. Kind. He would never touch his children like that, and he'd kill anyone who tried. If he'd had the chance, he'd have stopped those boys that night. But he didn't. He'd allowed the bullets to fly and the bodies to drop. She had no right to be angry at Seth, but that did not make the anger go away. She let the anger swallow the empathy. Anger was so much more comfortable. She pushed her teeth into her lower lip until the pain anesthetized her from any emotion.

Lisa awarded Tonya with a huge smile. "Tonya cannot change what happened to her. She can change how she deals with it. Some of you turn to drugs or alcohol or self-harm, purging, bingeing, starvation, or destructive relationships rather than face what you're avoiding. And that's not healthy."

"I don't do any of those things," Kathleen clapped her palm over her mouth, wishing the words would disappear out the window.

"Are you telling me you have healthy coping mechanisms?" Lisa was so fucking nice, so compassionate and so determined.

"I'm telling you I don't need to abuse my body," Kathleen said.

"Kathleen, we all have ways of handling stress and heartbreak. You may not drink to excess. But whenever we find ways to avoid suffering, it is unhealthy."

"You cannot tell me reading is unhealthy," Kathleen challenged.

"In and of itself, you're right. But, tell me, how much time do you spend reading? What do you miss in life or avoid or run from by reading?" Lisa leaned forward as if it were just she and Kathleen in the room. "It's not the reading. It's the avoidance. Reading for pleasure is wonderful. Reading for escape is good, too, when it's limited and intentional for rest. But..." Lisa paused and studied Kathleen for several seconds.

Kathleen would not give up the only friends she had even if they lived in the pages of her books. Lexie made her laugh. Krystal said things everyone wished they could. Eve lived an adventurous life all around the globe and she took Kathleen with her to places Marcia used to dream of.

"Let's back up a second. You don't have to accept the deepest, darkest things today. Maybe today you could accept that reading is a coping mechanism and as such is not healthy." Lisa nodded at her and then addressed the entire room. "What are you willing to accept *today*? Tonya is ready to look at her alcohol abuse and what her father did to her. She's ready to hold it. She shared in the safety of this space and with women who will understand and support her."

Kathleen looked again at Tonya's hands joined with the woman next to her. She looked at the greasy head sitting at her feet. She did not want to be touched or to share with these people. She didn't want to breathe the same air as a meth-head. Not wanting any connection, she pulled her leg out of Gloria's hold.

"Write down three things that you wish weren't true but are and will forever be true. For those of you who are new," Lisa looked directly at Kathleen, at Gloria and the other new residents. "You can start slowly or you can jump into the deep end. Listen to your body and be confident you'll get there when you feel safe."

All around her, people scritch-scratched on their paper but Kathleen didn't know where to start. Her family had been slaughtered while she did nothing. Her family bled out while she hid in a closet. Her family would never breathe or laugh or cry, so she couldn't, either. How could she put that on a piece of paper?

"*Mama*," Brice said, "*We'll start smaller. I'll get you started. You have physical scarring that will never go away.*"

Kathleen wrote the words as if she were taking dictation. Marcia had both loved and hated when Brice called her Mama. It was his "I need you to really hear me" voice. It was a voice that preceded bad news or some sort of admonishment.

"Our home in the mountains is gone," Brice added, and Kathleen wrote.

I will never see my best friend again. Kathleen wrote without Brice's help.

My family is gone. She couldn't write *dead* or *murdered.* The papers had called it a family annihilation, but that wasn't true. She was left to live. "After you've written three truths, identify and write down your primary emotion." Lisa said.

Without any help from Seth or Brice or Courtney or Lucas or Kiley, Kathleen filled the page, HATRED. FURY. HATRED. FURY.

"Often we accept something as true when it's not. Look at the list. Is there anything there that can be changed if you're willing to face the trauma?"

"Moms, Stephanie? She's the best friend you've ever had. Is she truly gone, or is it you that's gone?"

Kathleen forced her daughter's words out of her mind. Stephanie was the past and the past was dead. *DESPAIR.*

Two therapists slipped into the room and sat on the floor near the door. Their presence initiated a shifting of bodies and murmuring of voices.

"I'd like you to write down three things you can change but you think you can't. This list will require honesty and will likely create anxiety. Breathe through it and reach out if you need extra support."

Kathleen closed her eyes and pictured Matt's tall frame crammed into a closet just to be near her. She pictured him kissing her forehead and calling her "Love" and meaning it. She opened her eyes and wrote three things she'd like to change: *I sleep in a closet. I can't see a future.* There were so many things she refused to write. She hated touch. She was scared of people. She couldn't cry. She was frightened of who she was and who she would be. Fear had become a constant state of being.

I'd like to create something but I'm afraid of what that might be. Marcia had been a creative soul. But even that felt lost to Kathleen. If she let her creative spirit emerge, what horror would she create? Not pretty cards or photographs. Not a beautiful garden or a fancy meal. If she created a new self, a more real person, would she be a monster mired in contempt?

"*Remember when I decided to start running marathons?*" Brice said. "*You told me to start with a mile and then two. Of course, I was too full of myself to listen. I tried to run the twenty-six miles with no training. Remember the cramping? Mom, start with one mile and you'll reach the finish line.*"

"*You knew where the finish line was,*" Kathleen argued with the memory of her son.

"*You know where it is, too,*" he said. "*Pick one thing, start with a mile, but then you have to go the whole distance.*"

"We are going to end on a positive note," said Lisa. "You all have people or accomplishments or even things in your life that you don't want to change. These are things you can cling to when it's dark outside. We'll put them in black and white for you to see whenever you need encouragement. List at least three."

Matt. I enjoy his touch. I like hamburgers and swiss cheese and mushrooms. I managed to leave the beach and breathe.

"This week is about taking one step, not leaping across the chasm. Write down one goal for this week. You can use the lists you created this morning or you can come up with something new. It can be as simple or as hard as you want. Remember, this is a safe place to dip into courage."

Kathleen shifted her focus to the falling leaves. Marcia had loved to play with paper and scissors. She would have collected those leaves and used glue and glitter to create something beautiful or something ridiculous. Did Kathleen love that too? She could try. She could create something for Matt. Something that said *I love you*. She wrote *Create*.

"We have fifteen minutes left. I'd like you to work with a partner to develop a detailed list of steps you need to achieve the goal. If the goal is to eat a full meal, your first step can be as simple as gathering a fork, knife, and spoon. Debra, you partner with Joyce. Kathleen, you and Missy work together."

Kathleen could not have heard Lisa correctly. If Kathleen recognized a meth-head, then Lisa knew what Missy was and what that might mean for Kathleen. As Missy stood and came toward her, all Kathleen saw was her nephew.

"You need to back away," she said quietly. Kathleen imagined herself scraping her fingers down Missy's face. She pictured herself ripping Missy's ear off her head. She dreamed of watching the girl's blood pool at her feet like Courtney's had.

Whatever Missy saw or heard worked. She took one step backward. As she sashayed away, she tossed over her shoulder, "If I get in trouble because we didn't do this together, I will find you."

Unwilling to give Missy any more attention, Kathleen turned her chair toward the window. Missy didn't know that she had mastered being in a room and not being seen. She would remain hidden in plain sight and never share her family in this place, with these people.

Matt

Matt had to find a few minutes of peace. A few minutes that were not about Kathleen or Patti or Nelson Nelson and Jones. Ken was right on too many levels; life with Kathleen was daunting and frightening and confusing. In his professional life, he was the master of his universe. Now, he didn't even know what galaxy he was in. Part of him wanted to go back to the world where he was boss and there were no frozen oranges or sleepless nights in a closet. He'd settle for ten minutes of peace and a chance to be Matt Nelson, not the firm's and not Kathleen's.

    He found a place just five miles from The Center called the Buzzed Bibliophile. According to the internet, this place had excellent coffee and sandwiches. It was located in a run-down strip mall, but the interior was like stepping into a 1930s English country manor's library. Ten-foot ceilings made the room feel large and airy. Dark wood bookshelves lined most of the walls. Library ladders tilted into the room. An electric fireplace warmed the back corner where an array of leather wingback chairs was scattered. The front of the shop held what Matt labeled garage sale tables and chairs. No two tables matched. No two chairs matched. There were cane-back chairs, fancy dining room chairs, '60s-style rounded creations in strange colors. At least two tables were decorated with elaborate ink drawings. Another table was wallpapered in bumper stickers. On the right wall, there was a display case filled with sandwiches and pastries. A chalkboard listed a variety of drinks. It was charming and eclectic and so much better than Matt's normal Starbucks. He breathed in the luxurious smell of coffee, cinnamon, chocolate. Was he wrong to look forward to a meal where he didn't have to watch Kathleen or make sure she ate more than six bites?

He chose a table with names carved into the top. Before he could get comfortable, his cell phone vibrated. He dropped his laptop bag on the floor and pitched the notepad on a table. He dug out his phone.

"Unknown Number" flashed on the screen. Suddenly fearful Kathleen might be in crisis, he hit the accept button. "Matt Nelson."

"Matt, it's Jeff."

Fuck. Jeff Meyer was a client they never should have taken. He was too aggressive, too willing to dance in the grey areas of the tax codes and then blame NNJ for the blowback. He was not a thorn in Matt's side. He was a pointed spear.

"Jeff," Matt said. "How did you get this number?"

"Your sister. You haven't answered your business line in weeks even though you assured me you would personally handle my case."

Matt couldn't believe Patricia had given the Asshole his private phone number. "I've been busy with some personal business."

"That's what I keep hearing. But my case goes before the judge soon and *you* are my tax attorney."

"You signed a contract with NNJ, not with me." Matt's professionalism was slipping fast. Why couldn't Patricia handle this? Her name was on the damn door, too.

As if he were oilman-rich, Jeff used a Texas drawl that was so fake it would have been comical if Matt wasn't so pissed off.

Journey to Hope

"We spoke while you were on that vacation of yours and you gave me several guarantees."

Matt struggled to remember that call. He had just met Kathleen and would have promised this guy anything to get him off the phone. "Jeff, Patricia or one of the other partners can give you all the attention you need. I'll make some calls today and be sure someone else is up to speed."

"I do not want a flunky. I want the first name on the door. That would be you," Jeff said, enunciating each word as if Matt wasn't intelligent enough to understand him.

Flunky? This man had just called his sister, her husband and all the other capable people in his firm a flunky. "Mr. Meyer..." Matt paused, wanting to formulate the proper condescending response.

"Before you try to talk me into someone else," Jeff interrupted. "I have an email from you dated the day we last spoke. In it you explain you'll be back in two weeks and assume responsibility for my case. It's been four weeks. My patience is gone."

Matt didn't remember the email either. "Fine," Matt said, "I'll have the files in my hands within the hour. We can plan a conference call tomorrow at eleven a.m. with my team." Whether the Asshole liked it or not, Matt would transfer his case to someone else.

"Your team? I don't want a team. I want what I was promised. The managing partner. You."

Matt had no idea when the court date was. He did know that he would not leave Kathleen for this guy, consequences be damned. "Tomorrow, eleven a.m.," Matt repeated, unwilling to make any other promises. "And don't call this phone number again."

"Then answer your work phone," Jeff said, before hanging up.

For twenty-seven years, Matt had gone to the family firm, focused on winning cases and securing new clients. It hadn't been easy, but it wasn't emotionally challenging, either. He'd gone to sporting events and bars with friends. He'd dated, but never seriously enough for an emotional breakup. Now his yellow notepad wasn't filled with a to-do list but a page of questions and worries about Kathleen. Even though he didn't want to go back to the office, there was something comforting about feeling competent, about knowing what tomorrow would bring or what his role would be. He didn't feel that now.

Matt tossed the notepad and a purple pen on the table with a thwack loud enough to draw attention from the customers. He nodded with what he hoped was an apology and walked to the counter.

The barista was leaning over an algebra book. He was pulling at the roots of his hair with one hand while the other was furiously erasing a series of equations. How many times had Matt seen his nephews frustrated over a derivative? He wanted to pat this kid on the back and assure him that understanding how to solve for x was possible. He cleared his throat and almost laughed when the young man jerked as if Matt had tapped him with a taser.

"Can I help you?" He was wearing an apron that was two sizes too big. His name tag was upside down, but Matt could read *Ian*.

Matt searched the display. "A turkey avocado croissant, a bag of chips, two cookies."

This kid reminded Matt of his nephews. Jake and Joey had the same floppy hair young adults favored and parents hated. He'd loved it when they had both decided to enroll at the University of Minnesota. Matt had never thought about being a father, but since they'd been in Minnesota, he had relished his role as pseudo-parent and cool uncle. Jake and Joey made him laugh and forced him out of the office. They'd been so wonderful when Matt's mom was sick. They would spend one day a week with their Grandma Betty, watching TV or playing board games. If the tubes and bags bothered them, no one knew it. They had treated her like Grandma, not like sick Grandma, and she had appreciated that more than anything else.

Before he'd met Kathleen, Matt and the boys would spend at least one evening a week together, drinking beer, eating wings while they complained about classes or women. Frequently Joey, the partyer, would sleep in his spare bedroom after a night out drinking. Matt was their mentor and friend and he missed them.

Matt nodded at the boy's sweatshirt. "You go to UNC?"

"For now." He touched the book. "This is my second time trying to pass this stupid class. If I fail it again, my scholarship will be at risk. I live in a world of maximum rent, minimum wage and zero math aptitude." It was Ian's turn to nod at Matt's shirt. "What brings a Minnesota Gopher to Charlotte?"

"My—." He halted because he had no idea how to start. Girlfriend? Lover? Responsibility? Future? Partner? He frowned. How would he explain who she was? People would wonder about the scarf and the sunglasses, about how she wouldn't make eye contact, about how she leaned away from touch. What would he say? "Hi, this is my girlfriend; she was tortured and that's why she's so strange"? Would people look at him and wonder what he'd gotten himself into? Was Patricia right? Was normal out of reach?

As if sensing he'd asked the wrong thing, Ian said, "I'll get your food and coffee and bring it to the table."

Matt went back to his table where he was tucked in a corner with bookshelves on one side and windows on the other. He sat in the overstuffed chair and pictured Kathleen sitting next to him, holding his hand, smiling. He wanted to introduce her to Jake and Joey and hear her laugh at their debauchery.

He didn't know what would happen between him and Patti, but his nephews would embrace Kathleen because Matt loved her.

"Here you go." Ian put plates on the table. "Let me know if you need anything else." He moved away before Matt had a chance to thank him.

Matt ate his sandwich and let his eyes drift across the books. On the second shelf he saw one of the books Kathleen had bought yesterday. She'd lain in his lap last night without her scarf and sunglasses. He'd stroked her scars while he read to her. The main character was a sports agent who got himself sucked into mysteries. Matt had affected a New Jersey accent to match what he thought the character might have. Kathleen had grinned at him. When the character said something outrageous, she laughed. Actually laughed. Matt had to believe she would soon laugh at the real world. The hope and promise of her laugh were enough for him. He'd stay by her side and watch her return to life. He would redefine normal. He'd learn how to introduce her and how to ignore odd looks and inappropriate comments. He'd be honored to do it.

But first he had to deal with Jeff's shit. He pulled out his laptop and waited for it to boot up.

Ian sat at a table on the other side of the room. His apron was gone, but he wore frustration like a cloak. He ran his fingers though the messy flop and scratched something on his paper. He looked at the back of the book before he tossed his pencil down and banged his forehead on the table.

Matt laughed because Jake did exactly the same thing.

His computer dinged, alerting him to 162 unread messages. "Fuck that," he murmured. He closed the computer, shoved it away. He took one last gulp of coffee and walked across the room.

"Ian, I think I can help you with that."

Kathleen

Kathleen sipped a box of cranberry juice while she waited in Lisa's office for their individual session to begin. She resented that she had to drink out of a cardboard box. She wasn't going to hurt herself with a soda can or a glass. She was safe in a kitchen unsupervised. Maybe the other women needed protection from themselves. Not her.

As she waited, she kept replaying her earlier interaction with Missy. She imagined the two of them like animals circling each other, about to fight, both snorting and drooling, their jowls shaking with the urge to devour each other. She wasn't scared of Missy; she was scared of the violence inside herself. Missy represented all the evil that had destroyed her world, and Kathleen wanted revenge.

At least for now she was safe from Missy and Missy was safe from her. Lisa's office was at the end of Hallway B and as far away from the living area and Missy as Kathleen could get. Hallways A, C, and D were mirror images of this one. Each hallway had three bedrooms with one, two, or three beds. The last time Kathleen had been here she had still been in bandages, so she had been given a private room near the nurses on C. Instead of sleeping, she'd paced the hallways over and over and over again. The path from A to B to C to D was exactly six hundred twenty-four steps.

On each hall, opposite the bedrooms, was a locked bathroom. In the same way Kathleen didn't need boxed juice, she also didn't need a sentinel standing watch when she used the bathroom. She wasn't going to purge. The mirrors were some sort of reflective plastic. She didn't look in mirrors, but even if she did, she wasn't going to smash a mirror and use it to carve up her body.

The Center had everything; it was a self-contained world for twenty-four lost and wounded. There was a pharmacy, a mailroom, a laundry, a kitchen, and even a TV room. But Kathleen would need none of those things. She would walk out at five o'clock, embrace Matt, eat whatever she damn well chose with a knife and a fork, and go the bathroom without someone listening. She would never spend another night here listening to the middle-of-the-night crying.

She shifted her Curious George bag and the White Binder between her feet and looked around Lisa's office. It was a place she never thought she'd see again. It was still warm and inviting. She'd added stained glass ornaments to her windows. The sun streamed through the colored glass, sending shards of dancing color onto the carpet and walls. Pillows and blankets in bright jewel tones were tossed on the cream-colored couch. Courtney would tell her to add one dash of bright pink. Marcia's favorite color had been green, but what did Kathleen like?

"Sunset pink, Moms," Courtney whispered in her consciousness. "The best color of all."

Kathleen smiled. Her beautiful girl loved all shades of pink. But her favorite was a luxurious mix of pink and purple. A color only found in the sunset. At her beach, Kathleen had watched that sunset every night and pined for what she'd lost. Did people who'd lost it all ever feel whole, feel normal? Could Kathleen ever look at a sunset pink sky and not ache?

Journey to Hope

Shaking off the ache, Kathleen pulled out the notes she'd prepared and composed herself. One the main goals in this place was to meld the rational with the emotional and find what they called "wise" mind. Kathleen believed the wisest choice was convincing Lisa to keep Missy away from her, and she'd spent her free time planning her argument.

"Sorry, I'm a few seconds late," Lisa said as she breezed into the office and closed the door behind her. She plopped into her chair and smiled. "Since you've been here before, we can skip the 'welcome to individual therapy' speech. Let's talk about what happened in the group this morning. You reacted quite strongly to Missy."

"Her voice reminded me of Josh's," Kathleen said, proud of her calm honesty.

"Did it remind you of Josh or did it become Josh?"

She sucked on the straw until the tiny box collapsed in her palm, but she kept her tone placid and patient. She would stick to her plan, show dedication and progress. Admit some of her guilt and get rid of Missy. "I should have given him the money." That was the decision that plagued her all day, every day. If she'd given Josh the money, she'd be on her mountain arguing with Seth about how to cook the turkey instead of sitting in Charlotte ready to argue about Missy. "Seth and I had helped him before but I discovered he spent the money on drugs. I would only help again if he did a drug test. If I'd given him the money..." She stopped, rubbed her sternum with enough pressure to feel a bone bruise form. She took another breath, held up her notes. "I'd like to talk about Missy. It would be better for me if you moved her to a different lodge."

"You said 'I.' Did you make that decision without Seth?"

"The final decision was mine," she whispered. Did Lisa expect her to accuse her wonderful husband? He was dead and it was easier if it was her fault. "I'd like to talk about Missy, please."

"Was that a reasonable request?" Lisa asked.

Confused, Kathleen said, "I haven't asked anything yet."

"Was asking Josh to get a drug test a reasonable request?"

"Apparently not," Kathleen spat the words. She pushed on her bruised breastbone and used the discomfort to gather herself. "I'd like you to move Missy to another lodge."

"Why?" The question was genuine, as if Lisa didn't know the pain Missy would cause.

If Lisa hadn't acted seriously puzzled, Kathleen would have lashed out. Instead she answered with conviction and confidence. "I don't think I should have to be around someone like that."

"Someone like what?"

"She's a meth addict. I can tell. The smell. The look. The attitude. Exactly what my nephew disintegrated into. He went from this charismatic, goofy kid to a demon-possessed meth-head. I don't want to be reminded of him all day. It's not fair. You shouldn't expect that of me."

Lisa didn't speak for a long time. She repositioned herself and put the notepad down. These adjustments took seconds and felt like hours. Kathleen needed Lisa to say, "Of course, we should have considered that. I'll have her moved tomorrow." That was the only acceptable response. Instead, Lisa rested her elbows on her knees, bringing her face closer to Kathleen.

"If I remember correctly," Lisa started with that warm voice they were all taught in therapy school, "one of your primary goals this time is to live more fully in the real world. To not need to live in seclusion. Am I stating that correctly?"

"My world will not include people like her," Kathleen said. This time the words were slow and emphatic because this was an argument she could not lose.

"Describe for me the world you want to live in," Lisa said. "Do you want to be able to go out to dinner? Do you want to go to the movies? A mall? Duke games? Grocery store? Airplanes?

Journey to Hope

Do you want to be able to do those things and actually be there instead of in your fictional stories? Do you want to be able to look at people and be seen? Kathleen, do you want to be able to drive through the mountains without losing control?" The questions were rapid fire but kind and curious.

Kathleen wanted to visit her family's resting place and see Stephanie at least one more time. She'd like to take Matt to a Duke game, have a beer, and scream until her throat went dry. She'd like to go somewhere without needing sunglasses. But the world she wanted did not include drug addicts. That wasn't—couldn't be—too much to ask.

"The world is full of people we'd rather not engage. Missys are everywhere."

"But don't you think you can throw too much at someone?"

"Yes, we can. But that's not what this is. Missy is not too much. Recovery is a labyrinth. At each turn, we face another challenge. The goal is to learn to handle EVERY challenge you might face in the big wide world. You learn to understand yourself and respect yourself and your needs. Then you learn how to satisfy those needs in a healthy, constructive way. Missy is the first corner in your labyrinth."

Kathleen closed her eyes and pictured that marble game Lucas loved. The goal was to get a marble from one end of the maze to the other without dropping it through a hole. Her grandson would spend hours losing and starting again without ever getting frustrated. "I feel like I'm dropping into a hole," she admitted to Lisa.

"If it makes you feel any better, you will be a challenge to Missy, too. Your story—your presence—is a reminder of where addiction can lead."

Kathleen shifted to the edge of her seat and invaded Lisa's space. "Please forgive me if I don't care about how I might be able to help her."

If Kathleen's small act of aggression bothered Lisa, her tone and face didn't reflect anything but acceptance and understanding. "She's here for the same reasons you are. The same reasons everyone is here. You all want to be able to cope with difficult emotions and circumstances in a healthy way. Face down demons."

"It sounds like you're comparing us and finding us equal," Kathleen said. She gnawed on the inside of her lip until the metallic taste of blood hit the tip of her tongue.

"You are equal," Lisa said.

"Hell, no," Kathleen barked. She stood, letting everything fall to the floor so she could pace and flex her muscles. She slammed the juice box into the trash can, disappointed it didn't make a noise to match her mood. "Do not put me in the same boat as that girl. It was that type of person that turned me into this." She stopped at the window, placed both palms on the glass, and let the cool sensation wash over her.

"Do you have the same past? Did you make the same mistakes in life? No, of course not." Lisa moved to stand behind Kathleen. The two women made eye contact through their reflection in the glass. "But you both grieve. You both have anger and hate. You both have chosen unhealthy coping mechanisms. You both have amends to make. You both deserve something better. You are both here and doing the work. You both have stories to tell."

"When I look at her—hear her voice—I go back in time." Kathleen hated the plea in her voice. She hated sounding like a coward. Marcia and Seth hadn't been cowards.

"Kathleen, that's the point of this. It's time to go back there. This is not about Missy. It's about you. You are safe here. With or without Missy. Go ahead and fall through the hole. We'll catch you."

Light streamed through the butterfly ornament, sending circles of blue and purple onto the carpet. She used her big toe to trace the design and wondered if Lisa would change her mind if she knew Kathleen fantasized about gouging the girl's eyes out.

"*Mama, stop. We don't let bullies decide what we do, who we are, and how we behave. You'd kick my ass if I acted like you are now. This is not about her. It's about you and what you see when you look in the mirror.*"

Kathleen didn't have one mirror in her beach house. But that wasn't what Brice meant and she knew it. She was using Missy as an excuse to focus out and not in.

Her hour was far from over, but she'd found the end of her rope. She moved away from the window, picked up Curious George. "If you want me to fall through the hole, Missy will be happy to give me a shove. I hope you can catch me, because I think the hole might be an abyss." She turned the doorknob but Lisa stopped her with one more warning.

"Kathleen, next time we need to discuss how angry you are at Seth."

But she wasn't angry at Seth. She didn't need to be angry at him. She had a litany of other angers. Missy having power over her. Nothing positive to share with Matt. Losing her first battle with Lisa.

Most of all, she was angry because, maybe, just maybe, she *was* one of these people.

Matt

Matt arrived ten minutes before five and walked the path between the portico and the car dozens of times as he watched for Kathleen. Small groups of women walked in and out. Each group was trailed by someone with a clipboard. Some of the women gave him sidelong glances and he overheard one person say, "That's Scarf Lady's ride out of here."

He had spent an afternoon relearning linear equations, searching for Play-Doh, buying supplies, and worrying about how to handle Jeff. What should he expect from Kathleen at night? He had put a frozen orange in the room's tiny freezer but he had no idea what it was for. In three minutes, at least he could learn what she did here all day and how it was supposed to guide her through the nightmares.

The door swooshed open, a squirrel scurried away, and Kathleen stepped out. She halted as if trying to understand how she had gotten outside. Her eyes were tired and she looked as if the day had been a series of hard-fought battles. Her tote bag dangled from her hand and she had a thick white binder tucked under her arm. Her sweatshirt was wrinkled as if she'd been twisting and twisting the fabric.

"Kathleen."

Her confusion disappeared. She closed the gap between them and buried her forehead into his chest. "It's only day one and I'm so tired."

Matt kissed the top of her head, ran his hands along her spine. "Let's get you to the car." She wrapped her arm around his middle, rested her head on his shoulder, and held on tight. The binder jabbed his side, but he loved the way she leaned onto and into him. This is what he wanted—to be necessary.

He bundled her onto the preheated seats, tossed the tote bag into the back. He pulled her sunglasses from his pocket and placed them over her eyes. Gently, he closed her door and walked toward the driver's side.

The binder was heavy and exactly the type he used for active cases. The younger attorneys mocked him for his dependence on paper. But he got a fuller picture of the case when he spread out the documents like puzzle pieces. This binder held the secrets of Kathleen's day and the answers to many of his questions. Hopefully the binder, once spread out, would give him a complete picture. He would look through each page and analyze the information like he would a court ruling. His list of questions was generic, but with the binder he could develop questions specific to his Kathleen.

He sat in his seat, facing her. He stroked her neck from her shoulder to the bottom of what was left of her ear. Three bright red lines marred the skin where she'd scratched herself too hard. What had caused her to do that? Wasn't this place supposed to watch and intervene before she hurt herself?

She shivered and leaned into his touch.

"Love, how was your day?"

She pulled away and looked out the window. "It fucking sucked. How was yours?"

Matt flinched at her words and the stupidity of his question. If his day had been awful, hers had to have been worse. He needed to feed her, hydrate her, help her relax. He laced their fingers together and said, "I'm sorry. That was a ridiculous question. I found a great place this morning. Coffee. Books. Food. How does that sound?"

"I want to go home."

He didn't know if she meant the hotel or the beach. The hotel wasn't a home. It was just a place to sleep. The beach was a hiding place. Even in Minnesota, his condo was now an executive rental. It dawned on him that for the first time in his life, he had no home. The idea was disconcerting and exhilarating. He didn't know what he'd be doing or where he'd be doing it, but he knew his next home would be with Kathleen. "There's a park between here and the bookstore. Let's go for a walk before it gets too dark."

She released his hand, shoved her hands under her thighs as if she were cold. She moved to the edge of her seat, putting as much distance between them as the car allowed. "I told you in Minnesota that I don't need a babysitter. I'm a big girl. I'll eat when I'm hungry. Sleep when I'm tired. Exercise when I want."

She spit the words but they didn't carry any fire. It was if she wanted to be angry but didn't have enough energy.

What was he supposed to say? She had to eat and she needed some time in the fresh air. It was his role to take care of her, and if that meant being a babysitter, then so be it. A group of women walked past the car and Matt understood why some people wanted their loved ones to stay at The Center. Being what Kathleen needed was impossible if he didn't know what that meant.

"I'm sorry. I shouldn't have said that," Kathleen said. "Can you please drive? I want to get away from this place."

He rested his hand on her thigh, not demanding but hoping she'd take his hand. Had something happened to her, or was this normal? "We don't have to go, but this place I found is called the Buzzed Bibliophile. It's eclectic and charming. I keep thinking how much you'd like it. They have some strange hot chocolate. Salt caramel. Dark chocolate cherry. Bourbon brulee. Three of the four walls are bookshelves. I met this kid, Ian, he reminded me of Jake and Joey." Matt knew he was yammering, but tension was like a third person in the car, and it made him nervous.

"I just want to go home, take a bath, and go to bed. We are surrounded by people all damn day. I need some alone time."

"We can order room service," he said, but his heart sank. Another cold burger and warm salad in that generic room. Were they back to hibernating? And what exactly did she mean by *alone time*? He'd spent all day worried about her. Surely, she didn't expect them to go to separate corners now. Defeated and frustrated, he started the car.

"I saw you with Ken this morning," she said. "What did you talk about?"

The paranoia in her tone had Matt putting the car back in park. He turned so he could see her face and watch her body language. Her hands were still under her legs and she was facing forward. He wanted to reach across the console, but she'd built a wall he was unsure how to climb. "Mostly, he told me about The Center and gave me a walking tour. He mentioned you'd have homework."

"I thought you said you didn't talk about me. Did he tell you how difficult I was last time I was here? Did he tell you I never did the homework? Did he tell you to stand over me as if I'm five years old? What did he tell you exactly?" She no longer sounded paranoid. Instead she sounded accusatory, as if she wanted to find something to be mad about.

"It wasn't like that. I asked how I could best help you and he said to encourage you to do any homework." When Matt had pictured the evening, he'd imagined her cuddled in his arms discussing her day—the groups, the classes, the other patients, her time with Lisa. What he had not expected was to be a punching bag.

"Let me guess. He thought I should live here." Her accusatory tone became aggressive.

"I let him know that was not open for discussion." He forced the defensiveness out of his voice.

She jerked her head around to face him. "*Supposedly*, he didn't tell you anything. But what did you tell him? Did you tell him my best friends aren't real? Did you tell him about my bruises? The closet?" She swallowed and he prepared for one more cannonball. "Did you tell him how *you* freaked out at the restaurant?"

That was unfair. He was doing everything he knew to be supportive. She should be thrilled Ken had made time for him. Without that conversation, he would have been panicked leaving her. He closed his eyes and held his breath for ten seconds while reminding himself that his problems were small. "Kathleen, love, he told me about The Center. It was mostly a PR meeting. I won't share our private lives."

"This is not me." She spoke so softly he wasn't sure if the words were meant for him or for her. She removed the sunglasses and looked at him. "Marcia was never a bitch."

"You're not a bitch. You're a tired woman who has been so brave." He rubbed the worry from her forehead. "How about we go to the hotel. We'll get you in the tub and I'll order pizza."

She latched onto his forearm. "Lisa gave me a sealed envelope. It's like a snake in the backseat waiting to strike. I need to open it. Until I do, I can only imagine the absolute worst."

He tried to smile, to show her that he knew how to support her. "Ken told me to freeze some oranges. Do you know why?"

She rested the joined hands on her lap. "When the trauma starts to drown me, when the emotions claw and choke and try to kill, when the anger and shame grab me by the throat and twist, when the shaking and wailing won't stop..." The words raced out of her mouth like a high-speed train she couldn't hope to outrun.

She slowed, and her smile was sad and apologetic. "When I mentally leave the room and go into the dark recesses of pain—the orange, the coldness of it, helps to bring me back to the present. The cold draws the mind's attention away from the darkness."

He straightened his shoulders, pretending her words didn't frighten him. "I have one in the freezer."

"One? You might want to get more."

She said it flippantly and he couldn't tell if she was joking. "I'll take care of that tomorrow," he said carefully.

"Lisa wants us to do our first session together at eleven a.m. tomorrow."

Shit, he was supposed to be on a conference call with The Asshole at eleven. Patti would have to do it. "That's perfect. Tonight, I'll look through the binder and be able to ask intelligent questions."

Kathleen didn't release his hand, but her body tightened and a dark energy returned. "The binder is off limits. The envelope is off limits. My homework is off limits. I don't need a babysitter."

Matt felt like he was in a game of Truth or Consequences. Would the real Kathleen please rise? He heard his sister's voice: *You don't even know her.*

He had to believe he did know her. She was the warm, loving woman who shared his bed. The woman who leaned into him. The woman who loved the Blue Devils but who wore his Gophers shirt.

But what if he was wrong?

Kathleen

Kathleen sat in the king-size bed, wrapped in the blanket and the anger and the fear. To the rage and anger, she added a cloak of guilt. She sat on a bed Matt paid for, surrounded by office supplies he'd purchased, across from a closet he was willing to sleep in. She wore his t-shirt but she hadn't been able to tell him about her day. She'd wanted to, maybe even needed to, but how did she explain that the day had been a failure? After group she had spent the rest of her day ignoring the instructors, biting back tears, squelching her family's voices, and planning her argument with Lisa. An argument she'd lost. How did she explain to him that the rest of her life she'd be triggered by the Missys of the world? How did she tell him his sister was right? Normal was out of reach.

While she'd bathed, Matt had created a mini-office on the bed. Pens, pencils, post-it notes. Yellow, pink, and grey legal pads. Ruler, scissors, tape. Highlighters in every color. On the dresser he'd built a pyramid of Play-Doh. In the center of all the supplies sat a journal decorated with a gold-embossed tree. The pages were recycled paper and the ribbon was a fabulous teal. Any other time, Kathleen would have taken the time to marvel at the craftsmanship. But all the supplies in the world would not open the envelope.

The White Binder glared at her from the end of the bed. She didn't remember moving the feeling wheel to the front cover, but the primary colors swirled. She was playing Wheel of Emotions. The emotions would spin and click, click, click, bouncing from one to another. How did Lisa expect her to hold her emotions when she was nauseous from the whirling and swirling?

"It's fine to have every emotion on that wheel. But right now all we want is your courage. Courage breeds courage," Brice repeated a lecture she'd given him. *"You ignored us all day. But we were there. We're here now. Open it."*

Last time she was at The Center, she remembered every woman opening her envelope during "introspection" hour—that miserable hour where everyone was forced to look inward. The residents would scurry to a corner of the lodge, seeking that seat where they could hide in plain sight. Then, as if a conductor had raised a baton, envelopes were ripped open. Kathleen always found a trash can and shredded her unopened assignment.

"Oh, come on, catch the damn ball." Matt's shout reached her from the living area.

Marcia and Seth had loved Monday Night Football. No matter who was playing, they'd make a wager and rabidly defend their team. That last Monday they'd watched the 49ers stomp the Chiefs. She'd won a foot rub. She wanted to drink a beer, yell at the TV, win a bet. She wanted to high-five and cheer and scream at the referees. But the homework trapped her in the bedroom as effectively as any chain.

"Good lord, all you're doing by staring at it is getting yourself more worked up. Open it, do the work, and then hold Matt's hand while you watch the damn game." Brice's frustration was apparent in his tone.

"Maybe the contents will increase the suffering," she challenged.

"Moms, you've already survived the worst that can ever happen. I don't think the contents of an envelope could ever compare."

Before she could talk herself out of it, she snatched it off the table and endured the single shiver caterpillaring up her spine. "I hate that feeling," she said to the room.

"That's the eebie-jeebies," Courtney said. "I love those. It's a slightly painful tickle."

"You were always quirky."

"I was awesome," Courtney shouted in Kathleen's mind.

"Was." Kathleen's breath hitched at the pain in her chest. "Was." Past tense. Forever. Gone.

"Not there but not gone," her darling daughter whispered, and Kathleen would swear she smelled Courtney's rosemary mint shampoo.

Slowly she worked her fingernail under the flap. Holding her breath, she pulled out two sheets of paper filled with Lisa's elegant handwriting.

Kathleen, in the coming days, you will start to wonder how long you have to be here. In order to answer that, you need to answer the following questions. Remember the five-minute, twenty-minute rule. Read the question over and over again for five minutes. Then write for at least twenty minutes. Before you read the question, gather paper and a pen. Settle somewhere comfortable. Somewhere safe. ~Lisa

Somewhere safe? The curtain was open and the diamond lights of Charlotte sparkled beneath the shelter of the dark clouds. On the wall above the dresser was a picture of a frozen pond with kids playing. On their last Thanksgiving, she and Seth had taken Kiley and Lucas ice skating on the tiny artificial rink in Leeside Village. Lucas's little legs spread so far apart his little pants had split and his Batman underwear had peeked through. Seth had scooped the little boy into his arms and raced around the ice. Lucas had laughed until he peed himself. A memory too beautiful, too painful to share, but too difficult to handle alone.

Kathleen crushed the pages against her chest, scooped up a notepad and the package of pens, and bolted out of the room.

"Love," Matt said, obviously startled at her abrupt and somewhat frantic appearance. "You all right?"

She nodded, careened around the couch and fell into his body. She pressed against him, hoping to quell the eebie-jeebies. She was simultaneously hot and cold. Fevered and chilled. She wanted to run away. She wanted Matt to tell her she didn't have to read the question. She wanted to find a shredder and hide from the next page. Kathleen raised the crinkled papers. "This can't hurt me, right? It's a question. It's not a gun or a knife."

He looked in her eyes and then at the paper. She saw him push back the desire to ask to read the paper. He was her safe haven, even if she couldn't give him what he wanted yet.

Matt nuzzled his cheek against hers before coaxing her to turn so he could position her legs over his own. Tracing the darkening circles under her eyes, he said, "I'm here because I love you. I'm also here because I want to help. I don't know how to do that. But you do. So, tell me, how can I help you *right this minute*?"

"I have to do stream-of-consciousness writing. I don't censor or edit and I don't put my pen down. Most of what I write doesn't make sense, but it's like clearing out closets, I guess."

"Why is that so scary?" he asked.

"Do you think the question will be about fairies and rainbows?" She bit down on her lips until Matt gently tapped her chin. "I'm sorry. You don't deserve that. I can't seem to stop." One minute she was leaning into his warmth. The next she was balling her fists, wanting to lash out and draw blood. The Wheel of Emotion clicked and whirled, clicked and whirled.

He placed a tender kiss on her lips. "Don't apologize. I know it sounds like one of your romance novels, but I *am* a safe place and I can take your anger."

"Matt, what if she wants me to write about that night?"

He shifted so his back rested against the arm of the couch. He tucked her between his long legs, where she settled her head on his chest. With her wrapped in his embrace, he said, "I'll be right here. Would it be easier or harder if I turned off the game?"

"Leave it on. It's soothing." She sank deeper into him, raised her knees to form a table. She held her breath for five seconds, exhaled for eight seconds. "Let me know when five minutes is up." With shaking hands and surrounded by Matt's warm arms, she unfolded the second sheet of paper.

Why are you here? When can you leave? What does healthy look like for Marcia Kathleen Conners Bridges?

The question was future-focused and left that night where it should be—hidden at the bottom of her soul. Relaxing, she quietly repeated the questions over and over until Matt called time.

"What's your favorite color?" she asked.

"Gopher red."

"I like red. Marcia's favorite was green. But I think I like blue more." The question was innocuous, but the answer was important. A favorite color was a step into a new life. She picked out the blue pen and let her mind speak.

Matt

"One-hundred forty-eight, one-hundred forty-nine," Matt whispered, allowing the numbers to form in his mind. The nine added to the eight. "Seven carry the one. One, four, four. Nine. One, one. Two." He opened his eyes and added 294 to his sequence. He began again, 149+ 294 + 443.

"That's a unique coping mechanism," Ken's teasing voice startled him.

Matt sat at the table in Ken's office where he'd been waiting for fifteen minutes. Instead of a black leather couch, he found a duplicate of his own office. An executive desk with two visitor chairs. A conference table. Even a whiteboard. Matt's bookshelves held tax codes, law journals, and case histories. Ken's held therapeutic tomes. Matt's overlooked the Minnesota skyline. Ken's view was a pond. Different but the same. Matt understood this space.

"They're called Fibonacci numbers. It's just something fun I do from time to time," Matt said, flipping the pad over to hide rows and rows of numbers. He stood and the two men shook hands. Ken's tie had dancing watermelons and test tubes diving into a pool. Matt frowned at the lack of professionalism.

Ken stroked the tie as if it were precious. "The woman who sent me this was driving the car when she pulled in front of a truck. Both of her children were killed." He lifted a foot and displayed the matching bright blue shoes.

Ken's dress was not unprofessional; it was heartwarming and hopeful. Matt could not help feeling ashamed at his own arrogance. After last night, he needed to believe that Kathleen would one day buy Ken a ridiculous tie. "I appreciate you seeing me without an appointment."

"It's not a problem. Did you want to discuss something specific?" They sat at the conference table and Ken let his question simmer until Matt was ready to answer.

"Last night, after Kathleen did her homework, she settled next to me on the couch. We watched Monday Night Football and made small wagers. We had fun." It had been exactly what Matt wanted his future to be. She'd never told him about her day and she didn't show him the homework, but those worries were distant and insignificant this morning.

"And then," Ken prodded.

"I know she likes baths so we soaked in bubbles together. I told her about my nephews and Ian, a young man I tutored yesterday, and she told me a story about Brice. I read to her like I always do, and she fell asleep with her head in my lap. It was our normal." Matt took a deep breath to prepare himself for what came next.

"At two in the morning, she lurched up. It was like she'd been zapped with a cattle prod. When I turned on the light, her eyes were wider than I thought a human could manage. Her entire body was trembling. I kept calling her name, but she didn't hear me. I'm not saying she ignored me. She. Did. Not. Hear. Me. She kept screaming, louder and louder." Matt ignored the shiver blooming up his spine. "I tried to take her hands in mine, tried to pull her out of it, but she..." He had to stop. She'd been out of control. Wild with fury. He'd been frightened for her. But he'd also been frightened for himself.

It was in her eyes, in her tone, in her punches and scratches—she wanted to hurt someone.

Matt rubbed his arms, which were laced with ribbons of deep gouges. "She was like a feral cat. I kept trying to reach her. But she was gone. I tried to pull her close, but she used her head as a battering ram. I had to let go. I didn't have any choice." He hated the anguish and desperation in his voice but he needed Ken's advice and reassurance. "When she started to claw at her ear, I forced her hand away. It was not easy."

"How did she finally come around?" Ken didn't sound surprised or alarmed, which made Matt both mad and relieved. Someone should have warned him these terrifying nights were possible.

"I think she ran out of steam. Her screams became whimpers. Her body slowed. She dropped out of the bed and crawled to the closet." While she'd gone to sleep, he'd spent the night in the closet, wide awake, worried and powerless. "What the hell am I supposed to do with this?"

"When she was screaming, what did she say?" Ken asked.

Matt closed his eyes and forced himself back into the nightmare. "It started with 'Stop.' 'It's my fault. I'm the one that said no.' 'Did you hurt them?' That's when she started to whimper. She kept saying, 'They were innocent. They were just little babies.'" Her words began to make a sickening sense. "That's what she said that night, isn't it?"

"Probably," Ken agreed. "I know it sounds scary, but this was actually good."

"It was the stuff of horror movies. She thought I was the monster."

"That night is in her mind and body. Think of a 1000-piece puzzle. You can't see the picture unless you put pieces in the right place. All stories have a beginning, a middle, and an end. We don't read the middle, then some of the ending, then go back to the beginning. It's linear. Kathleen's story is disjointed, and because of that it never ends. Once we, or she, reconstructs the narrative into beginning, middle, and end, she can understand the Event—capital E—is over. Grieving and accepting are impossible until she does that. The story is stuck, and so is she."

"So the nightmares will continue." It was a statement, not a question. Nightmares in the world of therapy might be good, but in the real world they were difficult to endure.

"Yes. No. Maybe. It's not an exact science. The days and nights will be good or bad or great. Awful. Mediocre. Forward. Backward. She'll be furious one minute. Depressed or remorseful or happy or anxious or hopeful or despairing." Ken pointed to the feeling wheel painted on his wall. It was the same wheel he'd seen on her binder. "She will have every one of those emotions and they will cycle like a fast-moving roller coaster."

"Please, Ken, I need to know how to handle this."

He nodded as if this, too, was to be expected. "Since she goes home at night, we are dependent on your feedback. She will not be honest about her nightly experiences. Not because she wants to deceive, but because she won't see reality. She'll see it worse or better than it was. What did she say about the nightmare this morning?"

"Neither one of us mentioned it." He had been afraid to mention it, afraid it might trigger another episode he didn't know how to manage.

"My guess is that she doesn't remember. That's a coping mechanism. She's been doing that since day one. As far as we know, she's never told anyone about that night. Not the police. Not Lisa. If I remember correctly, she never spoke of it with her friend Stephanie. She's mastered closing the doors in her conscious mind. It's bubbling out. Matt," Ken leaned forward, "she has to remember. She has to get it out so we can help her.

Do you want us to discuss her staying here? We can approach the subject gently."

"Stop asking that," Matt barked. "I don't want her to stay here. I want you to tell me the best way to help her. I'm treading water and I want you to tell me how to put my feet on the ground." He could not remember a time in his life where he'd admitted being incapable, and the word tasted bitter.

Ken didn't say anything for several long seconds. "She stayed at that beach so she couldn't be triggered to remember or to feel. Here she'll be triggered over and over again. Why are you so adamant she not stay here? As I explained yesterday, families often need a break. We're having this conversation because this might be too much for you—for anyone."

"You know she wouldn't agree to that," Matt challenged.

"Actually, we don't know that. If we told her about your fears and worries, she might see the benefit for both of you."

He shook his head. This subject was a waste of time. He wanted her home at night. For her and for him.

"You do know that her needing inpatient care is not a reflection of you. It's not a failure of yours or hers."

When Matt continued to glare and not respond, Ken added, "You're exhausted. Pale. Did you get anywhere on finding someone to talk to?"

"I don't need to talk to anyone. I love her. I want to be there for her. I promised her and I made that promise willingly. I just need a plan, an intervention. This is not about me. It's about her." This was the first time he'd ever loved a woman, and his need to protect her was instinctual.

Ken settled back into his seat and traced circles on the table before he spoke to Matt in an I-need-you-to-really-listen voice. "We recommend the significant other be in counseling."

Matt shifted in his seat. "I get that Kathleen has to be here. Her problems are beyond what anyone could manage alone.

But I *can and will* handle it. You're missing the point. I simply need you to tell me how to wake her up."

"I'm not suggesting you sign up for intensive rehabilitation. I'm suggesting you find someone to talk to about you."

Matt shoved his hands through his hair several times. He was exhausted. He did have decisions to make. But right now he wanted to focus the conversation on Kathleen.

"I want you to imagine something, okay?" Ken asked and waited.

Matt didn't like the tone and he didn't like the subject change. But he could tell by the man's expression that there was no choice. He shrugged, not in agreement, but in acquiescence.

"A friend comes into your office and tells you he's leaving on vacation. The man hasn't taken a vacation, ever. And he's not *scheduling* a vacation. He is dropping everything and getting on a plane. He goes to a beach he's never heard of and on the first night meets a woman."

Matt tightened his jaw, but Ken kept talking.

"Not just any woman. A traumatized woman. Now, this man—your friend—is giving up his career, his home. Again, counter to everything he is, he's not planning—he's doing. Within weeks, he's unemployed, in a new city where he knows no one. No support system at all. Living in a hotel. What would you say to this man?"

"You aren't being very subtle," Matt braided the words with sarcasm. "But I would probably tell him he'd lost his mind."

Ken nodded. "You've made some decisions that speak more to your issues than to Kathleen's. Yes, you need help to manage Kathleen's trauma and recovery. Lisa will guide that. But, you, Matt Nelson, need help too."

Matt bit back the *fuck you* forming on his tongue.

"Why are you reluctant to get help?" Ken pressed.

"Because I don't need it. I'm not weak! Tell me what to do if it happens again."

For the third time, Ken let silence weigh the air until Matt felt the pressure between his eyes. "Is Kathleen weak?" Ken finally asked.

"God, no. She's the strongest person I know. The fact that she gets up every day is astonishing. But it's not the same. I've never—"

"Are the women here weak?"

"How would I know? I assume they're here because of some horrible event. So, no, I suppose not." Matt tried not to sound defensive.

"When was the last time you did that?" Ken asked, tapping the yellow notepad where Matt had been calculating Fibonacci numbers.

He ground his teeth together and quickly calculated the next number. Seven-hundred thirty-seven. "I started doing this in law school."

"Why?"

"The classes were boring." Ken was making way too much of a simple game.

"Why did you become a lawyer if it was boring to you?"

"It's what my dad did. It's the family firm." The choice to be a tax attorney was never made. It just was.

"Did you ever like it?"

Matt let the question roll in his mind. "I liked other things more," he finally admitted.

"But you became managing partner. The boss. And I believe you've been very successful."

Yes, he was successful. Since he'd taken the corner office, NNJ had opened three satellite offices, increased its billings, and captured several high-powered clients. "If you're going to do it, do it right or go home."

Ken raised an eyebrow.

"The family motto," Matt said. "I did it right."

"Do you do everything right?"

"I do," Matt said but as soon as the words hit the air, he knew that wasn't true, at least not lately.

"Do you do what's right for Matt or for others?"

Matt rolled his eyes. "I do not want a therapy session. What do I do tonight if Kathleen wakes up like a wild animal?"

"And you're afraid you aren't doing what's right with Kathleen?"

"Are you listening? Since I don't know what to do, how can I know if it's right or wrong? I want to understand why she pushes me away, claws at me, acts like I'm the enemy. Why can I not reach her?" He didn't shout but only because he caught himself in time.

"Have you ever given thought to what is right for Matt Nelson? Not for Kathleen. Not for the firm. Not for the family. For you. Have you ever wondered why you've never been in a committed relationship? Or why Kathleen pulls at your heart? Do you ever think about you?"

Before Matt could tell him to mind his own business, Ken pressed on as if he knew Matt was about to shut this all down.

"You're in Charlotte living in a hotel. You already admitted you didn't investigate this facility the way you normally would. Did you really want to leave Minnesota—the only home you've ever known? Do you have a plan for the future that considers what you want? Are you going to let Kathleen drag you around like your dad did? Who is Matt Nelson, anyway?"

Matt shoved out of his seat and prowled around the room. Ken's questions and accusations put him on the defensive. He would have walked out, but he needed Ken. He stopped pacing and leaned against the wall as if the distance from Ken would alleviate the discomfort in his chest. "I'll admit that I haven't managed all of this like I normally would. It's a different situation."

"What's changed?"

Matt crossed his ankles and tucked his hands in his pockets. "Meeting Kathleen changed my priorities."

"That's bullshit. Kathleen came *after* your impromptu vacation. Kathleen came *after* you disappeared and left your job without notice or preparation. Kathleen didn't ask you to give up your entire career, did she? This is you. You can't blame her."

"I do not blame Kathleen. My mother, who had just died, had asked me to take a vacation. It's not that complicated." Ken had a point, but it was a point Matt wanted to ignore. "Ken, what happened last night? Why was she fighting me like that?"

Ken shook his head like a disappointed coach before he rose from the table and walked to his desk. He opened a drawer and pulled out a blue ball, a little bigger than a racquetball, a little smaller than a tennis ball. He began to toss it in the air. "Lisa told you a flashback is re-living, not remembering." He tossed the ball one more time and then hurled it at Matt's head.

Matt's right hand shot up and caught the ball. "What the hell?"

"What just happened?" Ken asked as if what he'd done was totally reasonable.

"You threw a ball at my head and I defended my face."

"Imagine Kathleen in that kitchen. Those boys are taunting her. Her dead family surrounds her. They cut and burn and slice her. What do you think she does?"

Matt didn't need to answer. She defended herself in whatever way she could.

"When she's there, you're not Matt. You're one of those boys. She fights back. Next time, rather than touch her and get dragged into the re-enactment, take the time to get the orange."

"I was afraid to go to the freezer and leave her alone," he admitted, feeling foolish that he'd already been told what to do but had ignored the advice. He wasn't doing it right. He wasn't doing anything right.

"The few seconds it takes to get the orange will be worth it. That should help her return to the present. She'll come back to the present, but part of her will still be in that cabin. Touch might scare her."

Matt's heart broke at the thought that she believed, even for a split second, he was one of her tormentors. He wanted to be associated only with love and hope and protection.

"Matt, one day Kathleen will be functional in a healthy way. But aspects of her life will never be easy. That's the reason we have ongoing outpatient and family therapy." Ken trailed his fingers down the hideous tie. "It would be nice if you were healthy, too. That starts by admitting you are not fine."

Matt tightened his hand on the ball, filling the air with the squeak of plastic. "Do you take on new clients?" Matt whispered the question, partly hoping Ken wouldn't hear him.

"Not normally, but we've made many exceptions for Kathleen."

Matt picked up his notepad of numbers, shook the man's hand. If Kathleen could do the work, he could do it, too. Even if he hated it.

Kathleen

Kathleen stepped into the group therapy room only to find Missy sitting in what Kathleen thought of as her chair.

"What's the matter? Did you think you owned this spot?" Missy taunted.

Other than enduring a few of Missy's sneers, Kathleen had been able to avoid her yesterday. Now, she clutched the binder tighter to her chest and held the young woman's eyes. Missy's eyes were brown and Josh's were the same blue as her own. But they had the same mocking expression and the same rotting breath. The tiny sliver of peace she'd claimed in the morning yoga class melted. She wanted to race across the room and tear Missy's ear from the side of her head.

"Ladies, let's find somewhere to sit," Lisa said.

Kathleen blinked away the image. She was exhausted this morning, but it was the exhaustion of hard work instead of the weariness she always carried. She and Matt had woken in the closet, but she'd done the homework and writing had opened a release valve. For the first time in years, a tiny pinprick of light shone in her darkness. The light was at the end of a very long, very dark tunnel, but she would not allow the power play of some meth addict to keep her from that light.

"Yeah, bitch. Find a seat," Missy sneered.

Kathleen moved to the corner of the couch, kept her gaze on Lisa, and pretended not to hear Missy's infantile harassment. Missy was an insignificant gnat and Kathleen would not let a petty, pathetic child take away her hope. She had Matt. She had her family's voices. Lisa started as she always did. "Please tell the group the emotion you are currently experiencing."

Missy started with "satisfied."

The little twit who was attached to Missy's hip said "cheeky."

Kathleen looked down at her wheel and, sure enough, cheeky was a synonym for happy. Courtney would love that term.

"Kathleen?" Lisa prompted her.

"Prepared," she said.

Lisa nodded, turned back to all the other women in the group.

"Confident."

"Discouraged."

The feelings circled the room before Lisa said, "Thank you all for sharing. I feel expectant. Please get out the assignment from last night." She waited while the women shuffled and shifted to retrieve their journals. "Each of you thought about why you're here and what healthy looks like for you. I'm going to ask each of you to distill the answer to *one* primary thing."

Kathleen gazed down at her journal. Nineteen pages. Single-spaced. Tight, small handwriting. Blue ink. The first few lines were Marcia's handwriting but, as she continued to write, the words shrank, squeezed together, ran off the page, and became almost illegible. It was as if, as she wrote, Marcia faded away, leaving a jumble of confusion on the page.

When people started to mumble, Lisa added, "I know you have more than one answer. You probably have pages of them." She formed a triangle with her fingers. "A pyramid has a larger base in order to balance and hold the weight. I'm asking what forms the base of your healthy lifestyle. What *one* thing could you look to and say 'there, that's it. If I can achieve that, then everything else will follow'."

"Can you give an example?" a woman asked.

"Some of you may hope for reconciliation with family. That one goal is so vital to your happiness that you're willing to do all this work. Think of it as the reward you get when you face yourself in the mirror. The base of your pyramid must be achievable, something you *can* change."

For Kathleen the answer was the last sentence in the last paragraph on the last page. Seven simple words. *Love their stories. Love Matt. Love me.*

"Let's start on my right and go in a circle. Kathleen, that means you start us off," Lisa said.

"Maybe she can share why she gets to go home at night while the rest of us are prisoners. Or why she gets to cover her head when everyone else can't." Missy spoke, but Kathleen felt the entire room look her direction.

She sat straighter, clasped her hands over her homework, and said, "I'd rather not share." She didn't want Missy to know anything about them—not their names, not their hopes or dreams or fears. Brice and Courtney and all her memories were *her* treasures and *her* nightmares.

"You sound angry," Lisa said.

Kathleen knew the 25 words associated with anger, and for the first time she appreciated the choice of the exact right words. "I'm resentful, indignant, and provoked. I don't want to share with complete strangers. With people like her. I don't think I should have to." She modulated her voice in a vain attempt to convince Lisa she was in control.

"I didn't ask you to share with complete strangers. I asked you to share with the women here. They are not strangers to your journey," Lisa said without hiding her disappointment.

"This is bullshit," Missy said.

"Missy, what's bullshit?" Lisa asked with her calm let's-dig-deeper voice.

Missy snorted like a bull about to be unleashed, and any other time Kathleen would find the display humorous. She cranked her head around so she could see Missy and imagined a poison dart hitting the girl between the eyes.

Missy's behavior was proving her point. Why should anyone here know of Courtney and Brice's habit of talking in a horrendous British accent or learn that Lucas couldn't say his *Rs* or share in the memory of catching butterflies with Kiley?

Missy pointed at Kathleen. "What makes her more special than anyone else? What is her issue anyway? Did her daddy not buy her enough Louis Vuitton? Maybe she was touched by an uncle." Warming to her outburst, Missy wiggled in her chair as excitement bubbled over. "Drugs? Alcohol? Starves herself or vomits? Oh, I know, she's a sex addict? That explains that man. Either way, nothing happened to her that hasn't happened to one of us. She's here because her life is a fucked-up mess."

Those last three words landed like blows in Kathleen's chest. Josh had had one goal—to make her life a fucked-up mess. He'd said the phrase over and over as if it were the chorus to his favorite song.

"Oh, Auntie Marcia, when I'm done your perfect little life will be a fucked-up mess. Your family's dead because you're a selfish bitch."

Someone held a flame to the edge of her left breast. The smell of her burning flesh co-mingled with garlic and tomatoes.

"I wanted a few thousand dollars. I bet all these lovely rings will get me more than that." *He held out his palm so Marcia could see Courtney and Amanda and her own rings. He kicked her in the stomach, and she fought to hold back the scream and the vomit.* *"More,"* *he yelled to the boy with the lighter.*

Marcia scooted away from the flame, tried to grab the lighter but the blood from her severed finger made the hot metal too slippery. "More," Josh taunted as he tracked blood around her kitchen.

Cold. So cold. How could she be on fire and freezing at the same time? Kathleen tried to push the cold away, but someone forced her hands around it. "It burns," she whispered, hoping her nephew wouldn't hear. If he heard her, he'd relish her suffering.

"It's supposed to burn, you bitch. It's supposed to buuurrrn."

Kathleen pulled away, clamped her hand over her ear hoping to stop the lighter from touching her again. She scrambled backwards until she was trapped between the back of the couch and him.

"Kathleen," Lisa's voice penetrated her nightmare. "Put both hands around the orange and breathe."

Kathleen tried to shove it away but hands held hers and together they squeezed the orange. "It's too hot. Too cold."

"Kathleen, open your eyes. Tell me where you are," Lisa demanded.

It took several seconds for the directions to make sense before Kathleen opened her eyes and stared at the frozen fruit.

"Breathe," Lisa instructed.

Confused and frightened, she stared into Lisa's big brown eyes and followed her breaths.

"Thank you," Lisa said after several seconds of breathing together. "Tell me where you are."

Kathleen looked around the room. The faces were hazy, but she knew where she was, and she knew she needed to get out of here. "The group room."

Lisa was crouched in front of her and she heard women whispering.

"I want to go home. I want Matt."

"Hold on to the orange for a few more minutes," Lisa said.

Kathleen twisted one hand off the fruit and clasped Lisa's fingers. "Please let me go home."

"Kathleen, do you remember what I asked at the beginning of this session?"

She could focus her eyes, but her thoughts were still muddled as if her body had raced ahead and her mind was trying to catch up. "Why are you doing this to me? I told you I couldn't be around her. She can't have my family. They don't deserve my stories."

"The stories aren't for them. They are for you. *You* deserve the right to tell them. Don't let anyone take away your healing. Not in here and not out there," Lisa said. She waited a few beats and then continued, "Why did you come back here today? You could have simply not returned."

Kathleen thought of the nineteen pages of wishes and hopes and fears. She thought of her meanness towards Matt and his gentleness towards her. "My life is a fucked-up mess," she whispered. "Josh made sure of it."

"He can't get to you anymore. You have to take your power and your life back."

Kathleen's eyes darted to Missy, who was staring at her lap and picking at the frayed hem of her slutty shorts. "It's like he never stopped."

"We need to make him stop." Lisa tapped Kathleen's hand until they once again held each other's eyes. "What is the base of your pyramid? What will make all of this worthwhile?"

Kathleen could clearly see the blue ink on the pages. She'd started by writing their names and then she'd written of Courtney's wedding plans. Courtney had died eight weeks before the big day. Kathleen wrote the toast she'd never give, and a list of daddy-daughter songs that would never play. She wrote advice for Kiley on how to wear enough make-up but not too much. She gave Brice financial planning guidance because he had wanted a cabin near her and Seth. "I want to hold them the only way left to me. I want to love like I used to."

Lisa nodded and smiled. "You can have that, but you have to stay, keep working, keep enduring. You get to control your actions and reactions. Give us time to relearn." Lisa gave her hand another tight squeeze. Leaving the orange melting in Kathleen's hand, she rose and went back to her seat.

Kathleen held the orange, watched it melt, the water dripping down her arm and plopping onto the floor. Gloria moved closer, took Kathleen's arm and gently stroked her wrist. Stephanie had touched her the same way every day during those weeks in the hospital. Whether it was a need for connection or simple exhaustion, Kathleen didn't pull away. She lifted Matt's sweatshirt to her nose and held on to his scent. Rather than listen to the women around her, she listened to Lucas.

"Gwammy," Lucas shouted. *"Ki and I get to snap the turkey wing, wight? I've been pwacticing with chicken. I'm gonna win and then my wish will come twue."*

Kathleen was that turkey wing. In order for her wishes to come true, she had to snap.

"But you have to pull weally hard."

She looked at Gloria's hand stroking her arm. Could she try again? Could she tell this dirty, sad little girl about Kiley's love of puppies? Or Seth's habit of burning the chicken? Or the way T-Bone had loved to lick the yogurt cup?

Josh had succeeded in making her life a fucked-up mess. She had to unfuck it. In her homework she had explained to Kiley that nasty people only had the power you gave them. She'd given her power to Missy today. Tomorrow she would not. She had to find a way, find the courage, to take her family back.

Matt

The Buzzed Bibliophile's tinkling bell that had sounded so charming yesterday sent tingles up Matt's spine today. Yesterday, being surrounded by books felt like being surrounded by Kathleen. Today, the books reminded him of how little he knew. Why hadn't he gotten the frozen orange like he'd been told? He'd failed her. He did not—and never would—have the skills to guide Kathleen through her quagmire of pain and anger.

He had ninety minutes before he met with Kathleen and Lisa together. He had to tell Lisa about the nightmare and he hated Kathleen knowing he'd had an orange but didn't use it. While he ordered coffee and a cookie, he had the unwelcome thought that Kathleen's emotions were like rocks in a sling shot. If he didn't duck, she'd take him out.

When Matt's mother had asked him to take some time to himself, had she guessed that he'd be baffled by his own life? Had his mother seen his discontent when he couldn't? What would his mother think of Kathleen and this new situation he found himself in? When he was twenty-five and about to marry the wrong woman, his mother had sat him down and said, "Mattie, when you find someone to love you'll know it—it'll be the clearest pool of warmth. But it won't be easy. Love is the hardest thing of all. Wait until you find someone worth the fight. Then, like your dad and I have, hold on tight." Who knew he'd be fifty before he found that clear pool of warmth? Who knew it would be so damn hard?

He opened his computer and began to review Jeff's situation. It was simple. Jeff owed the taxes and the penalties. He'd played a game with the IRS and lost. Matt located the letter he'd sent warning him not to be so aggressive. Jeff wouldn't listen. It was a game to Jeff. A game he'd lost. Matt copied the letter in a new folder labeled *Jeff's an Asshole*. Without any guilt, he composed a terse email to Jeff telling him there would be no 11:00 a.m. meeting. He didn't give an excuse. It was none of the Asshole's business. He should make his clients happy, his sister happy, his employees happy. He should think about what Ken had said. Instead, he went to the bookshelves.

He pulled down a book he and Kathleen had listened to in the car. It was what he would have once referred to as a chick book, but he liked the male character who was an art restorer. He was surprised how much he learned about art and how much he enjoyed the fictional world. He opened the flap and discovered there were ten books in the series. He searched the shelf and found books two and three.

He wondered if Matt Nelson was a man who liked to read mysteries or a man who listened to mysteries because his Kathleen liked them.

Matt took the two books to his table. He sat and began to nibble on his cookie. He wore a University of Minnesota sweatshirt because he loved his Gophers. Until he'd met Kathleen, he'd not once missed a Minnesota Gophers home game. He had season tickets to the Twins and the Vikings and the Timberwolves and the Ducks. Normally this time of year, he'd spend Saturdays with his dad and nephews, going to Gophers games, and Sundays watching football, basketball, hockey. He didn't even know if the Gophers won last weekend or who they played next. He'd not watched one Timberwolves or Vikings or Ducks game. *Who was Matt Nelson?* A man who loved Minnesota sports.

And now, since he'd met Kathleen, a man who had to hide scratched arms.

Was Patti right? Had he used Kathleen as an excuse to run from a life he didn't like? Was she a project with a beginning, a middle, and an end? Did he love the real Kathleen or the broken Kathleen? Did he love the person or the project?

Who was Matt Nelson, anyway? Who did he want to be? He loved Kathleen. That was not in question. He wanted to make changes for her, for himself, for them. But how could they do that if he didn't know what he wanted? And what about her? Did she want to go back to the beach and into hiding? Was she working for a new kind of life or just a way to breathe while remaining isolated? Did she love him or was he just someone to cling to in the storm? Was she too broken to want anything?

He looked around for Ian, hoping for a distraction and an excuse to ignore his own problems. Except for Kathleen tucked next to him on the couch, the highlight yesterday had been helping Ian understand parabolas. Ian's problems were simple. One plus one equals two. *Who was Matt Nelson?* A man who liked math and who liked teaching others to like math.

The vibration in his pocket jerked him from his runaway train of thoughts. It was either Patti or Jeff. He needed to talk to both. He wanted to talk to neither.

"Jeff." He laced the greeting with a false combination of patience and apology.

"There is a lot I could say to you right now but what's the point? You do what you want and I'm getting jerked around. I chose your firm—and you—because word on the street is that you are not only excellent but you specifically are accessible and attentive. What the fuck is so important you can't keep an appointment you scheduled?"

With his free hand, Matt pinched the bridge of his nose. What would Jeff say if he described Kathleen, his girlfriend, as feral?

"Jeff, I've never asked. How many times have you been married?"

"Wife number three as a matter of fact."

"Number three. Why does that not surprise me?" Ten weeks ago, Matt would never have said such a thing. Today, the words tasted sweet on his lips. He let the words lie between them for several long seconds, secretly wishing Jeff was turning red with embarrassment.

"You are not taking my case seriously because of a woman?"

Matt did not know who he was, but he knew what to do. "I'm filing the last bit of paperwork today."

"File it. I want it in my email by four o'clock today." Jeff was an unhappy man and Matt smiled.

"Or what?" Matt asked, but Jeff was gone. Matt searched the company's database for a document that had been created by his father over forty years ago and, to Matt's knowledge, had never been used, called *You Gotta Go, Dickhead*. The document was five pages of single-spaced legalese that severed NNJ's relationship with a client. He pictured Jeff's face when he saw the last bit of paperwork and, for the first time in a long time, he enjoyed his job.

Kathleen

"What do you remember?" Lisa asked gently.

She and Matt were side by side, sitting in Lisa's office, where she'd hoped to tell him about Missy and her resolve to unfuck her life. But Lisa wanted to know about the night before, and Matt sat gripping her hand as if he was tethering her to the room. His tapping foot contradicted the calm look on his face. When she frowned at him, he gave her one of those encouraging smiles that wasn't encouraging at all.

"I did the journal activity." With her free hand, she pulled her journal covered in blue writing into her lap. "We watched football, we read, we made love, and we went to sleep."

"Where did you wake up?"

"The closet. But that's not unusual." She knew a bomb was about to be dropped. It was like all those times when the kids had some bad news and they'd dance around it. Their voices would either get louder and faster or softer and slower. Lisa's voice was slow and soft. Why couldn't Lisa just get to the point?

"You had a nightmare. It's my understanding that you woke screaming and clawing at Matt?"

A nightmare? Why had he not mentioned it? She turned to him and, with a tremor in her voice, she asked, "I did?"

"I'm fine." He stopped her hand from its frantic attempt to look at his arms.

She yanked her hand from his grasp and shoved the journal off her lap. "Fine? I have a nightmare that I don't remember. A nightmare you didn't tell me about. A nightmare that ended with you injured. And all you can say is *fine*." She had not yet fully recovered from her flashback in group, and now her calm snapped like a branch in a hurricane. She shuffled to the opposite end of the couch and glared at Lisa. "And how did you know I had a nightmare? I don't remember it, so you didn't hear it from me."

"Matt mentioned it to Ken and Ken called me." Lisa was learning forward, shortening the space between her and Kathleen. She had that same face Marcia used when she wanted her kids to relax and listen.

Kathleen swung her head and faced Matt. "Why would you talk to Ken and not me? You told me you were going to some coffee shop. Why did you lie? I thought I could trust you. I thought you were on my side."

"Kath, love—"

Lisa held up one hand. "Matt, I'd like you not to speak for a few minutes. I know you want to reassure and soothe. Anger is a healthy and helpful emotion. But not when it controls us. It's a tool, not a taskmaster, and I need to help Kathleen take back control."

"I don't want her to think I've betrayed her." His deer-in-the-headlights expression was a mix of "I'm begging you to let me explain" and "How dare you tell me what I can do?"

But he had betrayed her. What else do you call it when someone talks about you behind your back? Betrayal 101.

Lisa tapped her pen on the table until Matt's puppy-dog face looked at her. "Matt, I know this is hard, but one of the goals of family therapy is to learn when to step back and let our loved ones deal with their own emotions. Your job is to look at your own thoughts and feelings." She turned toward Kathleen. "And Kathleen, I'd like you to take a seat wherever you're comfortable."

Kathleen crossed the room several more times before her pace slowed. She picked up the binder where it had dropped on the floor. Keeping the coffee table between her and Matt because his touch might relight her barely-tamped rage, she sat in the chair next to Lisa. She kept her eyes focused on the floor, not wanting Matt to see how much his betrayal hurt her and not ready to see his apologetic face.

"Thank you," Lisa said. "Matt, we are going to walk through one of the Dialectical Behavior Therapy skills. DBT is a fancy acronym for a set of skills to help us navigate our emotions so they work for us and not against us."

"I don't want to," Kathleen said. "I'm more comfortable with the anger."

"What prompted your anger?" Lisa asked.

Lisa would keep poking and prodding until Kathleen participated. She bit her tongue until the pain relaxed her. "Matt told Ken about a nightmare instead of telling me."

"I'd like you to stop mumbling and look at me. I'd like you to own your emotions and tell me why this situation is so volatile for you."

"I don't remember the nightmare. God, Lisa, what else am I doing that I don't remember?"

"Pay attention to the sensations in your body. Would you like to add an emotion to your anger?" Lisa instructed.

"Hot. I'm very hot. My scalp itches and..." She rotated her shoulders in a figure eight. "I have ants on my skin."

"Name the emotions and grade the intensity. Remember the scale goes to 100."

"Anger was at 110. Now it's 75. Helpless is at 100. I'm jittery and out of control." She didn't want to do this exercise.

She wanted to run and keep running until her past quit chasing her.

"Let's keep working. Review the facts of the situation with me. Remember to stick to facts, not judgments."

She darted her eyes to Matt. He had moved to the edge of his seat and was watching the interplay as if he were studying an exhibit at the zoo. A red scratch mark was visible on his left wrist. "I apparently had a nightmare. I don't remember it. I clawed at Matt's arms. He told Ken. He did not tell me."

"Those are the facts. You feel angry and helpless. Do your emotions fit the facts?"

Kathleen blew out a long breath and waited for him to look directly at her. "No and yes. You needed to tell Ken or Lisa. But I'd like you to tell me first. I don't want to be blindsided. I have enough shit sneaking up and choking me."

Matt looked to Lisa for permission to speak. When she nodded, he rested his elbows on his knees, leaned as close as the table between them would allow. "I'm sorry. When you acted as if nothing happened, I kind of freaked. I was afraid to bring it up because I had no idea what your reaction would be. But I knew I wouldn't know how to handle it if you reacted badly. I was afraid to screw it up and make matters worse."

"Kathleen, can you understand why Matt didn't tell you? Can you step into his world for a minute?"

Her lip began to tremble, but she fought to hide it. "I understand why he had to wait. I wish it was different. I wish I was different."

"It—and you—will be. Give it time and patience," Lisa assured them both. "Do an emotion check-in again?"

Kathleen's chest still ached, and her throat still itched with unshed tears. But she could breathe, and the tremors were calmer. "Anger is at 20. Helpless is still at 100."

"We will continue to work with both of you. But, Kathleen," Lisa waited until Kathleen turned her direction. "You did a great job today. Can you be proud of that? You honored what your body was telling you and you found a constructive way to communicate."

Kathleen finally nodded but she didn't feel confident. Hurting Matt was a new low and she hadn't thought she could go any lower.

"Matt, you asked what she did here all day. This is what she does. We find these angry and painful spots. We expose them, lance them, and heal them. We teach Kathleen how to do this for herself without destroying the world around her."

"Was I wrong to tell Ken instead of her?" Matt asked.

"You need to take care of yourself. Her safety is important. So is yours. If you felt it was unsafe to talk to her without support, then you have to honor that. Your emotions and beliefs are just as important as hers."

He leaned forward. "I told you before, I can handle your anger if that's what you need."

"No," Lisa interjected forcefully. "We do not allow people—even people we love—to use us as a punching bag. Would you want Kathleen to allow someone to do that to her?"

But you let Missy treat me badly, Kathleen wanted to say. She stood. She was, as Courtney would have said, over it. Reaching for Matt's hand, she asked, "Would you walk me out?"

He stood and ran his thumb under her eyes. "I'll walk with you anywhere."

Kathleen breathed in the smell of turpentine in The Center's Art House. The piney scent opened a slideshow of memories. Like the time she and Seth had painted the deck, only to decide the color was hideous and start over. Or when she and Courtney had taken an oil painting class, only to discover they had zero talent. They'd hung those awful paintings in the cabin's guest bath and counted how many people complimented what was obviously awful. For the first time in almost four years, she regretted not being the one to decide what to keep and what to destroy. She'd let Stephanie make the choices, and she still hadn't had the fortitude to open one box.

Through journaling, Kathleen had discovered parts of Marcia that she wanted back. Kathleen would never have Marcia's confidence or trust in people, but she could reclaim Marcia's love of photography and her desire to travel. She wanted to see Asia and penguins and the Northern lights. She wanted to swim in Australia and drink *grappa* in Italy.

She wished there was a way to let Matt know that she was trying, that she wanted to get better. The nightmare, his frightened look, and the claw marks on his arms made her want to work harder. Never before in her life had she hurt someone physically. If she hurt him again, he'd have to leave. She'd make him leave. No matter how much she loved him and wanted to see the world with him, she would not stand by while he became her whipping boy. In this art class, she'd find a way to thank him. She'd get those three words past the hole in her soul.

"Ladies, before you get too involved, let's gather around," Allie, the art therapist, said. Her paint-splattered overalls, ratty UNC t-shirt, and messy ponytail disguised her skill as a therapist. Allie was a continual source of encouragement. The young woman's enthusiasm and constant energy reminded Kathleen of her Courtney.

"*Moms, I would never wear a UNC shirt,*" Courtney said. Kathleen could picture her standing there with her hand on her cocked hips. "*I'm glad she's still here, Allie's pretty cool.*"

Kathleen paused at the revelation. "*You were here last time? Why didn't you talk to me? Help me?*"

"*We tried, but you weren't ready to listen. You were having a pity party and you needed that. But it's time to move on.*"

Kathleen hesitated before asking the question that plagued her. "Courts, I've heard from Brice and you and even *the grands. Where is your father? Why is Seth not talking to me?"*

Courtney remained silent and Kathleen was relieved. Sometimes not knowing was less painful than the truth. Did Seth blame her? Hate her? Did he not approve of Matt? Did he think she should always live in despair?

Like a kindergarten teacher, Allie clapped her hands. "Before we go to our stations, one of you has asked for time to share her story through her art."

This was new and unwelcome. In the past, the women would do a private check-in with Allie and then get to work. Allie would play loud music and bop around to everyone. This had been the one place Kathleen could taste a little bit of Marcia.

When no one spoke, a restless energy invaded the room. The voyeurs searched for the source of the next graphic story. Others, like Kathleen, were impatient at the intrusion.

"Gloria," Allie's tone changed from that of a cheerleader to that of a kind and encouraging therapist.

Kathleen snapped her head to stare at the sad girl who had held her hand just an hour ago. She was about twenty-three years old and her face was littered with pimples. Her dress was a flowered concoction fraying at the hem and neckline.

Gloria held Kathleen's gaze and gnawed on her grimy thumbnail. She was seeking something from her but Kathleen had no idea what.

"Moms, nod at her. Smile. Make it easier."

"I'm not her mother or her protector," Kathleen argued.

"Maybe she needs one."

"What she needs is a bath." Guilt and embarrassment swamped Kathleen. She might not be able to swim in Australia or create a damn thing, but Kathleen Conners would not—could not—be mean. With a small smile, Kathleen nodded at Gloria.

"This is a coffin," Gloria pointed to a dark rectangle in her painting. She moved her finger and pointed to a heart painted inside the darkness. "This is a heart."

The painting was remarkable. At first the coffin was unclear, but after careful study, it floated to the surface through the myriad of dark colors. Gloria's pain was felt as much as seen. Gloria put her finger back in her mouth and her head hung on her shoulders as if it weighed too much.

"Who or what is in that coffin?" Allie asked in the same gentle tone Kathleen used when the grandkids were frightened.

It took several seconds of tense silence before Gloria swiped her hand across leaking eyes and answered, "My mom."

"Would you be willing to tell us more?"

Gloria shrugged, flicked her eyes at Kathleen before she looked at the table.

"We don't allow shrugs," Allie said. "That's the same as 'fine' and it's a bullshit answer." The words were blunt but empathetic. Allie didn't touch Gloria, but she did move closer, lending Gloria her warmth and security.

Gloria's terrified face hardened as if Allie had pushed her one step too far. "Me! It represents me. When my mom killed herself, I buried my heart with her." The words burst from her mouth at the same rate the tears burst from her eyes.

I buried my heart. I buried my heart. I buried my heart. The words—the power of them—the truth of them—pummeled Kathleen.

"Moms, what would you say to me if I said that?" Courtney asked.

Unable and unwilling to ignore her precious girl's presence, Kathleen answered, *"I would tell you that your heart still beats. It's got permanent cracks. But it's not buried. It's just waiting to be uncovered, dusted, and used again."*

"Tell her that?"

"Courtney, she's none of my business. There are therapists at every corner. I'm the exact opposite of what she needs."

"Or exactly what she needs. You just said you want to love. Can you love without having compassion?"

Allie thanked Gloria for her courage, clapped her hands again and women scattered to their chosen area. Gloria stood silently facing the window, her face toward the sun and her shoulders dragging the floor.

"Dammit," Kathleen muttered, but she walked to the girl, took her hand, and together they stared at the leaves drifting to the ground.

"My daughter could never decide on a favorite color," Kathleen said.

Gloria squeezed Kathleen's fingers, pinching them until pain shot into her hand. "My mom liked the yellow with the orange speckles," Gloria said in a small voice before she rested her head on Kathleen's shoulder. "She said they were like little leaves of fire."

Kathleen didn't respond. Sometimes words were unnecessary. Instead of words, you had to reach out, take someone's hand, and hold on. As much as she wanted to make Matt a card and find the words for him, she had to be in this moment, with Gloria and her suffering. For the first time in almost four years, it wasn't about her.

Matt

Sipping a black-cherry mocha latte with a shot of almond at the Buzzed Bibliophile had become Matt's second favorite activity of the day. His favorite, of course, was picking up Kathleen. Sometimes she came out almost smiling. Sometimes her shoulders were heavy and the circles under her eyes were darker. Every time—absolutely every time—she put her arms around him, dropped her forehead into his chest, and held on.

After a long two weeks of treatment, they had developed a routine. He'd moved them out of the hotel into a vacation rental. He'd discovered—and she'd rediscovered—that she was an excellent cook. On the days she was almost smiling, they went for a long, quiet walk and then made dinner together. When she wasn't smiling, he prepared them a nest in the closet. The nightmares hadn't stopped and she continued to add bruises to her body. But today Matt was especially excited because she'd agreed to join him for coffee this morning and meet Ian.

"Matt," Ian said when he walked over to the corner where he and Kathleen sat. "This must be Kathleen."

Matt stood, pulling him in for the type of man hug he gave his nephews. "Kath, this is Ian. Algebra student extraordinaire."

Ian rolled his eyes and extended his hand to Kathleen.

She froze. She touched her scarf and reached for her sunglasses. She cocked her head and her eyes lost focus for several seconds. Matt had seen her do that many times and he knew she was listening to her family. She liked to hear their voices and, from Matt's perspective, they gave her good advice.

Finally, Kathleen gave a quick nod as if she were agreeing, then she smiled, pointed at Ian's shirt, and said, "Please tell me you aren't a North Carolina fan. We're a Duke family and we don't like North Carolina. Brice and Courtney call that 'public bathroom blue.' We're having a hard enough time with the Gopher red." She jerked her thumb toward Matt's red Gophers shirt.

If Ian noticed Kathleen's strange behavior—and he had to notice—he gave no indication. He simply dropped his hand, smiled hugely, and said, "Go Tarheels!"

Kathleen laughed and Ian pulled up a chair, turned it backwards, straddled it, and started talking.

"Brice used to sit like that," Kathleen said.

It was Matt's turn to freeze. She had shared some anecdotes about her family with him, but he knew it was painful for her and it often sent her into a place he could not reach. He watched her carefully, ready to jump in at the tiniest hint of distress.

"My mom hated it," Ian said before he launched into a list of reasons why the Tarheels were better than both Duke and the Gophers.

Matt sipped his coffee and watched as Kathleen leaned closer to Ian and teased him. He watched as the tension in her body dissipated and the blue of her eyes shone brighter.

"Matt," she said, pulling him from his contented observation. "Ian has never been to a football game. Never." She acted as if this were a cardinal sin. "We have to fix that. Get on your phone and buy him a ticket. Get him a good seat, too."

"Yes, ma'am." Matt wasn't sure if she meant Ian and Matt or all three of them. Rather than ask, he opened his phone and spent a lot of money on three tickets for the NC-Pittsburg game this Saturday. He knew the football game was a risk. If she was triggered, they would be buried in a crowd of eighty thousand people. But right now she was laughing and eating and smiling and the risk seemed worth it. He bit into his scone and relished this step into their normal—Ian, coffee, and football.

"When football season is over, let's get tickets for Duke basketball," Kathleen was saying. "They always kick ass."

His Kathleen was planning for a future beyond the next few weeks. Duke basketball tickets were extremely expensive, but if a basketball game made her grin like she was grinning now, he'd buy the entire arena. They would have Ian and coffee and football and basketball. They would have normal.

The three of them bantered for several minutes before Matt stood and said to Ian, "I have to drop my Kathleen off and we have to get that brain of yours to add two plus two. Get your stuff out and I'll be back in fifteen minutes."

Kathleen's shoulders dropped but she rose, picked up her Curious George bag, and took his hand. "I'll cheer for your Tarheels until they play Duke. Then all bets are off," she said over her shoulder as the door closed behind them.

Twenty minutes later, Matt was back at the bookstore with a fresh cup of coffee and a bowl of fruit in front of him. Dropping Kathleen at The Center was no longer a torturous process. She kissed him, reminded him to be on time, and climbed out. She never looked back. Another sign she was getting better and their lives would begin soon.

Now Ian sat across from him, surrounded by pages of notes, two pencils, and a calculator. He wore his normal frustrated look, and that was another part of the routine Matt enjoyed.

"Back up two steps," Matt said.

Ian began the necessary corrections. "I know I sound like a middle schooler. But seriously, when will I ever need to multiply polynomials?"

"You probably won't need it, but you have to pass the damn class," Matt said with a smile in his voice. He'd heard the same complaint from Jake and Joey every time he tutored them, but his nephews were taking calculus and statistics. Ian was struggling to pass basic algebra. "If it takes us all day, every day, we will get through this."

"Easy for you to say," Ian muttered, but he started the steps for the second problem.

"Your final is Friday. We have four more days to finish this study guide." Matt flipped through the pages Ian had given him. "That's ten problems a day. I'll help you until you're bleeding $ax + by = c$."

Friday was a big day for all of them. Ian had his midterm. Kathleen would meet with her treatment team. They both believed she was making enough progress to set a discharge date. She hadn't yet remembered everything. She had yet to cry. At night, he saw where she pinched herself so hard that dark bruises trailed up her inner leg from her knees to the tops of her thighs. He hadn't counted, but he imagined there were twenty dark purple circles on each leg.

But Matt was beginning to believe that giving her a discharge date might help her move past those last obstacles. It was like tax season. Once April 15 was a reality, you buckled down and got the work done.

Matt and Ken had met two more times. Ken kept challenging Matt to think about what he wanted tomorrow, next week, next year. He was teaching him to ask, "What is the next best decision for Matt Nelson?" Not for Kathleen, not for his dad, not for his sister. For Matt.

For the first time, Matt actually had time to think about what he wanted. Every morning, he opened his work email and closed it without reading a single message. Eventually he would have to deal with NNJ and Patti. He simply could not make himself care. He was enjoying working with Ian during the day and chopping vegetables with Kathleen for dinner. His world was not perfect because she still had pain to suffer, but he was more content than he'd ever been. Kathleen would always be his next best decision, and he wanted to keep all other worries tucked in the back of his mind.

"Is that right, finally?" Ian asked, and Matt once again pushed the thoughts of Jeff and NNJ and his sister away.

"Told you it could be done. Listen, about the football game... The last time Kathleen was at a football game, she was with her family. This will be hard for her," Matt said. The game would be crowded. She'd be touched by the people next to her. A college football game would hold more poignant, painful, and wonderful memories.

Ian put down his pencil, sat up straighter. "What happened to her?"

Matt knew Ian would eventually ask. The boy wasn't stupid. He'd seen her missing finger and her frantic worry over her scarf. He'd seen her stare at the sunglasses as if they held the power to transport her elsewhere. He'd seen Matt's overprotectiveness. But how would he handle the truth of her? It was one thing to know his Kathleen was odd. It was another to know why.

"Her family were all..." Matt stalled out. The next word was *murdered*. He'd never had to say it before. The words were heavy and dark and frightening. Losing your family in an accident was tragic enough. But murder? He could say *killed*, but he knew the next question would be *how*. They'd expect a car accident or something more tragically normal.

Before he could decide how much to tell Ian, Matt's phone vibrated and skittered across the table. His father's name flashed on the screen and Matt smiled as he reached for it. His father had been a constant source of comfort and encouragement.

"Dad," he said. "Look, I'm working with Ian. I'll call you back in—" he paused, looked at Ian's work. "After he finishes two more problems."

Ian grunted but picked up his pencil and got started.

"Matt, you need to get back to Minnesota..."

"Are you all right?" Matt braced himself. The last time he'd heard this tone in his father's voice, he was learning of his mother's cancer diagnosis.

"Did you really fire Jeff? Without discussing it with Patricia? Without permission from the board?"

"I'm the managing partner. I don't run to the board with every decision, and Patti made it perfectly clear this was my problem." Matt gripped the phone so hard his knuckles ached and he had to fight hard not to sound like an arrogant dictator.

"You're the managing partner and yet you sit in Charlotte, ignoring emails and phone calls, tutoring a young man you hardly know."

"That's not fair. You were supportive of this. You understood. Why did anyone even bother you about this idiot? You're retired."

"Patti called me last night and gave me the entire story. She was hoping my intervention would satisfy the dickhead. I spent the morning talking to him and his team of lawyers."

"I can't understand why this is such a big deal. Maybe we could have scrounged out a few thousand more. Maybe not. We fired him, but we'd already done all the work." Matt had not been called on the carpet in twenty years and, while on some level he deserved it, he resented his illusion of contentment being smashed.

His father sighed loudly, as if he were talking to a recalcitrant child. "You use the pronoun *we*, but it was you. While you were at the beach, did you promise Jeff you'd handle everything? Did you send all those promises in an email—an email he can print and hold and shove in our faces?"

"I don't know what I said at the beach. Seriously, Dad, I had just met Kathleen. My world was rocking." And, he thought stubbornly, Jeff was an asshole who did not merit the time or the drama.

"Did you promise to check in *at least* once a week? Did you schedule calls and then cancel at the last minute?"

His dad waited, but there was no reason for Matt to answer rhetorical questions or jump to his own defense. He'd made the right decision for everyone.

"Jeff is screaming breach of contract, among other things. He's an asshole. He's enjoying himself. He's willing to take this as far as he can."

Matt walked away from Ian and into the parking lot, letting his fury rise and whip on the wind. He forced his voice to sound calm. "Let him. The firm has liability insurance."

"If we did nothing wrong, then we shouldn't roll over and play dead. That's not our way, and that will only bite us later with other clients. Our firm is built on integrity and we don't let anyone say otherwise." Joe said.

Matt blew out a breath and asked, "What more can I do?"

"You need to come home," Joe said.

Matt stopped walking. "I can't come to Minnesota. Not now."

"Let me put this another way," his father said. "You *must* come here and clean up this mess. I've tried. Patti has tried. If you don't come, the firm could suffer irreparable damage. I get you need to be with Kathleen, but she'll understand you need to spend a few days here. You told me yourself she's improving."

Matt paced the parking lot. It wasn't just leaving Kathleen or Ian. He did not want to step back into those offices. He was tired of doing a job he didn't like. Tired of working with people willing to steal and cheat to make a few bucks. The next best decision for Matt was not in Minnesota.

"This is the family firm, Matt. Patti's livelihood. Jake and Joey's future. You cannot leave us hanging when all it takes is your ass on a plane and a bit of eating crow."

"Things are better but I take her everywhere. I encourage her to do her homework. I hold her at night. And there's Ian, too. I only have a couple more days to get him ready for his final." He didn't mention frozen oranges and nightmares but he thought of those, too.

"I don't know what to tell you. All I can say is that I wouldn't be making this call if I had any other solution."

Matt stopped pacing and leaned against the car door. It was cold and getting colder. A sleet-rain was expected in the next hours and he had planned to light the first fire of the season tonight. Kathleen was planning to cook homemade tomato soup and grilled cheese sandwiches. According to her—and Seth—she made the best grilled cheese known to the modern world. He wanted the best grilled cheese in the modern world. "When would I have to be there?"

"We've already booked you on the seven p.m. flight tonight. We'll have twenty-four hours and a lot to accomplish in one business day. Jeff will be here at seven a.m. Wednesday, and he's expecting you to greet him at the door. Wearing Armani." Matt wished they'd all wear jeans and University of Minnesota shirts. Or better, a taco tie and Converse shoes. Jeff wasn't worth it.

"Tonight? Five hours from now?"

His dad didn't answer.

"What do I tell her?"

"The truth usually works."

"But I'm not sure she's ready to be left alone." Matt was repeating himself, but he had promised to be here. He could not leave her to face the nights alone. If he was gone, she would have to stay at The Center. There had to be a better solution.

"Matt, she's not a child. She cannot become dependent on you. That will backfire in so many ways."

Ken's warning from their last session reverberated in Matt's mind. *Don't become co-dependent. She must stand alone. You must stand alone. You lean on each other. You do not hold each other up.*

"How long will I be gone?"

"I have no idea. While you're here, let's go over all the accounts, meet with all the associates." He wasn't saying the words, but what he meant was come-home-to-do-your-damn-job. "You told me you trust Lisa and The Center. Call them."

Matt wanted to tell his dad no. He wanted to tell him that any other employee could quit, and he wanted to quit, too. It might be unprofessional to leave with no notice, but people did it all the time.

Matt wasn't people. Matt was a Nelson. Matt was *the* Nelson. The man in the big office, the man in the big chair, and the man with the big fucking problem.

"I'll meet Jeff tomorrow. That's Wednesday. I want a return ticket for late Thursday. I have to be here Friday." He had three hours before he had to be at the airport. He'd call Lisa and Ken. Then he'd speak to Kathleen. She would understand.

"I'd like you to stay through Friday."

"I have to be back Thursday night," Matt said. She could—they could—manage three nights. She'd understand. But he had to be here while Kathleen met with the treatment team. He had to be standing outside Willow Lodge on Friday. That was non-negotiable.

"It's not only the firm. You and Patricia cannot go on like this. You're both being childish. I lost your mom. I will not have my kids not speaking to each other."

"She is way down on my list of priorities," Matt retorted, letting some of his annoyance travel the phone line.

"Change your priorities and get on the damn plane."

"Dad…"

His father had hung up.

Until ten months ago, Matt could not remember a time when he'd not kept a promise. His father was right. If there was one word to describe NNJ and the Nelson family, it would be integrity. Matt had promised his mother he'd take care of his father by handling the firm. He'd promised Patti he'd not drop this in her lap. He'd broken so many promises with Jeff. And now, Kathleen. He would have to break the one promise with the greatest risk.

Matt fought the urge to throw his phone across the pavement. He looked into the Buzzed Bibliophile and saw Ian pulling at the roots of his hair. Ian was yet another promise he might not be able to keep.

What was the next best decision for Matt? Matt laughed an angry laugh. That question was a big fucking waste of time.

Kathleen

"Pia, do you still want to do this?"

The furniture in the group therapy room had been rearranged. Chairs and couches had been shoved against the wall, and pillows formed a large circle on the floor. It reminded Kathleen of church camp when she was a girl. They'd sit in a circle around a fire pit, hold hands, sing songs, and one girl would always give her testimony. Kathleen didn't want to sit in a circle and sing songs. She didn't want to do any of this anymore today. But she was trapped and had to face this last session. She folded her legs and found her place on the circle's edge. When Gloria sat next to her, she sighed. She had no energy for Gloria, either. She was tired and drained and weary and wanted to make soup, cuddle on the couch with a fire, and pretend this place did not exist.

"Pia has found the strength and courage and desire to share," Lisa said. "This is her time. And as her support system, we will listen and provide her a safe place. Judgment-free. And, as always, we ask that you honor your own emotions. Sit with it, hold it. Try not to block."

Pia was the girl who had to sit with a therapist at meals to prove she ate everything. The girl who couldn't go to the bathroom without supervision. The girl who weighed eighty pounds. The young girl whose collarbones were so pronounced Kathleen could grab them and swing her 'round and 'round. The girl whose hair fell out in clumps. The girl Kathleen wanted to feed and feed and feed.

Pia's lip trembled and, even in the dim lighting, Kathleen saw she was as translucent as tissue paper. The girl sitting next to Pia reached over and traced figure eights on her back.

"It started when I was six years old," Pia began. She held Lisa's eyes as if Lisa were the only person on earth.

Pia spoke of extreme wealth and privilege. Of life in Seattle. Yachts. Parties. Fancy dresses. Famous people. She spoke of her parents' three-month trip around Europe. Nannies. Two couples. One for days, one for nights. Duct tape. Tied hands. Tied feet. Locked closets. Money exchanged. Pictures taken. Videos. Pain. Blood. Bruises.

As Pia spoke, Gloria began bouncing her leg so hard and fast Kathleen felt like she was on an amusement park ride. Kathleen's hand shot out, applying pressure to Gloria's leg, forcing it flat into the ground. Gloria tangled their fingers together. Kathleen stared at their joined hands. At Gloria's dirty nails. At her own shredded skin.

The last time Courtney had held her hand, she was Marcia, Honey, Moms, Mama, Grammy. The day had been sunny and unseasonably warm. It could have been four years ago this very day. Wedding dress shopping. Just a mom and her daughter. Excited. Laughing. Joyous. For the first time since she was a child, Courtney had grabbed her mother's hand. They'd swung their arms up and back, up and back. "Moms," she had said, light leaping out of her brown eyes. "Do you think Dads can learn to dance well enough not to embarrass us all?"

"Dads," Kathleen whispered, still staring at her hand laced with Gloria's, and she understood Gloria's desire to end the day and rest until the poking and prodding began again tomorrow. But neither Kathleen nor Gloria could escape the horror of Pia's story.

"They made me wear this sequined red dress with those plastic high heels for little girl dress-up." Pia swiped at her eyes. "My panties were all the Disney princesses. They called me Princess Pia."

Seth had called Courtney *Princess Courtney-bug*. Kathleen's emotions—her anger and her empathy and her despair—were choking her. She clamped her eyes shut, and swallowed and swallowed and swallowed, begging herself not to vomit. She untangled her hand from Gloria's, wrapped her arm around her bent knees and rocked herself, trying desperately to stop the pain in her chest and the burn in her throat. She felt Gloria touch her shoulder and whisper in her ear. But she had to keep rocking or she'd rip her skin to shreds. After a while she heard the other women leaving the room but she kept rocking. She was in a fog and the only sound was Pia's keening and her own panicked breathing.

"Kathleen, let's talk," Lisa said, putting her palm on Kathleen's shoulder. "We're alone now. Keep rocking, but open your eyes so we can understand why you're reacting so powerfully."

"Go to Pia," Kathleen said.

"Pia's with her therapist. She's being taken care of. Let's take care of you."

Kathleen opened her eyes and bit her lower lip to stop any tears from falling. "She's the same age as my Courtney. Why is she ashamed? Guilt-ridden? Where are her parents? Do they feel guilty or ashamed?"

"We don't question her experience or her emotions. All we can do is honor them and her. But why did her story impact you so strongly?"

Kathleen rocked faster. The answer—the truth—was a horse waiting for the start gun to open the gates. "She didn't do anything wrong. She was so very innocent."

"Are you talking about Pia or Courtney or yourself?"

"Pia, Courtney. Both of them." In her mind, the words were a shout but they came out as an anguished whisper. "Pia. She's lost her childhood and her family and her health. But she's a survivor! She should stand tall. Her story is a story of strength. Why can't she see that?" She pleaded with Lisa to make Pia see, to make her understand, to make the beautiful Pia whole.

Lisa sat cross-legged across from Kathleen. Her look was so warm, so accepting, so welcoming that Kathleen almost lost her grip on the tears.

"Kathleen, how does your story parallel Pia's? You carry such guilt and shame. But aren't you a victim? Haven't you lost everything and still you survive? Isn't yours a story of strength, too?"

"But it was my fault. I am guilty."

"Guilty of what? Does guilt fit the facts?"

Lisa let the weight of the question hang in the air for several seconds, then she stood and left Kathleen to decide her own guilt or innocence.

Kathleen wasn't sure anymore. Lisa was right. She had lost everything, too. She had survived. Would she ever get over the guilt?

She straightened her scarf, scratched at her scars, and checked the time. She had a stress management class before her final session of the day with Lisa. But Lisa saw her weariness and Kathleen expected her to keep their session gentle, focusing on beautiful memories or future goals. Lisa knew when to press and when to pull back. Today was a day to pull back.

She had time to get a snack, compose herself, and then in two hours Matt would be here and she could go home. She'd be free to make grilled cheese sandwiches, throw their new Duke blanket over her legs, and let thoughts of loss and survival wait one more day.

Matt

Matt sat at Ken's table twirling Kathleen's blue pen in and around his fingers like a baton. Once again, he'd been waiting for fifteen minutes, and each minute only made him write faster. At his feet was the bag he'd packed for Kathleen—his sweatshirts, his shirt that she slept in, pajama pants, jeans, socks, underwear, toiletries, her sunglasses. But what if she refused to stay at The Center? She might smile and agree and then leave anyway. She had the resources.

He'd decided to leave his car at The Center, so Kathleen had tangible evidence that he'd be back. He checked his watch. He had under an hour before Ian would be there to take him to the airport. When he'd told Ian he had to leave for a few days, the young man had looked at him, then at his equations, alarmed but accepting. It was the acceptance that made Matt feel like an ass. On the drive to the airport, Matt planned to give Ian a strategy for recognizing mistakes before they became wrong answers on his math final. He also planned to check in with him via Facetime at night. The firm be damned. He'd find a way to keep his promise to Ian. But what about his promise to Kathleen? He was confident Ken would let him see her so he could tell her that he loved her and that he would be back on Friday morning. He wanted to see for himself that she understood and forgave him for this sudden change in plans.

"Good afternoon," Ken said, stepping into the room. "Is everything all right? We don't meet until later in the week and my secretary said it was an emergency."

Matt sat straighter in his chair and leaned over the table. "Can Kathleen stay here for a couple of nights?"

Obviously startled, Ken settled in his seat, rested his ankle on his knee and said, "Back up. Tell me what's happening."

Matt told him everything. "If you'll just let me talk to her. I promised her I wouldn't leave, and I want to explain myself."

"It seems you have made some promises that are mutually exclusive," Ken said.

"I didn't realize that at the time. But, yes, I suppose I have." Matt was defeated and disappointed in himself. Ten months ago, his life may have been uninspiring, but at least it had been easy. He was the lead attorney and that was his life. There was no need to have emotions and certainly no need to identify and discuss them. Everyone depended on him, but no one depended on him emotionally. He was used to a world where *fine* was not only appropriate, it was expected.

"I can't let you see Kathleen," Ken said.

Matt forced his fingers to loosen his tightening grip on the pen. "What will she say when I don't pick her up at five? She has to know that I couldn't figure a way out of this."

"And if she isn't good with this, what will you do? Break another promise?"

Ken's questions weren't judgmental. They were probing. Which, right now, was worse. Matt didn't have time to probe. He had a lover to see and a plane to catch and an asshole to soothe and a company to fix.

"We don't allow people to just show up and intrude on the resident's treatment. Can you imagine the chaos if family members could come and go as they please? This protective environment would lose its safety."

"But we aren't talking about the residents. We're talking about my Kathleen."

For the first time since Matt had known Ken, the man looked angry. "This place is not designed around Kathleen," he said slowly.

"But, come on, Kathleen's situation is different."

"Do you think she has bigger problems than our other patients? More to overcome? Do you think she's more special than the next woman?" Ken took a deep breath but with his next words Matt knew he wasn't calm. "One of the women here was raped by her father. Repeatedly. If that wasn't enough, her father pimped her out to his friends. Kathleen—and you—had healthy, loving families. This woman—many of the women here—have no one to love them. No support. They have no reason to want to get better—except for their internal bravery. Kathleen may have lots to work through, but she has something at the other end."

Matt's shoulders dropped and guilt swamped him. He *had* thought Kathleen was more special, more troubled. "I'm sorry," he whispered. "I love her and for me she is special."

"All the women here are special, and they all have freedom of choice. They can say no and yes. They can choose who is in their lives. I can't make Kathleen do anything. I can reassure her that she's safe here and you'll be back. In some cases I can force a psych hold—which I have no indication Kathleen needs. The choices are hers."

"Goddammit, Ken. She's not ready to be alone! Someone needs to stop her when she hurts herself." Matt couldn't believe he'd said that. He'd promised that was between them. Ken frowned. "Hurts herself?"

Kathleen had stopped digging her fingernails into her palms until she bled. She had stopped clawing at herself when overwhelmed. She'd assured him she'd stop the pinching too.

"I'd like this to stay between us," he said. He had opened a door and he had no choice but to walk through it.

Ken raised his palm. "No. You can keep your secrets from her. But when it comes to her well-being, you should have told us anything that was worrying you. This is why we are an inpatient facility. The women here—Kathleen included—use these dark methods to cope. We teach them a healthier way. What is she doing?"

"She pinches herself." Matt touched his inner thigh to indicate the location of her self-abuse. "She's covered in bruises. But I believe her when she says she can and will stop."

Ken leaned into Matt's space. His voice was both warm and matter-of-fact. "It's time for you to leave her here. The women here are forced to sit with themselves and their pain. They are forced to watch and listen as other women suffer and struggle and win. She gets to this edge—one toe in the abyss of her memories—and then she pulls back. She can do this because she goes home with you at night. She can hide in books or TV or even by making dinner. She gets twelve hours away and in that time she repacks the boxes."

"That's not fair. I'm helping her. We're facing all of this together." Matt sounded as defensive as he felt. He had to be helping her. That was his role, his duty, his privilege. It was one thing to fail the firm. It was another thing to fail Ian. But to fail Kathleen? No, he could not accept that.

"I know she wouldn't have even started this process without your presence. That's why we allowed her to be outpatient. But the time has come for her to stand on her own feet. She has to step into her story, and you are keeping her from doing that."

"But..." Ken was wrong; she was getting better partly because he was there. Matt was not keeping her from facing those memories. He was holding her as she faced them.

"Are you expecting to be with her twenty-four hours a day when she's discharged? Or are you planning to hire a babysitter? This is the codependence I keep warning you about. Do you think that's what she wants? You keep saying you want a normal life. Well, Matt, a normal life is not being attached at the hip. You—and she—will want to go places and do things without each other. You both will *need* to do that. You have to deal with a family situation. A healthy—normal—relationship is one where the partners understand and support each other in difficult situations. The fact that she doesn't know you've had this problem brewing is an indication that you are taking care of her but she's not taking care of you. That cannot last. It's a burden no one can bear. No one should bear."

"She's not a burden," Matt spat at him.

"Let's say that she refuses to stay here, what then?"

"She can go to Minnesota with me." Maybe that's what he should do, anyway. They were going to ask for a discharge date on Friday. Maybe they could just discharge today. Maybe he could find her an outpatient program in Minnesota. Even as he thought it, he knew that wasn't a viable option. She wouldn't want to start with someone new and neither would he. He'd come to trust The Center and Ken and Lisa. And he knew she wasn't ready. But what if Ken was wrong? What if leaving pushed her backwards instead of forward?

"And if she refuses?" Ken continued. "You can't throw her over your shoulder. And even if you could, are you going to have her sit in on meetings like a pretty, broken doll?"

Matt buried his face in his hands. He'd painted himself into two corners. "I don't want her to think I've abandoned her. I'll be back Friday morning. I promise." Matt winced at his choice of words. He hadn't been so good at the promise thing lately.

"If it makes you feel better, I think she'll stay without much of a fight. She knows, in her heart, that she keeps pulling back.

She's afraid and that's to be expected. She's been asked, 'Why do you want to suffer through this process?' Every resident is asked that repeatedly. Just as I've told you to ask and ask and ask again, she has been instructed to do the same thing. Her answers are always the same."

Matt held his breath. As he'd toiled with that question, the one constant answer was that he wanted to be with her. Even if she was never healthy—even if that meant a life hiding on the beach—he wanted to wake up next to her. Even if that meant sleeping in a closet. But what did she want? Maybe he'd never asked because he was afraid of the answer. If she didn't need him, would she still want him?

"She wants to experience the world in all of its wonderful colors. She wants relationships and a partnership. She wants to feel. Love is a feeling and she wants that. But she has to push through that final barrier." Ken touched his tie and said, "I chose this tie today."

The tie was decorated with ogres eating tacos.

Ken held up his leg and showed his sock. "I chose these socks today."

The sock was decorated with penguins and igloos.

"Kathleen wants to be able to laugh at my socks, at my tie. She's begun to smile. But she has to cry. Give her the chance to do that. Trust her to do that. She'll be a great partner if you let her in. She's told us about Ian. He's another reason I think she's ready to face her future. She likes that young man and she talks about how he reminds her of Brice and Courtney. It's painful for her but she's doing it."

Matt wasn't sure if he'd lost or won. If she had this breakthrough Ken was sure she was ready to have, then their lives could begin. This news was bright and comforting and something he'd carry with him to Minneapolis.

"My plane doesn't take off until seven, so I'll be at the gate, desperate to hear that she's okay and understands. Can you tell her to call me?"

"She can only call you three times a day—eight, twelve, and six. She will be allowed to talk for ten minutes."

"Fine." It wasn't fine but his time was running out. "Have her call me at six."

"Matt, just tell her the truth of what's been going on with you. She's not stupid. We carry our worries on our shoulders for our loved ones to see. That's the best part about relationships. My loads are heavy, but I get to share them with my wife. But I wouldn't want to do that if she didn't share with me, too."

"I don't want her to know what a mess I've made. She's supposed to be focusing on herself. I'm supposed to handle all the rest. I don't want her to worry."

"I want my wife to worry about me," Ken said. His desk phone speaker chimed, and his secretary said, "Ken, Mr. Nelson's ride is here."

Matt snatched his notepad and flipped to a fresh page. If he'd known he wouldn't get to see her, he would have spent this time writing her a letter. Quickly, he wrote,

My Kathleen—I love you. There is a situation at the firm that requires my personal attention, so I have to go back to the office for a few days. Please forgive me for breaking my promise. I will be back. We can pretend to be Tarheels fans on Saturday. I'll have my phone with me at all times. I love you—Your Matt.

He stuffed the note in the top of her overnight bag and pushed the bag over to Ken.

He might not be keeping his promises, but he made a new one, anyway. He promised himself that he would quit holding back from her. That he'd be a partner. He'd carried the burden of NNJ and his mother's illness alone. Beginning today, he'd lean on her, too. She was the strongest person he knew. She'd be there for him.

But first, he had to get on a plane and trust that she would not spend the night in the closet or require a frozen orange. He had to trust that she'd understand and forgive him for leaving, and that when he got back, she would drop her head to his chest and hold on tight.

Kathleen

"Good afternoon."

Kathleen's step faltered. Ken had never been part of her sessions with Lisa. Often he joined in during groups or classes. He even did yoga from time to time. But one-on-one therapy? Never. He stood near the window, the sun shining on his silly tie. She glanced down to see bright purple Converse shoes. Lucas would love those shoes.

She crossed the carpet and buried herself in the corner of the couch. She prepared herself for whatever bomb Ken was about to drop and said, "You're not here because you have nothing better to do." She didn't like the way Ken was looking at her. It was as if he could decide her level of insanity with just his eyes.

"Matt came by," Ken said. "He's had to go to Minnesota for several days to handle a situation at the firm."

Matt was gone? He hadn't even told her! He must have decided this was all too much for him. On some level, she'd known he would want something better but she never thought he'd abandon her.

Abandon her. Abandon her. The words ran on a loop going faster and faster, getting louder and louder. She clapped her hands over her ears but the loop played on. When he'd dropped her off, had he known he would never see her again? Had he held his kiss longer? Hugged her harder?

Moms, slow down. You're not listening to what Ken is saying to you.

"Go away!" Kathleen said, not caring if Lisa and Ken witnessed her madness.

"Kathleen," Lisa said. "I'd like you to access your feelings. "

"I need to find a place to stay. Can I use the phone?" She could focus on what had to happen next. Get a hotel for tonight. Get a car. Drive to the beach. Start over on nothing. She'd done it before. She'd do it again. And this time she wouldn't let anyone in. Ever.

"Matt has packed your clothes and toiletries. We are planning for you to stay here until he returns." Ken was matter-of-fact, as if that was the only option.

She couldn't stay here. Not again. Not in that tiny room with no closet. Isolated. Damn him. She'd gotten comfortable with isolation and then he'd come to her beach and given her something more. Goddamn him. "We all know he'd be a fool to come back."

"He'll be back Friday." Ken was insistent.

"No, he won't." She wasn't going to lie to herself and she wasn't going to let them lie to her, either. "You know, if Courtney or Brice brought home a person like me to spend their lives with, I'd take them out to coffee and tell them to run far away. He's done the right thing."

The woman in her wanted Ken to argue, to tell her Matt loved her so much he'd never leave her like this. The victim in her accepted her new reality and understood why he had to leave. She was taking too long, taking too many steps backwards and not enough forward. He'd been sweet this morning and she'd thought it was because he was proud of how she'd interacted with Ian. But maybe it was because his time in the purgatory of her life was almost over.

"What are you feeling?" Lisa repeated. She tried to locate something in her body. "I have been abandoned but I feel nothing."

"As hard as this is, we both believe this—his timing—is exactly right."

She interrupted Ken. "Did he pack my books?" She couldn't feel for herself, but she could feel for Lexi and Ty. She'd start in chapter 11—the breakup scene. Then she'd read about hope and struggle and happily ever after. Her fictional friends always got their happily ever after.

"As we discussed this morning, you are holding back. That's easier to do because you get to go home at night and regroup. Being here won't give you that escape hatch."

"Why didn't he have the nerve to tell me?" His leaving wasn't a surprise. The fact that he took the coward's way out was.

"He wanted to tell you. I wouldn't let him," Ken said.

"How dare you!" She could feel her face turning red. She could hear the blood rushing in her ear canals. "I don't deserve much in this life. But I deserved the chance to say goodbye. To say thank you." She hated the shrillness in her voice. Hated the way a breakdown felt. Her body was closing in on itself, shutting out the world and the pain.

"Say goodbye to who? Say thank you to who? Matt or your family?" Lisa challenged.

How many books had she read where the protagonist "saw red"? Until this moment, she'd thought it was only a colorful idiom, but she saw red now. The red of anger and retaliation. "Do not bring my family into this!"

Auntie Marcia. She can't bring your family into this. I killed them all.

Bile rose in Kathleen and her vision blurred. She had to get out of here. Josh was swallowing her whole, pulling her under, drowning her. He'd won. He'd taken her past and now he had taken her future.

"Are you going to put me on 72-hour hold or let me use a phone?" She heard the venom in her voice and lapped at it.

"Let's take this one day at a time. Stay tonight and then we'll talk again in the morning. We don't need to make permanent decisions when our emotions are hot," Ken said, but it wasn't a suggestion. It was a statement of what would be. Matt would not be arriving in forty-three minutes. Fictional Kate and Lexi would not be taking her to coffee or helping her shop for scarves.

She tried to focus on her choices. They would not let her leave until she showed them she was not in crisis. They held all the power and everyone in the room knew it. Her only power was in pretending.

"Will I share a room with that Missy bitch?" The rational part of Kathleen hoped not. The emotional part of Kathleen hoped for a chance to collect the rage in her fists and beat the girl to death.

"No, there is a bed in Gloria and Pia's room."

Only three people in her life didn't flinch around her. Matt, and he was gone. Gloria and Pia remained.

"But," Ken took over the tête-à-tête. "I'd like you to agree to go all in for the next few days. Really seek to put everything on the table. Until you open and release, you will not be able to function in the real world in a healthy way."

"Real world?" Matt was her real world. Outside these doors she had nothing else. Nothing except a hidden bungalow and boxes full of untouched memories.

"You have a life outside of here. A life to build. With or without him. This has always been about you—not Matt. Just you. Let's open those boxes, Moms. I want to see my thumbprint Christmas ornament. Or Kiley's self-portrait that looked like the dog and not the girl."

"Gwammy," Lucas chimed in. "'Member that snowman I made out of stywofoam balls? 'Member we made that little cawwot nose?" Kathleen couldn't see him, but she knew he was wiggling in excitement. "I wanted to put a wed nose like Wudolph but you said it was Fwosty."

"Matt's expecting your call during phone hours tomorrow. Give him the chance to explain. I know you'll understand," Ken said.

She pulled Matt's sweatshirt off, uncovering her Duke t-shirt. She folded the sweatshirt, placed it in Ken's lap. "Can you ship this to him?" She picked up her binder and the suitcase sitting next to Lisa's desk. "Where is my room?"

She'd been fine at the beach. But Matt had arrived and convinced her to make a life with him. He'd opened a door that was now closed. She wished she'd never met him.

Small bed. Scratchy sheets. Sliver of light. Kathleen lay in the bed listening to her roommates breathe and sigh and shift. The fragment of light seeping under the door and through the window allowed her to see the room's shadows. Four beds. Four desks. Four damaged women. Bed. Desk. Window. Bed. Desk. Window. Dickensian.

There were no closets. Where would she hide? Who would hold her when the nightmare attacked? When Courtney was little, a neighbor friend had stupidly let her watch a horror movie. Night after night, she'd climbed in bed and Seth had cradled her. Where was Seth now? She'd stuck by him for over thirty years. But he'd stood there when four men entered their home. He should have found a way to stop them. Wasn't that the husband and father's job?

She shook her head. This was not Seth's fault. Or Matt's. This was Josh's fault, her fault. She'd been selfish. She should have given the money to Josh and she should have worked harder for Matt.

She shuffled out from under the cover, repositioned herself to sit cross-legged in the corner. She had to stay awake and alert, otherwise the nightmares had easy access to her.

"Grammy," Kiley's tender voice entered the darkness. *"Why are you so scared? You used to tell me and Lucas there was no such thing as monsters."*

"Smell that, Auntie. That's your skin burning. You'll be so pretty when we're done."

In the darkness of the room, Kathleen slid to the floor and unwrapped her scarf. She closed her palm over her missing ear and began rocking. "I hate you," she whispered to her nephew's voice and to herself.

"Why don't you tell that brat Kiley the truth. You are the monster. You. You. You."

Yes, Matt was right to leave her here. She was a monster, an ugly, scarred, embarrassing, cowardly monster.

In the deep dark of the night, Kathleen jerked awake to Pia's quiet whimpers. Pia thrashed in her bed and pushed at the air as if fighting an unseen force. Her whimpers turned to moans. Her moans turned to pleas.

"No. Stop. Please stop!" Pia said. "I want my mommy. It hurts! Mommy!"

"Moms, get up!" Courtney shouted into Kathleen's awareness. *"Don't watch that girl suffer. Please, don't you dare just sit there and watch. That's not my Moms."*

She leaped off the floor and went to Pia. She held the girl like she had Brice and Courtney and Kiley and Lucas. She held the girl like Matt and Seth once held her.

"Shh," she whispered into Pia's nightmare. Stroking her hair, Kathleen said, "You're safe now."

Matt

"I hate dealing with shit like this." Patti threw her arm out to encompass the table where all of Jeff's documents waited.

From his fifteenth-floor office in Minneapolis, Matt ignored his sister's unspoken rebuke and watched the sky brighten over his city. Minneapolis was the only city he'd ever truly known. He loved it. Even the snow and the cold. He'd never seen himself anywhere else, but he liked Charlotte, the Buzzed Bibliophile, and Ian, too. Could Charlotte be the right place for him and Kathleen to settle? Matt turned away from the window, wondering what Kathleen was doing at that moment. Had she slept? Had she had a nightmare? She was so silent when she had nightmares, he was afraid that if she had one, no one would notice. He wished desperately that he could be there for her, but his father and sister sat at the polished walnut conference table, waiting for him. Patti was straightening the scattered papers, her nervous energy obvious. Until he caught his father studying him, Matt hadn't realized that he was pacing.

Joe looked first at Matt, then at Patti, then back to Matt. He watched as his father began to smile, but he had no idea what his dad was finding humorous in this situation. Suddenly Joe slammed his hands on the table, rattling the coffee cups and making everyone jump. "Let's just sell this place. It's worth enough for all of us to do what we want, when we want, where we want." His Dad rested both forearms on the table and spoke directly to Matt. "We can be with who we want."

Matt was stunned. He'd spoken to his father several times the day before and he hadn't mentioned selling. "Dad?"

"You want to sell NNJ?" Patti leaned back in her chair with such force she rolled backward several inches.

Joe nodded at Matt before turning to Patti. "I don't care. That's what I'm saying. For thirty years you've walked the path I set out for you. It's time to walk your path."

Patti clapped her hand over her mouth, but Matt could see the smile in her eyes. "Holy shit," she said. "Matt?"

The delight on his sister's face surprised him. Had she been as unhappy as he had been? They could sell NNJ. But should they? It was one thing to think about giving up his career. But to actually do it?

Within seconds, they all laughed. A laugh of forgiveness, joy, and a dose of hysteria. He'd not known the full weight of his responsibility to NNJ until he was offered this release. He didn't have to be a tax attorney anymore, and with this truth his priorities righted themselves.

"Well, that was easy." Joe was clearly thrilled. "Let's strategize on what we need to do, put together a timeline, separate responsibilities."

They each grabbed a yellow notepad and sketched a plan to dissolve or sell the firm. Patricia believed they should meet with each client face-to-face, even if that meant several trips across the states. His dad thought a call from him to the older clients would be sufficient. They all agreed one-on-on talks with each partner should happen quickly. There was a good chance the partners would want to buy the firm and keep the clients.

"It's already the end of day on Tuesday. That only leaves tomorrow. We can't have this all accomplished by Thursday night no matter how late we work," Patti said. She wasn't being difficult. She was offering tentative support, but the list of to-dos was long and required all of them.

"I have to be back in Charlotte Friday morning. I can take the red-eye, but it's not negotiable." Matt was going to be at that discharge meeting and he wanted to have the weekend of football with his Kathleen and Ian.

"I need you back on Sunday night." Patti said with expectation in her voice. "I'll get our administrative assistants to schedule a partner meeting and back-to-back appointments all day Monday and Tuesday. Then we'll work on the legal requirements and the other announcements? I want to support you and Kathleen, but we have things to do I can't do alone and some items need to be handled here."

Could he promise to be back Sunday night? He wouldn't make another promise he didn't believe he could keep. But he was confident Kathleen's discharge meeting would go well. And he did need to be here. "Kathleen should discharge in two weeks. I can be here on the weekdays, but I'll go back to Charlotte on the weekends. We'll need a break, anyway."

"We won't be done in two weeks. At least stay until the week before Christmas."

"No, I have to be with Kathleen in the days leading up to Christmas. You know that, Patti. If we work twelve hours a day, we'll have all the preliminary work done. That's the best I can do."

Patti's face dissolved from the aggressive tax attorney to the sympathetic sister who had always been there for him. "Today. Tomorrow. Then two weeks. All three of us. Right?"

Rather than answer her, he stood, held out his hand. When she got to him, he embraced her tight. "Thanks, Patti-cakes. I've missed having you in my corner."

They held each other for several seconds before Joe said, "Our first step is to stand together and let The Asshole know the Nelsons will not be bullied."

"I can't wait to see the dickhead's face. He's got balls when he's protected by the phone. Let's see if he has any now."

"Oh my God, Matt," Patricia said, shaking with laughter. "This is going to be so much fucking fun. The Asshole called me an underling."

The three smiling Nelsons leaned against the huge executive desk and waited for their futures to begin.

Kathleen

Kathleen sat in her corner of Lisa's couch. No one mentioned that she'd fallen asleep on the floor of her room or that she'd held Pia until the young woman got back to sleep. She'd showered and brushed her teeth. She'd eaten her breakfast like a good patient. They had scheduled this extra meeting this morning because they wanted to look at her the way a zoologist studies monkeys. She would give them nothing interesting to see.

When she'd put on Matt's sweatshirt this morning, his scent had pummeled her. If he was abandoning her, why hadn't he packed her something different, something of her own?

She hadn't called him during the morning phone time. What would she say? He was back where he belonged, in the corporate world, in Minnesota, with his family, and it wouldn't take him long to realize that he was better off without Kathleen.

"Good morning." Lisa sailed into the room, flipped on an extra lamp. A storm brewed outside and, rather than help the dreariness of the room, the light made the shadows darker and longer. Lisa had been playing in the art house. Her cheek had a streak of blue paint. Her black pants had patches of pottery dust. She looked like a young girl coming home from a birthday party. Lisa was so much like Courtney sometimes it hurt to talk to her. Sometimes it was the only bright spot in Kathleen's day. Today, Lisa's perkiness made Kathleen feel more tired and made pretending more difficult.

"My night went well," Kathleen said, jumping right in. "I didn't have a nightmare. I didn't search for a closet. I gave you the night, can we discuss my leaving?"

Lisa settled in her chair. "I'd like to leave that discussion for our afternoon session. Ken asked you to go all in. Do that today and we'll have more to discuss."

The monkey analogy became more apt. She would be placed in different environments and every therapist would study her and report back. Every second her resentment toward Matt grew. If he had given her more notice about leaving, she might not have returned. But now that she was here, Lisa held her captive. Damn him. She twisted his shirt—he'd only packed his shirts—wishing she was strong enough to tear the fabric.

Lisa continued talking, making it clear Kathleen's input was not needed. "I requested this extra meeting because the treatment team and I have made a change to your schedule. It's nothing drastic, but it is new for you, and I wanted to explain."

Kathleen rubbed her eyes. A new schedule? She was already in anger management and stress management and DBT and ACT and CBT and group. She went to yoga and brushed horses. She painted. What more could be expected?

"We've made some observations and believe a specialized group may help you move forward." Lisa leaned forward as if to emphasize the veracity of the new plan. "We'd like you to attend the noon Self-Mutilation Process Group."

Kathleen blinked. Lisa's words dripped in slowly, taking a long time to land and make sense. Once a complete sentence formed, she said in her new fake-rational voice, "I do not need to go to that." She shoved her fingernails through the plastic cover on the binder, twisted and ripped it from the stitching,

"I do not self-mutilate. I pick at my fingers when I'm bored. Do not clump me in with those people." She couldn't face another problem. Flashbacks, voices, Matt gone. If they kept finding problems, she'd be stuck here forever. "Kathleen." Lisa moved to stand next to her. She grabbed Kathleen's hand, stopping her from digging her nails into her palm.

Kathleen looked at where Lisa stroked her torn red fingertips, her scratched wrists and her blistered palm, and finally the blood blister on the tip of her index finger. Last night she'd used her thumbnail, running it across her palm over and over again, letting the friction's heat calm her.

"Matt told us you're pinching yourself. He says your thighs are covered in dark bruises. That's self-mutilation, whether you want to admit it or not." Lisa whispered the words as if the syllables had weight and substance and power.

Kathleen pulled her arm from Lisa's grasp. "When Stephanie told me about my family, she cried the entire time. She stroked my cheek and ran her thumb under my eyes as if to catch my tears. But I didn't have any tears." She looked straight into Lisa's deep brown eyes, trying to make her understand. "My tears are stored like wine. Deep in the cellar of my soul. Aging, fermenting. Waiting on me to pull the cork. Barrels and barrels and barrels." She leaned her head against the cool windowpane and away from Lisa's intense stare. A red leaf floated down and was drowned in the mud. "I pick at my fingers, scrub my wrist, scratch at my scars because that pain keeps the tears in their barrels."

"Why not just cry? There is no weakness or shame in tears. It's nature's release valve."

"I hear from them, you know. They talk to me. Guide me. Challenge me. Yell at me. If I cry, I'll turn on a faucet and they'll wash away. Like wine poured down a drain. I need their voices."

"Kathleen, tears won't wash them away. Maybe tears will make them easier to see and hear."

Before Kathleen could tell her she was wrong and that the risk was too great, something Lisa said landed and coalesced Kathleen's anger into a palpable ferocity.

"It's not a Twelve-Step program, is it?" she asked, knowing what the answer would be before she saw Lisa's nod.

"Narcotics Anonymous is a fellowship of men—" Josh said. "Thanks for coming with me, Auntie Marcia." He threw his arm over her shoulder, gave her a loud kiss on the cheek.

Marcia had been to several meetings with Josh. He'd come to the cabin or she'd go to Atlanta. She'd listened to him quote the mantras and say the prayers. She'd helped him make a list of people who deserved amends. Together they'd gotten on their knees and prayed for Josh's release from drugs. When he'd gotten his four-month chip, they'd celebrated with Seth's famous burgers, warm chocolate chip cookies, and blackberry ice cream. She'd trusted him. Believed in him. Believed in God's power to help him. And then he'd entered her home with guns and knives and vengeance.

"Courtney, cousin," Josh slurred the words. "I think this diamond will keep me going for months. But it seems to be stuck."

Marcia tried to shut her eyes, to block the sight of her daughter's dead eyes.

"Burn her again," Josh snarled. "Keep her watching."

Josh used his index finger to gather a glob of blood. He slathered Court's ring finger. He twisted and twisted and twisted. "Well, shit, Auntie, it's stuck." He flashed his hunting knife.

"No," Marcia pleaded. "Leave her alone now."

"But I like this ring."

Kathleen planted both palms on the windowpanes, letting the cold pull her from the sights and sounds and smells of that Christmas Eve.

Dante had it right. The last circle, the deepest circle of hell, is freezing. Every cell in Kathleen's body cooled and froze. Josh's voice turned into the whir of Satan's wings. Rather than the rhythmic *lub-dub*, her heart seemed to pause between each beat as if deciding whether to go through the effort.

"Can you tell me what's happening for you right now?" Lisa asked.

"My nephew—you remember him, right? The nephew that laughed while he danced in my Courtney's blood. He went to AA and NA and all the other bullshit *A*'s. He made his amends. The summer before he murdered us all, we stood together at one of those meetings and he publicly apologized to me." Goosebumps ran up Kathleen's arms, trying to melt the ice in her veins. "Within months he was asking for money again. Begging. Then threatening. Then killing."

Tears gathered in Kathleen's eyes. They weren't tears of grief. They were tears of rage. At Josh. At herself. At Seth. At Matt. At every fucking thing.

"I didn't know you had experience with Anonymous groups."

Kathleen drew knives and guns in the window's condensation. She spoke as if reading from the Big Blue Book. "The twelve steps require we admit we've done something wrong. The twelve steps ask us to make amends." She blew on the window, wiped it clean, drew more hearts, more dripping blood. "Lisa, do you think I did something wrong? Do I owe someone an apology for being forced to watch as my family was murdered?" The question was so sincere and the answer so dreaded.

"Of course not. But those groups are about more than that."

"The second step wants me to relinquish my sanity to a Higher Power." Lisa didn't understand what she was asking. Going to an Anonymous group would be stepping back into the past when she had hope for Josh and in God.

"Higher Power can be defined a number of ways."

"I was lying in a closet. Pieces of my ear were lying in blood. My finger dangled from a shred of flesh." She held up her hand, shook the bumpy flesh in Lisa's face. "I'd watched Courtney's eyes turn opaque while he cut her finger off. I could smell the iron of blood and the bar-b-que of human flesh. Guess what I did?"

Lisa gently took Kathleen's arm and led her to the couch. They sat facing each other. Lisa's expression was one of unconditional support. "What did you do?"

"I started to whisper Bible verses. 'Do not be afraid or terrified because of them, for the Lord your God goes with you; he will never leave you nor forsake you.' That's Deuteronomy. Oh yeah, and how can I forget, 'And we know that all things work together for good, to them that love God.' That's my favorite." She jerked the scarf off her head and turned her mutilation toward Lisa. "I did love God, and this is what I got in return." She wanted her sarcasm to slice through the room, through Lisa, through her.

With her eyes pinned to Lisa, she slowly re-wrapped the scarf. "I called on the Higher Power. I did the third step. The one where I agree to turn my will and care over to God. I learned a valuable lesson from both." She paused, wanting her next words to be clear and heard and acknowledged as Kathleen's deepest truth. "If there is a God, He-She-It doesn't give a good goddamn about Marcia Kathleen Conners Bridges."

She couldn't do this anymore. She needed a break. It was all happening too fast and too slow. She felt herself expanding like a balloon with too much air. She'd expected Matt to hold her when she exploded but he sat in his fancy office, thousands of miles away.

"Moms, don't you dare give up now. That's not fair to you. To us. Or even to Matt. This was never about him. It's about you being able to look in a mirror and see the Moms we loved and forgive yourself."

"I'm not giving up. I'm catching my breath."

"That is such bullshit." Kathleen couldn't see Courtney but she knew her daughter had huffed, stomped away and slammed her door.

I'm sorry, Courtney.

Kathleen turned to Lisa. "I am exercising my right to leave. I understand I have to wait seventy-two hours. I'd like the countdown to begin now."

Lisa couldn't hide her shock and disappointment. "This can't be about one group. That can be worked out. You're so close to breakthrough. Please don't lose the ground you've won."

Unless Kathleen became a danger to herself or others, Lisa would have to let her leave in seventy-two hours and they both knew it. The power was a hollow victory, but at least she'd taken back a small measure of control.

"I've relinquished control to you. To Matt. I have to stop depending on others. I have to stop needing a babysitter. I will be my own higher power."

"Is that your emotional mind or your wise mind? Those memories will keep attacking you."

"And I'll keep using my skills to combat the attack."

Lisa shook her head as if Kathleen was being a recalcitrant, short-sighted child. "Would you like to talk to Matt about this?"

"You're kidding, right? You do remember he dropped off a suitcase and bolted. As a matter of fact, I'd like to update my privacy guidelines. Beginning right now, I do not authorize any disclosure of medical information to anyone." He'd made his position clear. He needed a break and she would give it to him. If he felt like he had to call, then she'd release him from the burden.

"Moms, you are being such a bitch."

"Is that fair?" Lisa asked.

Kathleen held on to the hysterical laughter bubbling in her chest. "Not much has been fair in my life. But I will speak to him. When I'm ready."

"Kathleen, that means I cannot even tell him you're here."

"Matt's fine." He could stay in Minnesota and tell everyone he had done his best for the broken Kathleen. She didn't blame him. She loved him and that meant wanting the best for him. Even if that wasn't her.

Kathleen held her gaze. "I get to decide what's best for me. I get to have some control."

Lisa watched her for a long time, and Kathleen wouldn't shy away from the scrutiny.

"It's Josh and those memories that have control. I saw you have a flashback a few seconds ago. Do you think those will stop just because you walk out of here? You're shackled to the past. Josh and that night are your Higher Power."

Kathleen reared back and let the impact of those words slam into her chest. "That was a direct hit."

"Kathleen, why did you agree to come here?"

"Matt made me."

"Matt made a fifty-five-year-old woman climb in a car and drive to Charlotte? He makes you walk through those doors every day? He makes you participate in groups and in sessions with me? He *makes* you?" Lisa's sarcasm was tangible. And because it was so rare, the impact was so much greater.

Kathleen narrowed her eyes. "I don't like to be patronized."

"I don't like to be lied to," Lisa shot back.

"I have never lied to you."

"No, you lie to yourself and then spew those same lies to me. Did Matt *make* you come here?"

"We've got seventy-two more hours together," she told Lisa. "Then we're done." She stood tall and walked out of Lisa's office, leaving her binder on the floor.

Matt

"I'm ready for a break," Matt said to Patti, hiding his anxiety and hoping she'd take the cue to leave his office for a few minutes. Kathleen had not called at breakfast or at lunch. He'd tried calling but, again, it was not an emergency, so he couldn't get past the switchboard. He'd left a message for Ken, but he had not called yet. Now it was 6:00 p.m. and she should call any second.

Pat stretched like a cat waking from a nap. "The way our to-do list keeps growing, I'm not sure we can get everything done in two weeks." She said it conversationally, but her look told him she was trying to get him to agree to more time in Minneapolis.

Their dad had left before the skies darkened, admitting he was too old to pull an all-nighter. Matt's dress shirt was on his desk. Patti's high heels and Matt's shoes were across the room. Hell, he'd even taken off his socks. Papers were everywhere and his admin was exhausted from running around.

"Why don't I order some pizza? Pepperoni, mushrooms, extra cheese?"

"And a salad," Matt added. Like when they were junior associates, he and Patti would gorge on pizza and work alone until midnight and start again at six. Once all the other attorneys left for the night, rock and roll music would blast in his office and keep them both awake. If he weren't so concerned about Kathleen, he might enjoy this time with his sister.

"Salad? Since when do you eat salad?" She was teasing him, and the levity was a welcome break to the hard work.

He checked his watch for the thousandth time. Kathleen was missing the evening call, too. Desperate, he dialed Ken's office.

"Matt. I just got your message. I've been out of the office all afternoon. How are things in Minnesota? You're missing torrential rain here."

Matt had no interest or patience with pleasantries. "I haven't heard from Kathleen."

"I'm not allowed to discuss Kathleen with you." Ken's tone implied he wasn't happy with the new situation.

"What? That doesn't make any sense. Is she all right? God, Ken, tell me she didn't hurt herself." The idea that she wasn't safe overwhelmed him with an anguish so profound he had to hold on to the window ledge. What had he been thinking? How could he leave her without even talking to her? How could he have left her at all?

"Matt, she is not hurt. I'm very sorry but I can't tell you more. She signed the forms earlier this morning."

"What forms?" Matt heard Patti come back into the office and hoped she busied herself with work and not eavesdropping.

"She updated her privacy requirements. I can no longer discuss her with anyone. Not even you. I can't legally tell you if she's here or not."

What the hell was going on? Was she angry? Punishing him? She had no right to be angry. He'd adjusted his entire life to be with her. He'd sacrificed his job and had given up his home. She was intelligent. She understood what running a business meant. And it wasn't like he'd left her alone. He'd left her in the safest place possible.

He sensed Patti paying closer attention but this was too important to care about hiding his fear from his sister. "Ken, please don't leave me in the dark," Matt pleaded, and he never pleaded.

Ken hesitated and Matt listened to his own heartbeat. Could she not cut him some slack? He was doing this for them. Once he settled everything at NNJ, he'd be able to give their future his complete attention. He'd given her months. She could give him a few days.

"She said if you called to tell you, and I quote, 'Please tell Matt I said thank you.'"

"That's it?" Matt almost crushed the phone in his palm. Anger swept through him. He'd bent over backwards for her, changed his entire world. Shit, he was selling his family firm. All she had for him was *Thank you*? *I'm fine* had been wrong, but this was worse. She'd left him with no way to reach her. She had to know he'd be frantic.

Patti moved to stand next to him. She leaned against the window ledge and offered him a smile that was either support or *I warned you*.

"She said to tell you she understood your decision. She said she did this because she wanted you to find your next best decision without her as an albatross."

Which decision? To come to Minnesota? To leave her at The Center? How could she understand decisions he didn't understand himself?

"You did tell her I'd be there Friday? Can you please ask her to call me so I can explain it myself?" This had to be a simple miscommunication. Ken would talk to her and then she'd talk to him.

"I did." It was obvious Ken would only give him those two words.

"I'll be on the very next plane," Matt said.

He heard Patti's sharp intake of breath and could feel her revving for a showdown. Beginning right now, no matter what, Matt's needs would be first. And Matt's need right now was to hold Kathleen and not let her give up.

Matt threw his sister a warning look. He was here because Patti hadn't been willing to take the corner office and shut Jeff down. They'd both been too chickenshit to admit they wanted different paths than being a tax attorney. Not anymore. He'd do what he could to get NNJ on the market without too much damage. But that task would not be his top priority. Never again.

"Slow down," Ken said. "Even if you come, we can't let you on the property."

"Fuck that," Matt said. "If I have to, I'll wait outside the gates until I see her emerge. I have to see her for myself. Talk to her."

Matt darted around the room tossing random things in his briefcase. Yellow notepads. A calculator. The family picture he kept on his desk. Pens. Pencils. Post-it notes. He would not be back in this office ever again. No matter what happened, he was done with this job.

"Hold on," Ken said. "I'd like to tell you about our policies." Ken's voice changed. He was no longer the concerned therapist. He was the administrator.

Ignoring Patti's heavy breathing, Matt plopped down in his chair. With his elbows on his knees and his eyes on the carpet, he listened. He knew Ken was trying to communicate something vital. But his thoughts were muddled. He needed to be on a plane, and he needed to talk to Patti, and he needed to talk to his father, and he needed to organize all the shit on this table. He needed to do one thing fucking right.

"Residents often want to leave after a tumultuous session. Emotions are high and often feel uncontrollable. Realizations are made and those are frightening. And, like all humans, we seek to flee fear. That is often a more acute feeling in people with significant trauma."

"Are you telling me Kathleen had a tumultuous session?" And he hadn't been there for her. If she'd had a rough day, then she'd had a rough night. What the hell was he doing in Minnesota?

"Let's use a hypothetical case. Say we have a resident who has decided she wants to leave. She can do that, but she has to wait seventy-two hours before we allow her to leave the property. That gives us a chance to determine if she is a danger to herself or others. It allows time for a wise decision to be made. In that time, the resident has extra individual therapy sessions to determine her mental and emotional health."

"She asked to discharge?" They were going to talk to the treatment team on Friday about discharge planning. What had happened to Kathleen that made her feel so desperate she asked to leave now?

"Any patient can request a discharge. No one is a prisoner here."

It wasn't a direct answer, but Matt could read Ken's tone and the message within the words. His relief was so profound he wanted to lie on the carpet and breathe one full breath. "I'll take that as a yes, she wants to discharge and yes, she's there and she'll be there for seventy-two hours."

"A seventy-two-hour hold can be extended at the discretion of the treatment team." He was talking about policy. He was telling Matt everything he needed to know without violating Kathleen's privacy. Matt had liked Ken before, but now he wanted to kiss the man's feet.

"Seventy-two hours. I'll be there. Please, tell her that. Tell her I won't be leaving again." He had so much to say but he needed to see her eyes, hold her hands, kiss her.

"I know this is hard to understand, and more than I should share, but finally there is some light and hope for her."

Matt chewed on his inner lip hoping the tears didn't come. "Thanks, Ken. Please..."

"We will take care of her."

Satisfied Ken would do his best and that Kathleen was in the safest place, he hung up and resisted the urge to order a private jet. He had seventy-two hours to get his shit together and his words in order.

"Matt?" Patti said.

"I can't deal with you right now," Matt answered without looking at her. If she was angry or aggressive, he might say something he'd never be able to take back.

Patti put her hand on his shoulder and squeezed. "Are you all right? Is she all right?"

"I'm fine. She's fine." He grabbed Patti's hand, held it and made eye contact. "That's not true. I'm not fine. I'm fifty years old, in love for the first time, and it is fucking scary. I'm frightened I've fucked things up beyond repair. I'm frightened I've let her down with no way to fix it."

Like they did when they were small children ready to take on the playground, she laced her fingers through his. "I know you've felt guilty for working so much in Mom's last few weeks. But, Mattie, she understood."

She was right. Some of his fear was because of the way he'd not been there for their mother. He'd failed her and he'd never be able to fix it. "I have felt guilty. You stood by her, you picked up her hair as it fell out, you cleaned up her vomit and made sure her morphine was given properly. I couldn't watch her or you or Dad. It was too much for me. The powerlessness of it all. The hopelessness." Matt let a tear stream down his cheek and refused to be embarrassed.

Patti folded her legs and sat on the floor. She took both of his hands and waited on him to look at her. "She knew you loved her by taking care of Dad's firm. You were her rock by being Dad's rock."

Matt couldn't speak over the tears clogging his throat, so he nodded and held tightly to her hands.

"Please don't get angry, but with Kathleen, are you sure that's love and not some weird need to take care of her?"

"Oh Patti, there is so much I don't know. But loving her is my one constant. I'm her strength to face the past. She's my strength to face the future." He paused for several seconds before adding, "She signed a document not allowing me access to her."

Patti frowned. "Why are you smiling? That seems like a really bitchy thing to do after all you've done for her."

He went over Ken's words to him yesterday and a few minutes ago. "I don't think so. I think she's close to a breakthrough and running scared. Ken said that my taking her home at night gave her too much room to shut down. They are pushing her. But I do have to be there in 72 hours. I can't let her walk out of that door and not see me."

Relieved when a knock on the door and the smell of pizza sauce interrupted his confession, he said, "Two days, Patti. I have to leave here on the red-eye Thursday night. I want to be sitting at the gate before noon."

For a few moments they said nothing as they each ate a piece of pizza, popped open a beer, and watched the snow fall.

"Since I'm being embarrassingly honest," Matt said finally, "you were right. Kathleen will never be normal. She'll always have shadows lurking in her mind. She'll have bouts of withdrawal followed by an intense need for connection. It won't be normal. It will be ours."

"Matt, how will you explain her to people? Or do you plan to hide away with her?"

"Explain her?" He mimicked introducing her to someone. "Alex, this is *my* Kathleen."

"And if she shrinks away or refuses to make eye contact?"

"So what? I'd like you, Dad, and the boys to accept her just as she is. To love her if she's smiling or crying, laughing or screaming. To be sensitive and careful. But the rest of the world, I don't really give a fuck."

"That should be the new family motto." She handed him another piece of pizza and snatched one for herself. "Can you promise you won't leave me hanging? There is a lot to do around here, and, since we are being so disgustingly honest, it intimidates me."

Matt wrapped his arm around Patti's shoulder. "I won't make any more promises to anyone except myself and Kathleen. She loves me, Patti. She'll support me and give me the space I need to finish this. She'd have done that before if I hadn't been too prideful to admit I was fucking everything up."

"What if she won't see you?"

"I found her before. I'll find her again."

"And if she doesn't want what you want? What if she just can't?"

"My Kathleen is strong, so very strong. She can and she will." He'd been open with Patti, but he couldn't share his biggest fear. Kathleen could and would love again. But what if she chose not to love him?

Kathleen

Kathleen had never been in The Center's gymnasium. It was exactly like a church gym. Cinder block walls, a half court for basketball. A volleyball net was shoved into the corner. A basket of balls. An electronic scoreboard. Windows were located at equal intervals on three of the walls. The smell of lacquer, stale sweat, and rubber mats completed the effect. The only thing missing was the pullout stadium seating. How many evenings had Marcia and Seth spent in their church gymnasium watching Brice or Courtney playing games? Seth had been one of those parents who took the game seriously. Marcia had been the parent to pack unhealthy snacks. But together they'd cheered and loved life.

As the fifteen women from Kathleen's group entered the room, chatter stopped. Pillows were arranged along the circumference of the mats. The lights were dimmed. If they'd been expecting a group game, the room was clearly arranged for something different and something significant.

"Any idea what we're doing in here?" Gloria asked. She inched closer to Kathleen as if there was safety in numbers.

"No, but I don't think we're playing basketball." Kathleen wanted to lighten the mood, but her voice sounded too nervous.

Kathleen had fifty-one hours to go before she checked herself out. She'd been a good girl. She'd spoken in group about her life before that night. She'd talked about her isolation on the beach, about meeting Matt and his mother. She'd ignored Missy's rude comments. In art she'd painted an abstract version of her life. She would be sharing that painting tomorrow.

But she'd not been able to break through the final barrier. The details of that Christmas Eve were buried. She remembered walking with Stephanie that morning. The early dusting of snow, the dogs chasing a squirrel, the speculation about Christmas gifts. She remembered chopping peppers and onions, basil, and garlic. Courtney had been sitting at the island chattering about everything and nothing. Seth had smacked her on the head for painting her toenails in the kitchen. It was all so normal. So warm. So perfect. But that's as far as her mind would go.

Yesterday Kathleen had wanted to avoid the memories. Today she wanted to see if she could remember and survive. Lisa was right, she couldn't move forward until she put an end to that night. She couldn't carry anger and shame into a true future. She had to say goodbye to Marcia and embrace Kathleen. As the last stragglers entered and anxiety rose, Kathleen prayed whatever they were planning wasn't for her. She'd wanted to share with Lisa and Matt, but she never wanted to flay herself open in a group. She understood how telling the story was cathartic for some people, but not for Kathleen. Remembering and reliving was a private experience, a private suffering.

Several therapists stood against the wall like sentries keeping the captives inside. Ally, the psychiatrist, the yoga instructor, the kickboxing coach. Ken stood close to the door, wearing a Shrek tie and green sneakers.

With the palm of her hand, she rubbed the sand out of her eyes. Matt was likely standing in his office, being the boss, and wearing what he'd call a power tie. Would Ken tell her if he called? During morning phone hours, she'd sat in a phone cubicle, holding the handset. She'd dialed eight of the ten digits of Matt's number. But there was too much to say, too much distance. She couldn't call him until she had more to offer. It hurt to think she might lose him, but a broken heart was part of living. For Kathleen, a broken heart would be proof she could feel something other than hate and rage. A broken heart would be progress.

"Ken only shows up when things are going to get dicey," someone whispered.

Everyone started to talk at once as if talking would keep the session from starting. Women clustered together, eyes darted around and tension rose. The therapists smiled and nodded, but their attempts to soothe had the exact opposite effect.

"We'd like everyone to take a seat at the edge of the mat," Ally said.

Lisa stood at the head of the mat. She'd removed her high heels, revealing blue toenail polish. A color Courtney would choose. She took several minutes to smile at each woman, showing her pride and giving her encouragement.

"Today, we're going to use a technique called drama therapy. It's exactly what it sounds like. Storytelling, play-acting, improvisation. It can be very effective for giving victims of trauma a voice and pushing through blocks. It's a way to take the power back. To shift from victim to survivor."

Kathleen wouldn't let Gloria take her hand and she didn't make eye contact with anyone, especially not Lisa. She tried to disappear into a fictional world, but Brice wouldn't let her.

"Mama, if she calls your name, that means it's time. You always told us when a door opens—even if it's scary—we are to walk through it. You said doors open but don't stay open. It was cheesy but true."

"No. Not here. You don't understand, if I can't handle it, they can make me stay. Brice, I'm serious. I'm afraid for my sanity. A real insanity. A commitment to a psychiatric hospital."

She'd never admitted that fear, never let it become a conscious thought. If uncontained, her rage might be dangerous. If she was a danger to herself or others, then Lisa held all the power.

"Can we refuse this?" someone on Kathleen's left asked.

"Yes and no. You can refuse anything. You've trusted us this far. If you weren't ready, we wouldn't ask you to do this. But some of you are one step away from discovery. This method can help you over the barrier. Your stories need a beginning, middle, end."

Lisa had said those exact words to her just two hours ago. Beginning. Middle. End. Discovery. Barrier. Freedom. Life. Love. Lisa had promised all of that and still Kathleen resisted.

"If you can't access terrible memories, then they will continue to hijack you. Your body will hold all the horrors and keep you in a state of freeze, flight, or fight. That's exhausting, unproductive, and prevents you from ever being safe. Your brain is a vault, and burying the trauma is a coping mechanism. We open the vault and your system can calm."

Kathleen shot her eyes around the room. Each door was guarded and every window closed. She wished Matt were here. She wanted to run to the safety of his arms, to have him run away with her.

Stop being such a chickenshit. We have been with you through everything. We will be with you through this. I'm here. Court. Amanda. Kiley. Lucas. Even Matt's mom.

But where's your dad? Where's Seth? Kathleen did not understand where Seth was. He'd stood beside her through a life of ups and downs, joys and pains, successes and failures. But he'd been silent since that night. Was he disgusted with her? Ashamed at how she'd given up? Courtney and Brice talked to her. Even the grands had been helping her. Where was the man she'd created a beautiful life with?

"Mama, do this. We are all asking you to do this."

Seth might not speak to her, but she'd do this for the rest of her family. She'd make them proud even if she collapsed under the weight. She closed her eyes and pulled Matt's sweatshirt to her nose. His smell was already fading. If she wanted it back, if she wanted to open that closet and see her family's faces, she had to walk across this mat. She stood, walked to Lisa with a determined gait, knowing that if she paused, she'd run. "This is for me, isn't it?"

Lisa's gaze was an anchor in the storm. "You are ready. I promise you. We are all here. No one will let you crash. Breathe in through your nose, pause, breathe out through your mouth."

"Just start." Kathleen swallowed the bile in her throat and forced herself not to self-harm.

"Close your eyes. You told me that your family tradition was lasagna on Christmas Eve. Can you smell it? Onions. Peppers. Basil. Garlic. There would be a Christmas tree, stockings on the mantle, a blazing fire, maybe a football game on the TV. Can you see it? Where is everyone? What do you hear? Put yourself in the room."

Kathleen's body quaked, but the door opened and the memories slithered out.

"Amanda and Courtney are ripping lettuce and talking about wedding plans. Lucas is under the tree, digging through the presents, hoping to find one for him. Seth and Brice are sneaking cookies and making wagers on the football games." Not recognizing her own voice, Kathleen heaved in a deep breath and forced her feet to stay still.

"Where's Kiley?" Lisa guided her into that night.

"She is stuck to me, watching me cook, whispering about school and friends." Her granddaughter would have smelled like peaches and bubblemint.

Kathleen closed her eyes and stepped back into the nightmare.

Marcia stroked Kiley's head. "I think your curls are gorgeous. But it's hard when people make fun."

"Please don't tell Mommy and Daddy. I don't want the bully speech."

The TV was soundlessly showing the Minnesota-Chicago game. Christmas music filled the house. Marcia stepped to the corner of her kitchen and watched her family talk and smile and laugh. "Rudolph the Red-Nosed Reindeer" began, and Lucas scooted from under the tree and started to dance and sing. A perfect Bridges Christmas Eve.

"He's a goof," Courtney said.

"Marce, honey. Quit lolly-gagging. We're hungry," Seth kissed her cheek. He smelled of pine and soap and chocolate-chip cookies. "And Lucas is going to destroy our tree if we can't keep him out of it."

"Gwammy, does the 'sagna have any gween?" His voice was muffled because he was back under the tree with only his jeans-clad rump sticking out.

Marcia smiled. "No, honey. But there's salad, and you'll have to choke down six bites."

The song changed to Elvis's "Blue Christmas" and everyone but her groaned. From his perch on the sofa, T-bone barked, announcing the knock before it came.

"I'm not sure why Steph is knocking, but can someone let her in?" She peeled the foil off the lasagna, pulled a piece of cheese from the top, and offered it to Kiley.

Brice opened the door, bringing in wind and leaves and Josh.

"Auntie. Merry Christmas."

Marcia stilled. The room went quiet except for Lucas's singing. Kiley's arms tightened. Everything about this was wrong. His arrival. His voice. The look on his face. The brightness of his eyes. The jitters in his body. He was a man hyped on meth.

"Look at this," Josh said. "A Hallmark Christmas."

The cabin was one large open space. A large fireplace dominated the left wall. Lighted garland was draped over the mantle; white reindeer and silver ornaments were artfully displayed. On the hearth was a family of deer. The tree was ten feet tall, covered in special ornaments. But Josh's energy filled the space.

"Kathleen, open your eyes. Tell me what you see."

She blinked her eyes open, startled to see the gym and Lisa. As if she were controlled by a puppeteer, her legs folded underneath her. The mat felt cool through her pants and Kathleen imagined the coolness lowering the heat developing in her chest.

Lisa sat with her. "You're safe. Body, soul, and mind are all safe." Lisa looked at her closely and, when apparently satisfied, she said, "Go back. What are you wearing that night?"

Body, soul, mind. But what about her heart? "We all wore our Duke shirts," Kathleen said. "Lucas added a blue Santa hat. Every year, after dinner, we took a picture in front of the tree. Always in Duke Blue." She wiped her cheeks and ignored her burning eyes. "There are thirty years of Christmas pictures at my bungalow."

"Look down, what's on your shirt right now?"

She looked at her chest, surprised to see a dark red shirt with a big gopher on it. "Matt," she whispered.

Lisa nodded and then guided Kathleen deeper into the dark. "Josh is now in the house. What's happening?"

Kathleen let her eyes drift closed, let the smell of lasagna and Lucas's off-key voice take her backward.

"I brought some friends, Uncle Seth. You always told me I was part of the family. Come on in boys," he yelled out the door, his words were slurred, and his excitement was palpable. Three boys entered the house and stood behind Josh like they were dogs obeying their master. Two wore menacing smiles. They were dirty, skinny. They had the same wild eyes and restless

energy as Josh. The third danced from foot to foot, keeping his eyes pinned to the polished hardwood.

"Josh," Marcia said from her spot near the stove. She put her hand on Kiley's head and subtly moved the girl behind her legs. Out of the corner of her eye, she saw Brice and Amanda's alert faces and the cop stance of their bodies. Brice patted his back, but his gun had already been locked away. Elvis stopped singing and Bing Crosby started.

"Another slow song." Lucas whined and wiggled out from under the tree, a small package clutched against his chest. "Gwammy, can we find better—"

"Lucas, come over here," Amanda barked at him. She reached out for Lucas, but he was frozen, eyes wide, confusion covering his entire face.

"Come on in, boys. Spread out. My Auntie and Uncle have a fancy house. Three big TVs, custom furniture, fancy art. My Auntie and Uncle have plenty of money, but they won't share." As if choreographed, the three boys moved to the corners of the room.

Marcia looked from Seth to Josh. Kiley's hands tightened on her legs, but Marcia was too frightened to soothe.

Brice took one step forward.

"Oh no you don't, Brice. One move and they all die." Josh pulled a gun, aimed it at Lucas.

"Daddy, who's that?" Lucas's innocence tore through Marcia. Lucas knew Josh but Josh was so wired Lucas didn't recognize him. "He shouldn't point that at me. It's not safe."

Run. Hide. Run. Hide. Marcia tried to scream the warning, but her throat was clamped closed.

"Josh, what are you doing?" Seth was so calm, always so calm. "I think you should leave, and we'll all sit down after the holidays."

"Oh, Uncle. I can't leave until I get what I came for." Josh jumped from foot to foot, cackling like a demented clown.

Slowly, as if finally understanding the threat, Lucas tiptoed to his mom and hid behind her legs.

Time froze. T-bone, the sweet dog, jumped off the couch and began to bark and turn in circles.

Josh lifted his gun.

The bullet was loud. T-bone's body thudded to the floor as if someone had dropped a shoe. No one screamed. It was as if everyone thought it wasn't real, that this wasn't happening to them, couldn't happen to them.

The boys behind Josh laughed and cheered.

Brice rushed Josh. The bullet hit the center of his chest. Brice's large body buckled and crumpled. Blood bubbled from a perfect circle. As if moving through molasses, Brice lifted his hand to Amanda. His fingertips glanced off her ankle before his bright blue eyes died.

"Brice," Amanda whispered.

"I wouldn't move if I was you," Josh warned Amanda.

"What do you want?" Seth demanded, his calm replaced by rage and impotence. Marcia could see the veins in his neck pulse. It was Seth's fear that ripped Marcia from her trance.

"What do you think I want?"

"We don't have any money here," Seth said.

"Oh yes, you do." He used his gun to point at Courtney's finger, Amanda's finger, Marcia's finger. "Those diamonds will do."

Courtney gasped, covered her engagement ring as if hiding it would keep Josh from taking it. Tears dripped off her chin when she looked at Seth, her eyes pleading him to stop this.

"Josh, we can talk about—" Seth moved quickly, stepping between Josh and Courtney.

Another shot. Another collapse. Josh laughed and spun around on his toes as if he was celebrating.

Kiley screamed. Lucas screamed. Courtney screamed. Marcia was frozen, wondering why Seth wasn't bleeding from the circle in his forehead. This was her home. This was

Christmas Eve. They would have lasagna and garlic bread and warm chocolate chip cookies. The kids would open one present. The adults would drink wine.

Amanda scooped Lucas into her arms, tucked his face into her neck, cooing at him. His scream became whimpers and sniffs. His arms so tight around Amanda, her face was turning red.

"Auntie, make them shut up." Josh said it like he was asking for a glass of water.

"Please don't hurt them. You've done enough. We'll give you the rings." She barely heard herself. Screams were like waves in her ears, blocking her own voice.

"Josh," Courtney pleaded. "What are you doing?"

Josh stepped over Brice's body. The blood under his feet squished as if he'd stepped in mud. He caressed Courtney's face with the gun. She pulled back but Josh just followed her. "How much did that man of yours spend on that ring?"

Tears poured down her face and still Marcia didn't move. Couldn't move.

"This is your perfect Mom and Dad's fault. I asked your Mommy-dearest for some money. She said no and here we are." The reasonableness in his voice was menacing. The gun kissed Courtney's mouth. "Now behave, Cousin Court; Andy is looking at you like you might be his dessert."

Courtney leaned away from the gun, darted her eyes to the boys, to Seth's body, to Brice's body and then to Marcia. "Moms." Her precious girl looked at her, begging for rescue. And still Marcia didn't move.

Lucas dropped to his knees, keening at Brice to wake up.

Another shot. Silence. Lucas fell into his Dad's body where he would stay.

Amanda screamed and raced toward Josh. She clawed down his face, but he was stronger, faster. The back of his hand landed on Amanda's cheek before she could get another swipe. He hit her one more time and she fell to the floor, her face landing in the blood. Another shot and Amanda was quiet.

Josh wiped the blood from his face. He waved his gun at the tallest of the boys. "Mikey, grab that screaming brat."

Before Marcia could move, the boy had Kiley by the arms.

"Grammy! Grammy!" Kiley screamed and kicked and struggled. The boy growled and threw her little body into the wall with enough force she dropped to the floor and didn't move.

Marcia sank to her knees, crawled over to Kiley. She was breathing but remained still. Marcia scooped her granddaughter into her lap, hiding her as much as she could.

The boy who had been unwilling to make eye contact stood in front of Josh. "We came for jewelry. Not this."

"Shut the fuck up." Josh waved the gun at his companion. He seemed scared now, as if he was just understanding what he'd done and what that might mean. "We can't leave anyone alive. They'll know who we are."

Marcia wrapped Kiley tighter, hoping and praying that if she was quiet the boys would leave.

"I'm not leaving without those diamonds," Josh said, determined and commanding.

No one spoke for several seconds and Marcia could almost hear Josh's mind seek a solution. She held his eyes, silently imploring him to see reason, but the meth had him by the throat.

Josh walked and stood over her. He let a line of saliva trail out his mouth, land between her eyes. "You told me you couldn't support me anymore. You told me I had fucked up my life. I guess you were right. So, let's fuck yours up, too."

Another shot. Kiley spasmed and Marcia knew she was gone. Marcia screamed.

Kathleen screamed.

It was cold and hot. Hot and cold. Burning and freezing.

She opened her eyes, looked at the orange in her hand. Her body was in the gym, her mind was trapped between past and present. The smell of burning flesh and the feel of warm blood pooling in her ear still haunted her. She could hear the knife as Josh sawed through her ear. She could smell his sweat and see his dirty fingernails. She dropped the orange, reached out to take Lisa's arm. "Lisa, while they sat at the table and ate the lasagna, I crawled to the closet."

Kathleen felt fury rise in her. Lisa had been right; she hurt herself because she was the object of her own hate. She needed a new, more satisfying, target. Like the wicked Ursula in *The LIttle Mermaid*, she rose and walked across the mat where she stood above Missy. "Get up."

Lisa stood over Kathleen's shoulder and Ken moved in behind Missy. "Kathleen, where are you?"

"I'm right here. In this place. On this mat. Facing this bitch." Her fingers twitched, demanding to form fists and lash out. "It was her—her type—that took everything away from me. I want her to see what she did."

"Kathleen, Missy didn't do anything to you."

"You said we are supposed to help each other face our past and our problems." She sounded rational but it was her emotion guiding this confrontation. "Let me show her the future if she doesn't get her fucking act together. Stand the fuck up."

Missy's face shifted from fear to defiance. She stood, thrust her chest out and dared Kathleen with her eyes. The two women were three feet apart, each protected and observed by a therapist. But Kathleen didn't need Lisa or Ken to protect Missy. As much as she wanted to strangle Missy, to watch the light fade from her eyes as it had from Kiley's, Marcia Kathleen Conners Bridges was not that. "They decided to leave me alive because they thought I'd suffer more like this."

"Take it off," Missy challenged her. "I bet that scarf covers up nothing. That scarf is all about attention." Missy's eyes were glued to Kathleen as if she was waiting for a corpse to be revealed.

Kathleen unwound the scarf, let it fall to the mat. She heard murmurs of shock, whispers of pity. "Look, Missy. Look closely. You want to know how they did it?" She ran her fingertip over the rough edges of her ear. "He started with a hunting knife. Told me that without an ear maybe I'd listen better."

Missy didn't speak or blink.

Like a mannequin on display in a department store window, Kathleen turned slowly. She heard the mutters, but the faces were a blur. Everyone saw the carnage, the tufts of hair that peaked between scars, the burn marks and the slices, the mountains and valleys of her skin. "He told me if I cried, he'd just keep hurting me. He told me tears were for the innocent. He told me I was guilty."

The tears started as a trickle, a tease, a slow drip off her jaw.

"Don't stop the tears," Seth whispered.

That was Seth's voice! Her Seth! A sob burst from her lungs and her tears poured. She closed her eyes. "Where have you been? You've been so silent, and I've needed you." She spoke to him aloud, unable to care if people listened.

She folded her legs and let gravity and exhaustion pull her to the mat. She wrapped her arms around her knees and rocked. "Seth, are you angry with me?"

"Marcia, honey. I have no reason to be mad at you. Do you remember our number one rule when we needed to have an argument? I've been waiting until you were no longer angry. If I came too soon, you'd say something you regretted and you'd hurt more."

In their first year of marriage, they'd decided to wait until they were no longer angry before they tried to resolve any argument. Anger, they'd learned the hard way, caused you to say things you didn't mean. "But, I'm not angry with you."

"Marcia, please stop lying to yourself and to me. You're furious I left you."

She could hear the women quietly leave the gym. She opened her eyes to see Lisa facing her, holding out her scarf. Kathleen reached for the scarf and with practiced ease she wound it around her head. When the door clicked and Kathleen knew they were alone, she said, "Seth says I'm furious with him."

Lisa remained silent, letting Kathleen come to her own conclusions.

Choking on tears, Kathleen said, "I hate them all."

"Who do you hate?"

"Josh and his posse."

"Who else do you hate?"

"Myself."

"Why?"

"Because I survived. Because I keep surviving." How could she face herself when her family died, and she did nothing? What if she'd held tighter to Kiley? If she'd sent them to the basement to play? If she didn't have the rule that guns had to be locked away? If she hadn't insisted on Christmas at the cabin? If she'd not assumed the knock was Stephanie. If. If. If.

"Who else do you hate?"

"Isn't that enough?" She swiped under her nose, but the tears kept coming, soaking her pants and leaving the world a watery blur. "I hate Marcia. For standing there and not doing something." She tried to take in a full breath, but her lungs were stuck behind the tightness in her chest, behind the tears yet to fall. She'd expected freedom from anger when she'd told her story. But the anger was rising again, scalding her throat.

"You can admit the rest, honey," Seth whispered. *"We love you and that won't change."*

Not wanting to see Lisa's revulsion, Kathleen closed her eyes. "I hate all of them. Seth. Brice. Courtney. Even the grandkids." She'd said it and now she awaited the fall of the guillotine.

Journey to Hope

"I know," Lisa whispered. "This was the real truth you had to uncover."

"I'm a terrible person. I deserve to be alone and isolated. Why would anyone want to be anywhere near me? Who hates their family for being murdered?" Josh was only partially correct. It wasn't the damage to her skin that kept her suffering. It was the destruction of self and soul.

"Hate is easier than despair, easier than guilt and shame. But, Kathleen, you hate because you love."

"How do I keep going? Why would I try?" She forced the tears to stop. She couldn't cry for herself. She didn't deserve such a release. She deserved to hurt.

"You don't hate them. Or yourself. You hate that you are alone. You hate that your dreams died with them. You hate that their pictures and their memories come with both joy and sorrow. You hate that your life has to change. You hate that you have so much love and it was taken away." She reached over and touched Kathleen's arm. "They aren't gone. They live inside you. You love them so much that you hate life without them."

"I want to see them, hold them."

"You have to accept that's not possible."

Through the windows, Kathleen watched the sky darken. She watched as the women walked up the hill toward the dining hall. Many were bundled in coats against the cooling air and the high winds. Some ran. Others walked as if carrying bags of sand.

"I miss them. We used to laugh and cry, play games, fight and forgive. I'll never have that again." The tears restarted and warmed her face.

"You can't have Marcia's life back. But you can have Kathleen's life. Love. Laughter. Joy. Sorrow. You already do. You have to stop feeling guilty for it. You cannot embrace love and carry guilt."

"Marce, you weren't at fault. None of us were. It's time to let us go, let us rest, let yourself rest. We'll always be in your heart. Open it—you've always been so full of love. If you let Josh take that from you, then he will have taken it all."

Seth was right, as he always was. She'd given Josh exactly what he wanted. But he hadn't taken it all, had he? She was the one who had forced her best friend to leave her side. "I hate Stephanie."

"Do you want to do something about that?"

Could she face Stephanie? She could make amends with her family by living again. But could she look her best friend in the eyes and tell her the truth? She had to try. She owed Stephanie that much.

"You owe yourself that much," Seth said.

"I need to see Stephanie."

Kathleen wouldn't let Josh take it all. She wasn't sure where Stephanie fit in her new life, but Kathleen needed to speak her truth. They both needed closure and forgiveness. They both needed that night to end and a new story to begin.

Matt

Matt was standing on the portico outside the administrative building, braving the cold wind. Ken's secretary had invited him inside but he needed to move. He couldn't wait to see Kathleen smile, feel her arms wrap around his waist and her forehead land on his chest. He wanted to tell her he was no longer an attorney and that he and Patti were on firm ground again. He wanted to plan their first true vacation together. She'd mentioned Scotland. He was willing to taste haggis, and Scotland was close enough to Ireland, they could go drink some fresh-brewed Guinness. The football tickets were in his pocket and a new Duke shirt was in his car. Tomorrow they would cheer, eat pretzels, and drink beer.

Ken turned onto the sidewalk, but before Matt could speak, Ken held up his hand. "Matt, I need to tell you. Kathleen left early this morning."

Matt stared at him, not understanding, then pushed at the sleeve of his sweatshirt and looked at his watch. "You told me she'd be here for at least seventy-two hours." He held his arm out, tapped the watch face as if Ken couldn't tell time. "That's two hours from now."

"I wanted to call you and explain. But privacy laws wouldn't allow me to. I told you we could make her stay for seventy-two hours. But the situation changed, and we allowed her to leave earlier." Ken's tie was caught by a gust of wind and whipped around his face.

Matt's eyes were drawn to the silly image of Tom and Jerry spiraling up the tie, the cat never quite catching the mouse. The tie mocked him. Was he the mouse, always being chased by his broken promises, or the cat, never able to catch what he desired?

"What the fuck? You told me to get here within seventy-two hours, and I'm here!"

Ken captured the tie and stuffed it inside his shirt. "Matt, I never specifically said that. Let's go to my office and I'll give you a better explanation."

A group of women walked toward them, all bundled in coats and sweaters. Matt leaned around Ken, searching for Kathleen in the gaggle of women. He wanted Ken to be wrong and for her to be here and waiting for him. "Where is she?"

"When a patient requests a discharge, we have the right to hold that patient for..."

"Goddammit, Ken. I don't want the brochure read to me. I want to know where Kathleen is."

Ken opened the portfolio he always carried and pulled out a standard-sized white envelope. "She left this for you."

Matt snatched the envelope. His name was written in a lovely script, and he recognized she'd used his pen because the ink was always thicker on the first word. The heft suggested it was only one page, and he couldn't decide if that was good or bad. Both *come find me* and *it was nice knowing you* would only take a few lines.

"Ken, what the hell happened? You can't just hand me an envelope and not tell me what's going on."

"Do you believe I'd have let her leave if I didn't think she was safe?"

"No, I don't. But didn't you tell her I was coming?"

"I did tell her. That's what prompted her to write that letter. But she was impatient to leave and do what she needed to do."

"Which was...?"

Ken shrugged, leaned against one of the pillars, and answered in his therapist voice. "I'm sorry I can't tell you more. But one of our policies before a patient leaves is to pre-arrange outpatient care. Everyone who leaves here needs ongoing support. You don't leave an intense treatment center and go straight into life."

"So Kathleen has some sort of follow-up care arranged? Where?"

"One of our policies before a patient leaves is pre-arranged..."

"You don't have to repeat yourself. I get it." He smacked the letter against his palm, the slap-slap filling the air was not nearly as satisfying as shaking more information out of Ken would be.

Ken placed his hand on Matt's shoulder. "I know this is hard. Recovery is never a straight path, and many survivors have journeys they must take alone. But this is a good time for you to think about you. To put yourself first. Have you decided what Matt Nelson wants?"

He jerked away from Ken's reassurance. "How dare you ask that? What I wanted, left, and the one person who could have stopped her, didn't."

Matt stomped to his car holding the letter tightly in both hands. Ken could have made her stay a little longer—it was a few fucking hours. Couldn't he have made her go to art or yoga or pet some damn puppies? And, damn her, she should have at least let Ken tell him something helpful. He understood she was pissed and hurt he'd had to leave, but this was not fair. She—his Kathleen—was better than this.

He had to find a place where he could be alone and calm before he read Kathleen's letter. If this was the last thing she said to him, he wanted to be in a state of mind to listen and try to understand. As he pulled his car out of the parking lot, he turned on Led Zeppelin as loud as the car speakers allowed and pounded the steering with the drumbeat. He was torn between wanting to hit something and wanting to cry. Part of him wanted to throw the damn letter out the window. Part of him wanted to stop the car in the middle of the road and devour her words.

He'd driven twenty miles towards nowhere when the pressure building in his chest stopped him. He pulled into the McDonald's parking lot, found a space in the back corner. He shut off the car but let Journey keep him company. The letter sat on the console, mocking him as surely as Tom and Jerry had.

When he'd received the letters from his mother, he'd resented that she'd opened up to him only after she'd died. She'd asked him to look at his life, his relationships, his priorities, his wants and dreams. She asked him to go to a nowhere beach and to sit at a specific restaurant. She'd known he'd see Kathleen and she'd known his heart would open.

He turned the volume louder, letting the bass beat through him. He forced the seat backward and opened both windows so the wind surged through the car. Nervous energy had him punching the radio scan button, seeking something not available on a radio. He stopped when the Eagles' "Hotel California" filled the car.

His mother, like all mothers, had complained about his and Patti's music when he was a teenager. She hated Led Zeppelin and AC/DC. But she liked Glenn Frey and Don Henley. "Desperado." "Take It Easy." "Peaceful Easy Feeling." Her favorite had always been "Hotel California." She'd sing every word at the top of her lungs, with a hairbrush or spoon as a microphone. His mother absolutely could not sing. He turned the volume down, rested his head against the seat, and enjoyed the refrain. *Welcome to the Hotel California. Such a lovely place. Such a lovely face.*

He'd been sitting in this same seat, buried in Minnesota traffic, when his father had called to tell him his mother was gone. Matt had never heard his father cry, and his dad's choked voice had him pulling over to the shoulder of the road. He was seven miles from his parents' house when she died. Both Patti and their dad had been with her. Matt had not.

He'd sat in his car that afternoon letting guilt and shame and despair roll over him until a policeman sent him on his way. By the time he rolled into his parents' drive, her body had been picked up. He never saw his mother again. He never got to say goodbye, or a last *I love you.* She never got to see him with Kathleen.

If he'd left the office twenty minutes earlier he would have been able to hold his mother's hand, kiss her cheek. He could have held Patti while she cried and helped his father say his goodbye. He'd been too late then, and he was too late now.

He picked up the envelope, put it to his nose, hoping to smell Kathleen's lavender bath oil. In the weeks before she died, his mother had written him ten letters, and those letters had smelled like sickness. Kathleen's letter smelled like nothing. His mother's letters had sent him on an adventure where he had found the love of his life. Would Kathleen's letter end it?

While he traced his name written in Kathleen's script, he whispered, "Mom, I wish you were here."

He slipped his finger under the flap and opened the envelope. Treating the page like spun glass, he pulled out Kathleen's message.

Her handwriting had changed. The words weren't smashed together as if her mind moved faster than her fingers. The sentences no longer sloped off the page. This handwriting was beautiful and unique. Curlicues and swirls.

Matt ~

I started this process choking on anger and hatred. I thought it was anger at Josh and the evil he brought into my home. But it was deeper and darker. My mind was keeping me from facing that night but also protecting me from the root of my suffering. I hate that you left, but Lisa was right—if you had stayed, I would still have been stuck in the mire.

I know you wanted me to share—and one day I hope I get the opportunity—but how do I tell a man I love that I hated my husband for dying, for not stopping the monsters in the house? That I hated my son for locking his gun away? My grandchildren for not going to the basement to play? Courtney for having such a nice diamond ring? I hated myself for standing there paralyzed, watching my family fall one by one. I did nothing except survive, and I hated myself for that, too. I hated them because I loved them so much and they left me.

I wanted to hate you, too. For leaving me here. For telling Lisa about my bruises. I wanted to scream and hit you for betraying and abandoning me.

It was so much easier to blame you than look at myself. You did not abandon me or betray me. You loved me and carried me. I understand you have responsibilities—a life—beyond me and my drama. I am proud you claimed your own truth and went home.

Am I fine? No, never fine. I'll never be the world's version of normal. I'm worried and anxious—about you and about my next steps. I'll always struggle with sadness, anger, guilt. People will always make me nervous and look at me funny. And yet I'm hopeful. I can rebuild now. I can face the next obstacle and the next.

I get to create this Kathleen who loves hamburgers and swiss cheese, whose favorite color is green, who likes to paint but has no talent. I can do that because of you.

How do I explain what a gift you've been?

Matt, you gave me my family back.

I'm going to return the favor. It's okay to go back to Minnesota and the corner office. It's your turn to figure out who Matt Nelson is and who he wants to be.

My love for you will never stop no matter where life takes you. Love is in the heart and soul. My love does not create a responsibility for you.

No matter who Matt Nelson becomes or where he goes, he is loved. Deeply. Thoroughly. Always.

I love you. That is my gift to you. And also to myself.

You are free.

~ Your Kathleen

Matt crumpled the letter in his hand. Why did *I love you* come too late? Why was it safer to say *I love you* in a letter? If he'd been here—if he'd put his Kathleen before the firm—would she have had the courage to tell him? Did she love Matt Nelson or was he simply the man who helped her? Was his love one-sided?

He'd stood by Kathleen, slept in a closet with her, held her when she had nightmares, rubbed ointment where she'd hurt herself. If he gave her courage, she should have used that courage to face him and not run away. He deserved more than some ink on a piece of paper.

He flattened the paper, and re-read the letter once, twice, three times. He twisted around and reached into the back seat, where his mother's letters sat in their box. He pulled the box to his lap and rested his palm on top, remembering. No, his love was not one-sided. His Kathleen—like his mother—had poured her love on the page. Her courage was bold and beautiful, shining through the blue ink.

His mother and his Kathleen had given him more than words. They had given him purpose and passion. In the space of one page, his Kathleen had handed him her heart.

He started the car, pointed his Escalade east. She'd promised to give him his family back. He would find her and hold her to that promise. Kathleen was his family now. He'd handed her his heart. And he was not taking it back.

Kathleen

Kathleen wound her way up the curvy roads in Leeside Mountain Estates. Her Curious George bag and Matt's pen, along with her to-do list, sat on the seat next to her. Not for the first time in the last four hours, she wished she'd waited for him. She wished he was holding her hand and telling her everything would be all right. But she had to do this alone. Marcia needed to make this last journey so Kathleen could begin again.

"One step at a time," she reminded herself. The decision to leave The Center had nearly overwhelmed her. She had needed to find a car, a place to stay, money. All things Marcia would have accomplished easily. Now, she had to fight off Josh's mocking voice and remind herself that Kathleen was alive and capable of making this trip.

"Snow weather," she said to the empty passenger seat. The last time she'd made this left turn, her car had been filled with the ingredients for lasagna. From the top of her drive, she had been able to see one of the Christmas trees twinkling in the A-frame log cabin. White lights traveled across the deck and over the bushes wrapping around her porch. Smoke had twirled from the fireplace, and a light snow had dusted everything. A picture postcard.

Her basement would have had the kids' tree—flickering multi-colored lights and homemade ornaments. Stockings for Santa and sleeping bags ready for the kids in their never-ending quest to catch a glimpse of the fat man and his reindeer.

She had known Seth was making his famous pancakes for brunch. She knew she'd find egg and pancake batter on every counter and splattered on the floor. Bacon grease would have spread from one end of the stove to the other. At least one broken eggshell would have missed the trash can. Courtney would be in her footie pajamas, yammering to Seth about her wedding plans.

She'd walked in laden with grocery bags to find Seth and Courtney laughing so hard that all activity had stopped. She hadn't stopped to admire the beauty of her husband and youngest child.

She'd stuffed the groceries around Seth's mess, kissed both their cheeks, before she and T-bone joined Stephanie for their daily hike. She didn't recall their conversation. Was it frivolous and fun? Was it about their worries and hopes? Or the book they were both reading? Kathleen wished she could reach across the years and grab hold of the words, the smells, the view. The anticipation of having her family together, of Christmas morning, of wedding plans. She had accepted those were gone to her.

Stephanie's house loomed on the big knoll overlooking the creek. Smoke billowed out of the chimney; lights from the first floor made her feel both safe and vulnerable. Through the window, she could see the big-screen TV showing a football game. How many football games did they watch together over the years? She looked down at the Gophers sweatshirt. It was Matt's, and she could still smell his soap. No matter how much she hoped to watch a game with Matt, she had to accept the sadness that that dream might never be. She held the sadness before letting it roll over and through her.

Journey to Hope

She parked the car above Stephanie's driveway and out of sight of the windows. Sitting in the warm car, she closed her eyes and remembered the last time she'd seen her friend. Steph was the one who was at the foot of Kathleen's hospital bed whenever she woke. She was the one who yelled at the nurses when they wouldn't let her sleep or didn't give the pain meds in time. When that doctor told Kathleen he could fix all her problems by giving her a new ear, Steph was the one who told him to go fuck himself. Stephanie was the one person Kathleen could tell anything without fear of judgment. She had a deep desire to roast marshmallows and drink a beer with her, the way they used to. Not quite ready to face her, Kathleen tiptoed down the gravel driveway, hoping the crunching didn't stir the dog to bark. Halting at the bottom step, she wiped the cold mist from her face. The steps were both achingly familiar and strange.

The kitchen light cast a soft glow onto the darkened porch as Kathleen strained to hear voices. What if she wasn't home? What if she had moved? She leaned back and glanced up the hill. The cabin she and Seth had so meticulously designed and decorated sat two miles from where she stood. She did not want to walk those miles alone.

"Mom," Brice's voice spoke. "Count the steps."

Five steps.

You can do anything five times.

She put her foot on the first step and jerked it back. She looked back at the car. She looked at the kitchen window. She looked up the hill.

"You need to walk up that hill. You need to see where we are," Seth's voice intruded on her fear and loneliness. "You've got things to say, things to feel."

"Why? You're not actually there. Your ashes blew away a long time ago."

"Take the walk, Marcia," Seth said. "You have to go back and then forward. To do that you have to climb these steps and knock on that door."

Kathleen closed her eyes. "I need Matt."

"No, you don't. You are strong enough now. You have never been dependent on anyone. Reclaim that part of yourself. You can bring him back at another time," Seth encouraged.

"Not if he doesn't come back to me," Kathleen challenged.

Seth had no answer to that. She wrapped her arms around her waist, hoping to quell the tremors. She took a deep breath, counted to five. What if Stephanie didn't want to see her? What if Kathleen had destroyed the only thing left?

"Make this amends," she whispered to herself.

She opened her eyes and there stood Stephanie.

"Marcia?" her best friend said.

The two women stared at each other. With a shaky voice Kathleen said, "Please don't call me that. I go by Kathleen now." Her tone was wrong. She wanted to be gentle but the words left her mouth sounding harsh.

"I'm sorry. I know. Are you going to come in?"

Kathleen looked at her car.

"Don't run. Please."

Avoiding Stephanie's eyes, Kathleen watched her feet mount the first step, the second step, third, fourth, fifth. She stopped and looked at Stephanie, praying her friend understood what she needed.

Stephanie smiled sadly and nodded. She walked the final ten steps across the deck and pulled Kathleen into a tight embrace.

Kathleen jolted at the touch, but Steph held on tight. Marcia had to hug, and Kathleen would fight to reclaim that, too.

"Not this time," Steph whispered into her ear. "You don't get to pull away this time."

Kathleen relaxed into her friend's arms. She heard the door open. "My girls," Steph's husband Mitch said in a choked voice. He pulled both of them into his barrel chest and Kathleen felt his kiss on the top of her head. "Come on now. You both need to get out of the cold."

Kathleen pulled away, swiped at her face. "I have to go there." She reached out, slid her hand into Stephanie's. "Please don't make me go alone."

"Never," Stephanie said. "I may not have been there in person, but you've never been alone."

Mitch disappeared into the house, returned with Stephanie's coat, two hats, two wool scarves. He pulled a cap down over Kathleen's scarf, wrapped the wool around her neck. He did the same for Stephanie. He kissed each woman's forehead and silently went back into the warmth of their home.

Without a word the two women held hands and started the long, cold walk toward hard memories. The walk seemed like the thousands they'd taken before. Steph pointed at each house, updated her on the latest neighborhood gossip.

"How can nothing be different? It's as if we were never here. Did our tragedy make no impact?" Kathleen asked.

"Marci—Kathleen—everyone was changed by what happened to you. Doors are kept locked. We have a communication system if strange cars drive through the neighborhood. The neighborhood watch program that was once just a sign at the entrance is taken seriously. We no longer fight over stupid stuff. The board meetings are actually pleasant." Steph took an audible breath and continued, "Every Christmas Eve—." Stephanie stalled as if waiting for permission to go on.

"What happens every Christmas Eve?" Kathleen asked the question in a whisper because the tightness in her chest prevented anything more.

"We—the entire neighborhood—walk down the street, carrying candles. When we reach your property, we form a circle and sing silly Christmas carols. We make a bonfire, share apple cider." Kathleen didn't look at her dear friend, but she could hear her fight to not cry.

Kathleen let the image form in her mind, let it warm the coldness blooming inside. "We used to go caroling. Remember how badly my family sang? Not a one of us could carry a tune."

Stephanie laughed. "If you'd call what we did caroling. Thad could not believe you talked us into that."

Kathleen joined her laughter. "Lucas never got the concept of singing, did he?"

"No, but that boy could scream 'Jingle Bells' loud enough for the North Pole to hear him."

Lucas. Kathleen sobered. She tried to hear his voice, his laughter. They walked in silence as the snowflakes began to drift around them.

"Kathleen, we remember." Stephanie squeezed Kathleen's hand. "Am I allowed to ask how things are going?"

"I'm better. I've been forced to remember and that's good. I'm able to talk about them without crumbling. But I've got a few more hills to climb."

"Like this one," Stephanie said as they started up the last hill.

"Coming here. Seeing where their ashes were scattered. Opening the boxes you sent."

"You never opened those?" Stephanie was incredulous.

"They've been stored away."

"Kathleen, I wouldn't have sent them if I'd known that would be so painful."

"No, no. I'm glad I have them. I'll open them soon. One mountain at a time."

"Can I admit that I'm sad you still wear the sunglasses?"

"I don't normally. But today I felt like I needed them. Please don't ask me to take them off." She wanted to trust Stephanie to see her more deeply. But Lisa had encouraged her to take whatever steps were necessary and not worry about other people's needs or opinions.

The weight on Kathleen's chest increased but she refused to swallow her words. "We used to be able to talk about anything. No worries about judgment or hurt feelings. Every day it seems I stumble on something else I lost."

Stephanie pulled Kathleen to a halt, stepped in front of her. She cradled Kathleen's face just like Matt used to do. Kathleen stiffened and then forced herself to relax. This was Stephanie; this was safe.

"Kathleen, you still have that. You can tell me anything. Give me a chance to learn what's safe and what's not. Okay?" She leaned over, kissed Kathleen's forehead and added, "You didn't lose me. You can never lose me."

Kathleen kept her forehead against Stephanie's lips until the ache in her chest lessened. She clutched Stephanie's hand like the tether it was and put one step in front of the other.

They crested the last hill. This time Kathleen forced them to stop. She stared down the hill toward her old mailbox, her old driveway. She wasn't ready. This could wait. This mountain would not be gone tomorrow. "I need to turn back."

Steph blocked Kathleen's view of the property. "You will do this. You have no choice. It's time, my dear friend, for you to face this." She used her thumb to track the tears on Kath's cheeks. "Come." Steph re-laced their fingers. Together they started down the hill.

"You said you all come here on Christmas Eve. What do the new owners think of that? What kind of house did they build?" Kathleen raced on as if asking the questions was more important than the answers. "Do they have kids here or are they retired? Do you like the woman? Do they have a dog? Do you and she walk together?" This last question was choked out. What if Kathleen had been replaced? Part of her wanted that and part of her resented the idea that she was replaceable. She let the contradictions have their place. "It will be what it will be. I can feel what I need to feel and then survive," she whispered the mantra over and over again.

Rather than answer, Stephanie gently guided her closer to the past.

There was no new house, no new family. Instead Kathleen saw an empty lot where the house once stood, and what she knew would bloom into a magnificent garden. She dropped Stephanie's hand and, as if in a trance, she maneuvered down the drive and followed the mulch trail. She wound her way around eight circular gardens. In the center stood a Japanese maple. Marcia's favorite tree. And Kathleen's favorite.

In each garden was a bench and plaque. As she walked along the path, Kathleen stooped, touched the names and read aloud.

"Lucas. Learning his R's in Heaven.

"Courtney. Making Angels Eat Right.

"Amanda. Putting Up with Brice Forevermore.

"Brice. Quietly Watching Over What's His.

"Kiley. Finally Happy With Her Curls.

"Seth. Guiding and Loving From the Stars.

"T-Bone. Making Friends and Sniffing Butts."

Standing in the last circle, she found no sign. "The last circle?"

"Marcia—Kathleen, you lost seven souls you loved with all your being. I lost them, too. But I also lost you. That makes eight circles. Walk around it."

Kathleen stepped off the path and around the circle. Instead of a sign and a bench, there was a plaque nestled in the ground. "Marcia. Always In Your Corner."

Journey to Hope

    Kathleen was crying so hard she could not speak. Stephanie had always been in her corner and Kathleen had pushed her away without explanation. She'd treated her exactly as she had Matt, cutting both of them off like a severed limb.

    "Each circle is planted with a different flower. They bloom at different times so something is almost always in bloom."

    "When? How? Why?" the questions sputtered out of Kathleen.

    "When I got your lawyer's letter to sell the property, I couldn't quite do it. Tearing the house down was easy. But..." Stephanie paused, drew Kathleen to the center. "Your home was always open. When the kids were young, the neighborhood used your house as Grand Central. Even the adults never felt the need to knock. Mitch and I agreed that openness and welcoming spirit needed to be recreated."

    "You hate to garden."

    "Funny, huh. You always wanted me to garden with you and now I do."

    "Do people come here?" She had no idea what answer she wanted.

    "All the neighbors spend time here. Walking, meditating, tending the plants. The project was written up in the paper. For a while, there was a constant stream of people. Every kid you ever taught came by. Many of the parents. Seth's employees. Courtney and Brice's friends. On and on. Most of them left letters and cards. We left the mailbox because we still get cards addressed to you. They are all in a box in my attic whenever you want them."

    "I already have boxes I won't open."

    "I'll hold on to them as long as you want." Stephanie rubbed Kathleen's shoulders.

    "See those wild-looking bushes? Can you tell what they are?" Stephanie asked.

Together they clambered up the hill. Kathleen ran her hand along the bare branches. "Yellow bells."

"Your favorite. In the spring, the area is such a bright yellow it can be seen all the way to the main road."

Kathleen sank to the cold earth. Stephanie sat beside her. With her best friend's arms around her, they both cried.

When her tears slowed, Kathleen said, "I'm sorry I tossed you out of my life."

Whispering, Stephanie said, "Why did you do that? I never understood what I did wrong. I showed up to find you'd dropped me off the approved visitors list. Then I received a letter that sounded like an attorney talking."

Kathleen took a deep breath, raised her head and stared at her mountains covered in clouds. "I couldn't stand to look at you."

"Why, though? You'd been looking at me for months."

"You know the stages of grief include denial, guilt, anger, depression and acceptance. It's not linear. I can experience them all in a five-minute time span. Except acceptance. That one has taken longer." Considering her next words, she began to trace circles in the dirt. "I never had the luxury of denial. When you watch them die, when you smell the cordite and watch as the blood pools around you, denial is impossible. Instead I got a double or triple dose of anger and guilt." She removed her sunglasses and looked at Stephanie. "I hated you."

Stephanie flinched but she did not look away. "If you'd not come that night, if you'd not found me, if you'd not called an ambulance, then I wouldn't have been in such anguish, such pain. I could have gone with them. I blamed you for saving me."

After a long silence, Stephanie said, "That wasn't fair."

"What about this was fair?" She barked the words and then said, "I'm sorry. I didn't mean to sound like that."

"Do you still...." Stephanie's hurt voice trailed off.

"Do I still hate you?" Kathleen asked the unfinished question. "No. I hate those boys. I still struggle with hating myself. But I don't hate you. I love you, and in the back of my mind, I held on to the truth that you would understand and forgive me." She turned once again to look at her friend. "I realized you did exactly what I would have done. It wasn't you. It was my need to channel everything somewhere, anywhere. You were convenient." Kathleen scooted closer to Stephanie and leaned her entire body into Stephanie's body. She kept her gaze on the mountains when she asked, "Can you forgive me?"

Stephanie snaked her arm around Kathleen's waist, pulled her closer and asked, "Forgiveness is not needed but if it was, or if you need to hear the words, then yes, my best friend, you are always forgiven."

A silence descended around them. A light snow started to fall.

Stephanie squeezed Kathleen's waist and asked, "Did you at least miss me?"

Kathleen considered lying but knew truth was the healing choice. "No. I refused to think about you, about any of this. I lived the life of a recluse. I exercised to stave off insanity. I ate. I read and read and read. Shit, Steph, I paid an attorney and accountant to handle everything so no one could find me. My only contact with the outside world was to order books and to go to that restaurant. I stayed in a fictional world. I refused to let the ghosts visit. I refused to feel anything. Only at night could it all creep in." She shrugged, looked again at the mountains she used to admire every day. The clouds rested on the tops and within the valleys exactly as it was supposed to be in the Smoky Mountains. "Then, Matt arrived. He wouldn't let me read all the time. He wouldn't let me hide. He forced me to feel and then he joined me in the nightmares."

"Do you want to update me on Matt?"

In the before, Kathleen would have ached to tell every detail—the way Matt ran his thumb below her missing ear when she was anxious and the way he kissed every one of her scars before he made love to her. She would have told her about the letter she wrote him and let Stephanie call her a coward. That intimacy was dead, too. "Matt has had to go back to Minnesota to handle some things at the family firm." She'd never once lied to her friend, but that half-truth was enough.

"Will I see you again?" Stephanie asked.

Kathleen pulled her arms away, stood and kissed the top of Stephanie's head. Gently, she put her sunglasses in Steph's palms. "In the hospital, you brought me my first pair of sunglasses because I needed to hide. I won't be hiding anymore." She kissed her head once more and added, "I love you no matter where I am."

The snow blew harder as they made their way back to the car. For the first time in a long time, Kathleen was proud of herself. She gave Stephanie one last hug, then climbed into her car and drove in silence to an unknown future. A future she could face. Even if she had to do it alone.

Matt

Matt trudged through the sand, unable to take in the magnificent waves or the warm sun. He'd arrived at Kathleen's beach four days ago, expecting to find her sitting on her deck, staring at the ocean. But she wasn't there, and her phone continued to go unanswered. He'd called Ken and they hadn't heard from her, either. At the end of day two, he'd found Stephanie's number and, after an awkward conversation, she'd told him Kathleen had come and gone. Where was she? What was she doing? How did he find her? Did she want to be found?

He made the turn to her bungalow and stopped. His Kathleen sat on her deck, no sunglasses, no scarf. A book sat on the floor next to her. She held a water bottle and his eyes. She didn't smile or frown. When he'd pictured this scene, he had imagined the romance novel ending. They'd run to each other. He'd scoop her in his arms and twirl her around while she laughed. Instead, they both seemed paralyzed. Did he cross the sand or wait on her?

"Kathleen?" He knew the wind and waves prevented his plea from getting to her, but he needed a hint. Was he welcome? Wanted?

She shifted to the edge of her chair and Matt held his breath. Would she walk into her bungalow, close and lock the door?

She stood, never taking her eyes from his.

She took two steps forward and stopped at the top of her stairs.

The surf sloshed around Matt's feet, leaving white foam on his calves. Three months ago, he'd crossed this space day after day, shoving himself into her world, forcing her to decide on life. Until this very moment, he'd planned to do it again. But, as she stood there staring at him, he wanted—needed—her to go first. If they were to have anything, he couldn't chase her anymore.

A seagull swooped between them. Kathleen watched as it darted in and out of their bubble. When it flew away for the last time, Kathleen cocked her head as if she were wondering what was taking him so long. She raised her hand, palm up, and smiled.

He reached her in seconds, gathered her in his arms. "Love."

She wrapped her arms around his neck. "I was hoping you'd come back." Speaking into his ear, she said, "Because you lent me your strength, I'm ready to open that door. I'm strong enough to face it alone, but I'm grateful you're here."

He kissed her, a kiss of apology and relief and promise. He cradled her chin in his palms and kissed her nose. Did he need to explain why he'd left? Did she understand and believe that he would never have—and never would—abandon her?

"This is what I am." She touched the side of her head. "I won't stop being the victim and the survivor. I won't ever be fully free from what happened to them and to me. Can you live with that?"

He rested his hand on the back of her neck with his fingertips brushing her jagged hairline. He leaned down and placed his lips on hers. A romance novel could never accurately describe the love he felt in this moment. He breathed in the scent of her shampoo and let the warmth of her skin relax him.

She dropped her forehead into his chest. "I have to climb the ten stairs, open the door and see their faces, tell their stories. I have to carry them into the future with me. I couldn't do that without you."

He took her hand in his. "*We* have to climb ten stairs. *We* have to open a door, see their faces. *I* get the privilege of hearing their stories."

He led her into the house and to the top of the stairs. He felt her body tremble and heard her intake of breath. She traced the tick marks on the wall. "It's been one thousand four hundred seventeen days."

He waited. He would stand here, hold her tight, but she had to use her own courage and strength to flip those locks.

The click of the first lock was as loud as a starting gun.

She squeezed his fingers with her damaged hand and unlocked the remaining locks.

She dropped his hand and walked into the room. Three windows poured in sunlight. The room was quiet, as if this event required reverence.

"Fairy dust," she whispered and the awe in her voice sent shivers down his spine.

Placing both palms on a box, she took in a deep breath, let her head drop between her arms. One tear fell, hit the box and spread. Her shoulders rose and fell. He stayed at the door even as that lone tear turned into sobs. She choked and coughed and shook. Tears poured, leaving an ever-growing stain on the box. Matt desperately wanted to go to her, to stop the pain, to collect the tears. But he waited. This was her time, her space, her suffering.

His heart twisted, and still he waited.

Her sobs slowed and her body relaxed. His Kathleen was not a pretty crier. Her cheeks and nose were bright red. Her eyes were bloodshot and dripping. She'd never been more beautiful. She swiped her arms across her cheeks and under her nose. For the second time that day, she extended her hand, inviting him into her future.

Kathleen's face was buried in the third box. Pictures, awards, childhood art, homemade Christmas ornaments were strewn over the floor. A Barbie doll creation leaned against one of the boxes. She'd traced their faces, sobbing or laughing. She talked so fast he barely understood the words.

She held a picture to his nose, blurring the image. "Look at them." She sounded like a little girl holding a tiara.

Matt gently took the picture from her hands. It was of the entire family smiling with their arms around each other. Even the dog smiled at the camera. Seven smiling blobs of mud. Only their bright eyes and white teeth proved they were human beings.

"It started when they were washing the cars. Seth agreed to feed everyone his fancy roast beast but only if they earned it." Her voice was filled with glorious laughter and profound sadness. "It started to pour, and I heard Seth shout, 'Run.' They laughed and screamed and tackled. Mud was smashed into faces and ears. I tried to stay out of it, but Brice carried me off the deck. They wrestled me to the mud puddle and pelted me with mud. Stephanie showed up and took this picture." She held the picture to her chest and stared into his eyes. "This is who we were. Laughing. Teasing." She shook her head in delight. "And so friggin' loud."

She shifted to sit on her knees, and with a kid's excitement, she said, "I used to have this wall. Ten feet tall. Every inch covered with a picture. No frames. Just pictures tacked up. Every few weeks, I'd change some of them. The kids loved it. Their friends loved it." She shook her head and continued more softly, "I think I'll do that again. Wherever we end up, I'll hang these." She dropped the picture, grasped his cheeks, kissed him, and said, "Would that be all right with you?"

"We will find a place where you can hang each picture in the place of honor it deserves." He had done a lot of things in his life because he felt obligated. Creating a space for all of Kathleen and her family would be the first great pleasure of their new life together.

She bounced up and down a few times before she dug into the box again. "We can add Jake and Joey. Patricia. Your dad. Ian. Those damn Gophers. Wall after wall of love."

He stood up and began to put the pictures in neat rows so she could add more. He put the trophies and the kids' art around the walls.

She still had her face in a box when the energy in the room changed. She was no longer laughing and bouncing. She lifted her head. Her eyes were wider and bluer than he'd ever seen.

"Kath?"

Her bottom lip began to tremble as she lifted out a long box with a red ribbon. "It's from Seth." New tears pooled in her eyes.

Should he go to her? Or leave the room and give her privacy?

"Can I sit in your lap?" she asked with a tone that bordered on a plea.

With long strides he moved to her, sat, and pulled her tight against him.

She held the package up to his eyes so he could see the paper clearly. The paper was faded snowmen sledding down a hill. Fat snowmen. Skinny snowmen. Snowmen with hats. Snowmen with long pants. "Seth always wrapped my packages in snowmen paper."

She twirled the package in her fingers. "The last gift I'll ever open from him."

Matt squeezed but he didn't speak. This was her moment; all he needed to do was be there.

She moved the package from hand to hand. "Seth always had to hide my presents because I was impatient. I'd beg and beg to 'just open one.' I was horrible." She tore through the paper, unveiling a blue jeweler's box. Carefully, she opened it and pulled out a necklace. The silver pendant twirled in the sun, causing the colorful stones to create a kaleidoscope on the walls and floor. "It's a family tree."

She let it rest in her palm. She touched the blue stone. "That's me. Sapphire." She touched the orange. "Kiley." Her finger moved to the two green stones. "Brice and Lucas." She tilted her head back. "The diamond is Courtney. She always said that was proof she was a princess." She held the gift between their faces again. "Purple. Seth and Amanda."

Nestled together, they watched the jewelry spin and the sparkles dance.

"What is the light blue?" Matt asked.

Kathleen held the necklace closer to her face. "That's aquamarine. March." She shrugged. "T-bone, I guess."

Matt swallowed past a sudden lump in his throat and let a liquid warmth infuse his heart. "I was born in March," he said into her neck, and he could almost hear his mother say, *I told you you'd know her when you found her.*

Kathleen

"It's snowing hard. Do you think they can get here safely in this weather?" Kathleen peered out the window into the darkness of Joe's backyard, where the light from the greenhouse was a beacon glowing through the falling snow. A lighthouse guiding Kathleen to this new life. In the greenhouse, the broken pots were gone, and several plants were sprouting new life. The Christmas lily Kathleen had almost destroyed all those weeks ago sat in the center of the kitchen table. When she looked at it, she still ached. She'd always ache. There was a hole in her heart that would never mend. But she could breathe now.

"We're in Minnesota. This is nothing compared to February," Matt said.

They sat in Betty's kitchen at the long butcher block island. Above the island, shiny copper pots of all shapes and sizes dangled. Instead of a coffee pot, Joe used a press, exclaiming that good coffee should require effort. Every day, Joe told her, he chose a different coffee cup from Betty's vast collection. He would sit at the table overlooking the backyard and talk to his wife about the origin of that particular cup. Joe mourned and yet he lived. Kathleen would, too.

Kathleen took a sip of the apple cider from the mug with Matt's four-year-old buck-toothed face. She traced the painted *MOM*.

Matt sipped from a blue mug that said, "You Don't Have to Be Crazy to Live Here. We'll Train You." Kathleen knew it was the last mug he'd given his mother the Christmas before she died.

While she cleaned the breakfast dishes and began prep for dinner, Matt was updating Joe on all the happenings in Charlotte. "We're making our way. It's hard and easy and wonderful."

Her family had been taken from her one thousand four hundred sixty-two days ago. Today she'd focus on the good times, on her amazing family, on the love she carried within. Today was Christmas Eve.

Matt never asked if she was fine. Sometimes the sadness was so thick she'd go into her fictional world for relief. But she told Matt she loved him several times a day, and in many different ways. She reached for him in the night. He held her when she cried.

He never said he was fine. He never pretended this was easy. He never pretended he knew what he was doing. He still loved his yellow notepad and calculating the Fibonacci numbers. He wasn't clear what his next career would be, and the unknown was fun and exciting. He told Kathleen he loved her several times a day, and in many different ways. He no longer hovered, but on this Christmas Eve, he stayed closer. He'd watched her and touched her and let her know he was available.

"Our new therapist is excellent. She helped us develop strategies for today," Matt said to his father.

"Merry Christmas," Joey called. A cold breeze swirled in with Matt's youngest nephew. He stood in the kitchen doorway, snatching his hat off and shaking snow onto the floor.

In the last several weeks, Jake and Joey had come to North Carolina for two football games, teasing that all the Blue Devil blue was making them sick. On both trips, they'd brought Gopher décor—a blanket, a pillow, even sheets. It wasn't until she'd seen Matt and his nephews together that she understood how much Matt loved the boys and wanted them in his life. It surprised her how much she, too, wanted Ian and Jake and Joey in her life. She'd have thought being around young adults so much like Brice and Courtney would be too painful. But the boys made her laugh and gave her back a love for sports. Instead of being a reminder of what she'd lost, the boys reminded her of all that was now hers to reclaim.

For about ten seconds, their first meeting had been tense. Joey, so much like Courtney, had looked from Kathleen to Matt and then he'd swooped over, given Kathleen a short, sweet hug, and said, "Tell me you like the Minnesota Vikings and not the Charlotte Panthers. I can survive Duke, but that's all my patience will allow."

Jake breezed over to Kathleen, swiped a kiss across her cheek. "K, you better not have one of those ugly shirts under the tree with my name on it." Knowing it would annoy both Jake and Joey, Kathleen had chosen a sweatshirt and scarf with the Duke logo and a sneering Blue Devil. She couldn't suppress a grin of mischief.

The kitchen was overtaken by noise and people and hugs. Flakes of snow fell from shoulders, leaving dots of water across the floor. Everyone selected their cup of the day and filled them with Joe's cider. Betty's kitchen looked nothing like Kathleen's cabin, but it was exactly the same. The hub of all family activities.

Patti scooted closer, wrapped her arm around Kath's shoulders and pulled her from the room. "Before dinner, we decorate the tree in the basement. Mom called the tree on this level the 'department store tree.' The one in the basement she said was 'family beauty.' Which meant it wasn't pretty at all."

"Handmade ornaments?"

"Yep, and let me tell you: Mattie has no talent."

The family tromped down the stairs, teasing each other, letting the excitement build.

The den was a large space with dark paneled shelves of games and well-worn novels, a huge television, a pool table, and a blazing fireplace. Just like her cabin, it was warm and comfortable and perfectly messy. In the corner, Joe had put their unadorned tree. Sitting on the large leather couch were unopened boxes labeled *Christmas*.

Someone turned the stereo on, filling the space with Christmas music. Someone else muted the TV on today's football game. The family dove into the boxes and, as if they had designated roles, each person began to decorate. Matt started on the tree lights. Patti hung the stockings above the fireplace. Jake and Joey laughed at homemade ornaments before putting them on the tree.

Kathleen moved to the corner and watched the spectacle of Christmas, trying to stay in the moment and not surrender to the past. Seth had always hung the lights. Brice had put the star on top. Courtney's job had been to put the stockings up. She always put her own stocking in the center, and every year, Brice would make fun of her vanity.

"Moms," Courtney whispered. "*Tell them about our favorite Christmas tradition.*"

She leaned back into Matt's chest and did as her beautiful girl suggested. "We had this weird Christmas tradition. Every year, Seth would buy us the ugliest footie pajamas. You know, the ones with a butt flap. One year we were all abominable snowmen."

For a long while no one spoke. No one moved. Not even Kathleen. The smiles on their faces, their willingness to hear her stories, their obvious love for Kathleen's family helped her share the blessings and heartaches.

"That last year, he'd bought these beaver suits. Complete with the huge tail. The tail acted as the door to the butt. Lucas would have loved it. Courtney would have snarled. Kiley would have chewed her thumb in embarrassment." Kathleen did not try to stop the tears that fell. She did not try to stop the memory. "I wish I had that picture."

She touched her new scarf—Gophers dressed as elves. Earlier in the week, she had sent Ken a tie with Blue Devils dressed as Santa. Matt had added one with skiing Gophers. They didn't add a note. Ken would know who they were from—and what they meant.

"I bought you this," Patti said with obvious worry in her voice. She handed Kathleen a snowman gift bag with puffs of white tissue paper. "You don't have to open it. You don't have to use it. But I saw it and I thought you should have it."

"I love snowmen," Kathleen whispered as she turned the bag around and around. Kathleen and Patti had tiptoed into their friendship over a book they were both reading. Now they talked about books and TV shows and, of course, sports. Patti knew all about Courtney's wedding plans, and Kathleen knew Patti did not like Joey's girlfriend.

Patti stepped away, leaving Kathleen alone with her first Christmas gift.

Marcia had been the type to tear into a package, leaving piles of paper to clean away. Kathleen, she decided in the corner of Matt's family's home, would be different. She carefully tugged out the tissue paper, folded it into a square before reaching into the bag. Inside was an exquisitely detailed quilted stocking. Five snowmen and a dog all wearing reindeer horns and angel wings.

She stepped to the mantle, put her stocking next to Betty's. "Betty," she whispered so only Betty could hear. "Thank you for sharing your family." Turning, she saw Joe watching her with wet eyes. He looked at the new stocking and then back at her. With a big grin, he held her eyes for several seconds before he winked and went back to the revelry.

As she watched Matt's family play together, she ran the pendant—Seth's final gift—along the chain, letting the zip-zip soothe her. Seth's voice joined her in the beauty of the moment. *"Marcia, you are the gift. You've always been the greatest of all gifts. Merry Christmas, honey. We love you. Keep moving forward,"* Seth whispered. "We're not going anywhere."

When she went silent or let the tears fall or shared a memory, Matt's family embraced her, but they never flinched. They never flinched.

Kathleen felt her despair turn to hope. She let the laughter extinguish the last flames of anger.

Then she made lasagna.

Leeside Mountain News
February 14, 2017 ♦ Leeside, NC

An Update on the Bridges Family

Most, if not all, residents of Leeside Mountain remember the tragic events of December 2012 when the Bridges family was the victim of a family annihilation. The lone survivor was Mrs. Marcia Bridges.

Recently, our news department received the following announcement:

*Marcia Kathleen Conners Bridges
married
Matthew Joseph Nelson
on January 31.
The couple held a private ceremony on Rosamund Beach and plan to settle in Charlotte.*

Local resident Stephanie Culberson stood beside the bride as she took her vows.

The couple was surrounded by Mr. Nelson's family, the Culberson family and many of the people who helped Marcia Bridges heal.

According to Mrs. Culberson, the venue was decorated with pictures of the Bridges family and flowers from Mr. Nelson's mother's greenhouse.

Acknowledgements

I must start with Kathleen and Matt. My protagonists are as real to me as anyone. I thank both of them for not letting me rest until I heard and presented their authentic world. I can't tell you how often Matt whispered in my ear, "That's not what I would say. Please rewrite it." I have been shocked to discover that Matt has one more story to tell us in *The Secrets of Hope*.

My husband, kids, and grandkids are always in my corner, and I thank them for letting me steal tidbits of their lives to weave into my characters. Hailey's sweetness, Lleyton's silliness, Brian and Sydney's horrible British accents. And Dave, thank you for pretending everything I write is awesome even when it's awful.

My writing coach, Tammy Letherer. She would not let me give up (and I wanted to several times). She pushed me to understand Matt and Kathleen deeper. She forced me to make every situation they faced harder and harder. She challenged me to rework sentences and scenes. I think she might know Kathleen and Matt better than I do. I could not have done this without her. Tammy, ready for the next book?

Emily Aborn at She Built This is the most positive person I have ever met. She keeps me focused and handles all those pesky social media details most authors hate. Because she manages my "presence," I could write and not worry about what a # is.

Lisa Norman and Heart Ally Books created my website and agreed to stand behind *Journey of Hope* with her publishing house. Not only does she believe in me, she makes me look good. And she's already encouraging me to finish Book #3.

Lori Brown at Grammarwitch is amazing. Most authors will tell you that the editing process is the most tedious and exhausting. Lori was so detailed and thorough; I could just sit back and polish my nails (or write *The Secrets of Hope*).

I have the wonderful privilege to be involved in two critique groups. Both groups find ways to make me better every week. So, thanks to Barry, Bob, Carol-Ann, Cheryl, Don, Donna, Judy B., Judy M., Kathy, Marissa, Patricia, and Robert. Write on.

If you loved *Journey to Hope*...

Please consider leaving a review on Goodreads and with the vendor where you purchase books.

Turn the page for the first chapter of Matt and Kathleen's story from *Decide to Hope*.

Courtney

Kathleen stepped on the top step, shook the sand from her sandals and forced herself to walk the few feet to her front door. Placing her forehead against it, she fumbled for the keys buried in her pocket and breathed in the salty humid air. With the moon obscured behind storm clouds, she had to use her index finger to guide the key into the first lock. The first click helped slow her heart rate. "Almost safe," she breathed into the wind. Click. Click. Every time a lock slid open, her heart rate decreased.

A loud clap of thunder shook the boards underneath her feet. Startled, her fingers opened and the keys thunked to the deck. She spun around in time to see the lightning streak above the ocean. "Lighting," she whispered at the evidence of nature's power. "Lighting," she said again before she crushed the smile that threatened to form. Another boom vibrated through her body. Another flash brightened the sky.

Forgetting for just a minute her need to get inside and hide, she allowed one of the doors in her mind to slide open. The Before Door. Against the increasing wind, she gripped the headscarf she always wore and moved toward the lounger nestled in the corner of her deck. After settling back in the cushion, she tipped her face to the storm moving in her direction. While she slowly unwound the scarf, a memory seeped into her consciousness.

"Mommy, please come inside," her four-year-old pleaded. "Daddy, the lighting is gonna struck her. Make her come in." The round face squished against the glass door. All ten fingers created sweaty evidence of the girl's fear.

"It's light*ning*, not lighting," she corrected for the hundredth time. "I'm fine, honey. I like the lightning. I'll come in before the rain hits. Go cuddle with Daddy. I'll be there in a few minutes."

Courtney stuck out her tongue and danced it across the glass until the next blast of thunder sent her scurrying to Seth's lap. Even from a distance of twenty years, Kathleen heard the frustration as her daughter settled into her father's lap.

Kathleen traced the rough edges of skin normally hidden by the scarf. "I'm sorry I made you stop saying 'lighting' and 'struck'," she said, turning to the empty lounger beside her. In her mind's eye Kathleen saw the gorgeous young lady tighten her ponytail and harrumph. She imagined the words her daughter would say. "Mom, please, you're worrying about stupid stuff again. I can't be twenty-four years old and still saying 'lighting' and 'struck'. I already get made fun of for this southern accent you saddled me with."

Kathleen closed her eyes and reached over the space between the two chairs. Her fingers traced the iron armrest, pretending it was Courtney's arm. She made believe she could touch her daughter. She acted out a conversation that could never occur.

"It smells here," the mirage said.

"That's the storm stirring up the sea life. You smell the ocean." Holding the image behind closed eyes, Kathleen pulled the scent into her nostrils. Salt. Sand. Marine life.

"Why did you choose this beach?"

Decide to Hope

Keeping her eyes closed and the picture intact, Kathleen said, "Because I hoped you'd visit."

"I'll come anytime you want. We all will. You just have to let us in."

The person and the dream sat in silence as Kathleen continued to stroke the armrest.

"Did you do it today?"

The sad sigh emerged all the way from Kathleen's chest. "No."

In Kathleen's imagination, she listened as Courtney shuffled to sit upright. Courtney crossed her legs and settled her arms over her chest. "Mom, do I have to make you pinkie swear?" An imaginary arm pushed out with a pinkie extended.

"Pinkie swear," Kathleen whispered into the wind. She lifted her arm and her pinkie. "I swear I'll plant one plant before the end of the week." She wiggled her small finger, continuing to pretend her daughter's skin touched hers.

"Remember, Mom. Pinkie swears are sacred. I've had to do a lot of crap because of this."

With her finger still moving in the empty air, she answered, "I know. This week. One plant. Do you have one in mind?"

"That's your area of expertise." The sweet voice paused and added, "Things are going to get better. The days will get easier."

Kathleen dropped her hand, letting her fingers trail on the deck. "I don't think so."

"You used to tell me I had to do my share. Well, back at ya. You have to try harder."

A new boom of thunder catapulted Kathleen into the present moment. Jerking her hand back, she watched one more stripe of lightning play across the darkness. With the same pinkie, she traced the path of the lightning. "I don't want to try."

Swiping the single tear that trickled down her face, she laced the scarf through her fingers and moved back to the door. In the utter darkness of the porch she groped on the deck until she found the keys. Three more clicks, and she entered her version of safety.

Once inside, she stood in the darkness, not needing to look at the pictures to know where one of Courtney hung. Top row. Third from the left. A black-haired pixie-sized toddler popped out of the water with a huge snaggletooth grin. "I hoped you'd visit, but I can't let you in," she repeated to the empty room. She slid all the locks back into place. Dragging the scarf behind her, she moved to her bedroom.

As she went through her bedtime routine, she slammed the door on the past. She climbed into bed, burrowed into her pillow, and waited for sleep to relieve her.

Bolting awake, she clamped her knuckles in her mouth to stop the scream for help. Dropping to her knees, she began her nightly crawl across the cement floor. Tucking herself deep into the corner of her closet, she rested her head on her shoes, forcing her breathing to slow. Phantom pain began at the left side of her head and moved in tiny increments, stopping just below her hip. The pain she liked. The pain she deserved.

She huddled in the closet, listening as the powerful storm pounded the surf. She imagined the scattered debris and the wave-ravaged dunes. As she tried to find sleep, she was unaware that tomorrow her own life would also be reshaped.

Made in the USA
Columbia, SC
27 August 2020